The Voice Inside

Adrian Eller

This is a work of fiction. Names, characters, places, and incidents are products of the author's imagination or are used fictitiously and are not to be construed as real. Any resemblance to actual events, locales, organizations, or persons, living or dead, is entirely coincidental.

Ellian Publishing

Copyright © 2016 Adrian Eller

Cover artwork and photographs by Samantha Fortenberry

Cover design by Adrian Eller and Canva

ISBN: 0692827021
ISBN-13: 978-0692827024

DEDICATION

For my friends.

Thorn
Introduction

Elegrant Penitentiary   August 13, 2018
Three Rivers, California   9:00 a.m.

A silver-haired man in a brown blazer swung open the door to the hallway and nodded to an inmate sitting in the waiting area.

"Trevor, it's good to see you again."

The man hunched over in the plastic chair raised his head. It was evident that he was once handsome, with brown hair, an angled jaw, and clear blue eyes framed with long lashes. But the years were not kind to him. Dark bags under his eyes, deep facial scarring, and the restructured bones of a face victim to many fists caused his face to look like a Picasso painting.

Trevor smiled, the misaligned flesh of his face twisting in opposite directions. He tried to move the lower half of his body, but his legs gave out.

The psychiatrist moved towards the man in an attempt to help, but Trevor put up a hand.

"I got it, Dr. Bryan. I'm not decrepit yet."

The doctor stepped back.

After struggling to his feet, Trevor walked towards the door. His steps were short and staggered, but he made it past the door frame. Trevor's eyes wandered over the familiar shapes and colors of the room, the dim lighting, the smooth wooden floors lined with purple and red chairs, love seats, recliners, and pillows. But what comforted him was the soft jasmine scent.

He would never know that the scent was designed by K-Pharma to instill trust and openness between psychiatrist and patient. All Trevor knew was that he could be himself and reveal his deepest, darkest secrets in here, without fear or judgment.

A safe place like this was hard to come by. After all, he was 45-year-old Trevor Harding, notorious rapist, kidnapper, murderer, drug and human trafficker, and listed organ donor. His rap sheet includes thousands of charges, hundreds of convictions, hundreds of denied appeals, and a prison sentence of two thousand years.

Trevor sat down on one of the sofas lined with pillows and winced as he favored his right knee.

Dr. Bryan sat across from him, placing himself in a black rolling chair.

"What can I help you with today, Trevor? You sounded quite frantic."

"I had that dream again, Dr. Bryan."

"You know you can call me George. We're all informal in here."

Trevor waved a hand across his face. "I know I know, but I'm used to doing it already."

Dr. Bryan nodded.

With that same hand, Trevor rubbed it roughly up and down his face. "It happened when I was on that spree four... no, three years ago. When I was mainly running women.

"So... on our little trips, we'd occasionally filter through the streets, to see if there were any just hanging around, eager to be taken. Our normal method, we were doing all the work, so whenever we could, we looked for easy prey. We got about a third of our girls that way…"

Trevor licked his lips.

"Anyway, we were just heading back after dropping off a really good payout, twenty women from these fucking stupid-ass battered women's shelters, and one of my boys sees this girl standing on the sidewalk, next to a park fountain. She was alone. There was no one around."

He paused. "I don't know what it was about her. It was about three in the morning, even the police were fucking napping. It would have been the easiest steal of all, just a single girl. But I just felt so… off… about the whole thing. She was this pretty young thing, tall with boobs and hips, nice hair. Looked like a money cow." Trevor stopped.

Dr. Bryan nodded, prodding him to continue.

"I had my boys drive closer to her. Everyone felt weird about it. Despite the booze and drugs." Trevor's eyes took on a gleam of reminiscence. "So we drove closer, and the feeling didn't go away. It seemed like she was wearing a nightgown, standing absolutely still, even though it was the dead of winter. Maybe it was a trap, or she was bat-shit crazy. I decided I'd grab her."

"You're the leader. Why risk it?"

"Hell, you try being the leader of a group of bloodthirsty, hormonal fucks. Sometimes you still had to show them who was boss. That I could fuck them up if they got out of line. I sure as hell wasn't going to back away from something, especially when it involved minimal effort– did you know sex trafficking is the cheapest shit to do, since women are a lot easier to transport than thousands of pounds of coke? So I had my boys drive to the curb. I got out." He patted his pockets. "I had my guns. They've never failed me before.

"She was just standing there, hadn't moved a muscle. The nightgown was fluttering around her, and it was goddamn cold – swear almost thirty degrees – and she was just standing there, facing the fountain.

"So I walked up behind her and said, "Hey, how you doing?" which was a classic. They respond positively, we grab them. They start running, we grab them. This girl, she didn't respond at all. Didn't move a muscle. So I walked to stand beside her and asked the same thing. Still nothing. At this point I was getting mad, so I yelled "Hey bitch" right into her face. She finally acknowledged my presence, as I saw her take a breath. She tilted her head up so I could see her eyes…"

Trevor stopped to look at Dr. Bryan.

"Her eyes were dead. Empty. A pit of nothing… I wasn't sure if anything appeared on my face, but…"

He gestured with his hands.

"It's hard to describe what it felt like, but I was paralyzed, rooted to the ground, almost. It was dark so my men didn't notice my reaction… All they knew was that I stopped moving after I got close to her." He rubbed his arms, as if to warm them up. "She just stared at me for a good two minutes."

"Describe those two minutes."

"I was… Powerless. Drained. I pride myself on my ability to be in control, to not let anything get in the way of business." He rubbed his hands together. "But this…I still have dreams… nightmares about what could have happened that night."

Dr. Bryan nodded.

"So… she finally broke eye contact with me. I'm not sure what she was looking for, what she was trying to see in my eyes, and I'm not sure if she found it. But she looked down for a brief second, and all I saw was a flash of steel."

He shook his head.

"She had this kitchen knife in her right hand. None of us saw it, and if she hadn't looked down, I would never have known. Her eyes... I drew my guns and pointed them at her.

"Put it down!" He raised his hands, simulating his reaction at that moment. "Put that fucking thing down!"

"She didn't react to what I said. I don't know what she was seeing in her head, but God knows she didn't see the guns."

Trevor was panting, and a drop of sweat gleamed on his temple.

Dr. Bryan made a comforting sound. "I'm sure she would have reacted if she still could."

Trevor nodded furiously, his hands balled into fists at his sides. "You know what she did? She smiled at me. She FUCKING SMILED AT ME. Not just a grin or a snicker. But a full-blown, white-as-fuck teeth, I'm-the-happiest-person-in-the-world smile. As if everything was great. As if she wasn't about to be kidnapped and sold! I couldn't move. I could only take small steps back, put distance between me and her." His hands clenched and unclenched.

Dr. Bryan kept his hands on his lap, clasped together, his feet spreading a little further as he leaned in.

"She lifted the knife. With that same smile on her face. I knew, if she took a step towards me, even if she leaned an inch towards me... But even then... I don't know... I don't..." Trevor's eyes took on a glazed look, as if lost in that particular moment.

The clock ticked softly in the background.

With a shake of his head, Trevor was back. "She said, "Thank you.""

Dr. Bryan furrowed his brows. "You've never told me this before."

Trevor waved that comment to the side. "I've always forgotten about it. It was always those eyes. Always thought that was scarier than what she said." He pursed his lips. "Although now that I said it out loud, what she said was more fucked up."

The psychiatrist did not comment.

"Yeah, she had this sharp ass knife in the air, about to stab the shit out of me – I thought. And she says "Thank you." Her smile was still there, white and clean. And then she plunges the knife downwards. It was so goddamn fast that I didn't see where or what.

"For a brief second I thought she had shoved it into my stomach, that was how out of my mind I was, but then she fell to her knees, the smile still on her face. My eyes finally left her creepy, terrifying face, and I realized that she stabbed herself. In the wrist. Vertically. Along the vein. I don't know how, but she had stabbed with so much force that the tip of the knife stuck out from the other side. I guess she missed the bone? But there was so much blood. So much FUCKING blood."

Dr. Bryan lifted his hand and faced his palm towards the agitated inmate. "It's okay. We don't have to go through this if it's causing you distress."

Trevor shook his head. "No... I need to get this in the open. It's the only way, maybe, that I can sleep in peace." He rubbed the bottom half of his face. "So she falls to her knees. Her left wrist was just impaled on a chef's knife. The smile is still on her face. Her right hand is pressed to the ground, to keep her upright, but there is a pool of blood under her hand... spreading larger and larger.

"One of my boys got out of the car and was next to me, saying something like "T, T, are you alright?" for the past thirty seconds, but I didn't even hear him. He asked me if we should dump the body, so I slapped him and told him to get back in the car."

"Why did you slap him?"

"I... overreacted. But if we moved the girl it would have left evidence. I wasn't willing to risk that. And this death we weren't even technically responsible for!"

Pause.

"And?"

Trevor pressed his lips together. "I didn't want to touch her."

Dr. Bryan nodded again.

"I mean, not just because of the blood – we've gotten rid of blood and body parts and all that shit- but this was something else. And I didn't want any part of that." He turned to face the wall, his hands hanging loosely at his sides.

All of a sudden his hands clenched into fists.

"So what did you do?"

"I went back to the car. We drove off. We drank and smoked and fucked and partied." Trevor glanced at the doctor. "Yeah, we just left her there. We're fucking criminals, not boy scouts. It was the first and only time ever we didn't grab the girl."

Trevor leaned back into the sofa. "And it fucking only takes one time for me to have nightmares forever." He rubbed his temples with his right hand. "I just don't understand why."

Dr. Bryan leaned back in his chair. "Something about her must have triggered you."

"I don't know, doc. I've never been the same." Trevor looked up, his gaze thoughtful. "You know, I think it was because of a bad flashback that I got caught up with the pigs in the first place. That bitch got me locked up."

Thorn

Room 1662
The Ritz-Carlton
Malibu, California

August 13, 2018
11:45 p.m.

The body was so heavy.

As she dragged the dead man from the balcony to the bathroom, Thorn touched the scar on her left wrist. It throbbed.

She regretted not planning this a little more, perhaps killing him closer to the bathroom. But there was no use thinking about that now, especially since the police were already on their way. While she had no doubt she could eliminate them without an issue, involving outsiders was unnecessary.

Use your legs, not your back. VOS murmured in her head.

She always thought that "voice of subconscious" acronym that AEX gave it seemed a little obvious, but the name suited the androgynous speaker.

Thorn pulled the 250-pound black-haired executive of Kamden Banking and Securities inch by inch, hindered only by the plush expensive carpeting in his apartment.

Forty feet had never felt so endless. She looked at her twitching left hand. No matter how many times she went through this, the post-mission adrenaline never went away.

Thorn...

To give the guy some credit, he fought with a fierceness that she hadn't expected. He was quick on his feet and knew what he was doing.

Thorn's eyes flicked over the broken lamps, glass frames, kitchen knives, and random utensils scattered around the room.

Thorn, it's time to get a move on. Delay any more and you'll have witnesses. You know what that means.

Yes, did she. AEX code for witnesses was no witnesses.

Someone in the building reported the commotion, which meant AEX's typical clean-up crew wouldn't have time to arrange Kamden's untoward death before the cops showed up. Leaving the official "cleanup" to Thorn.

She didn't mind. It wasn't like the police were going to be looking too hard. She just needed to make it passable.

With a wistful glace at the ten feet between the body and the bathroom, she grabbed onto his lapels. She only had a few more minutes to create the scene of an accidental suicide.

Four more feet.

A memory flashed into her head, a memory she couldn't exactly recall, but she felt its impact in her body. The bottom of her stomach dropped out and she felt a cold fist in her chest. Her face felt hot. Oh no, not now-

She heard a small click and a wave of silence. Coolness washed over her. The panic and anxiety faded from her mind. She could concentrate again.

VOS.

The target's $3,000 suit remained soft but sturdy in the vice-like grip of her hand.

Three more feet.

The jacket flap opened, and her gaze fell on the Amber Mist in a little see-through plastic baggy in the jacket pocket. He enjoyed the recreational substances when he was alive... and to everyone else, he will have died from it. Full circle.

VOS definitely knew how to plan.

Hurry. I can hear the sirens.

Thorn dragged his body into the shower. She peeled off his coat jacket, hung it up on a hanger, and took the packet. Making sure not to leave marks in the bathroom, she quickly walked back to the dead man, unbuttoned his shirt, took off his pants and boxers, and threw them in a pile right outside the shower.

Thorn's eyes raked his naked frame. No visible marks.

Definitely passable as suicide. If he had gone for a weapon, she wouldn't have been able to pull her attacks, and the disposal of the body would have been a bigger problem.

She got lucky that he was arrogant enough to think he could beat her with his bare hands.

She opened the packet of concentrated powder and poured it into his nose and mouth. Tilting the body up against the wall, she turned on the shower, soaking his body from the waist down.

Leaving evidence for the police to find in his facial orifices.

There they were. Sirens. She could hear them now, even though VOS picked up on them minutes ago.

With one last look back at him, she took her jacket from the couch, the bottle of champagne they both drank from, and her purse from the coffee table. She turned towards the hotel balcony.

Thorn... Five seconds.

Just as the door burst open, the top of her head disappeared over the ledge.

When one suspicious officer looked over the edge, all he saw in the beam of his unflattering white flashlight was a twenty-story drop.

Two floors below, Thorn took a deep breath. She closed her eyes briefly and thanked VOS. To this day, she still didn't know exactly how to fight, win, and escape, but the voice knew what to do, and how to "make" her do them. It's gotten her out of more situations than she could count.

She opened her eyes and withdrew an electronic notepad from her pocket. His face appeared on the screen.

Hunter Kamden, CEO, owner, founder, and investor of Kamden Banking and Securities. Step-son of the President, husband to the third wealthiest woman in the United States, drug addict.

250 counts of premeditated murder.

As she stared at the handsome face staring back at her from his picture, she wondered how the rest of the world lived in such delusion. Politicians, public figures, his family... They all knew about his ambition, his greed. They knew how far he'd go to expand his business. How could they let all of this happen?

She turned the notepad off.

The answer was clear. The disease called familiarity made people blind to reality, making even the smartest individual weak.

Her lip curled as she swung off the balcony.

Khara
Introduction

December 5, 1992

I, Kharavera, promise to be the best daughter ever.
To never let down my mother, who died giving birth to me, and my father,
who from this day I will call Alann.
He has given me everything, and I will prove my worth to him.

I am unstoppable.
Khara (6)

December 5, 2002

I, Kharavera Terraza, do accept the five-million-dollar parting birthday gift
from Alann. With this money, I will give my life to create an empire that will
change the world and will not stop until I am dead.

From this day forth, I will not contact my siblings.
From this day forth I will not permit emotions to get in the way of true power.
I will not have contact with my father or his affiliates unless it relates to
business.

This contract is bound by no law except that of my word and my life.
Khara (16)

Khara

Office of Kharavera Terraza
9th Floor, K-Pharma
Casmalia, California   (Four years ago)

Dr. Evelyn Wells opened the top folder. She removed the paperclip and spread out the four sheets of paper on the desk between her and the CEO of K-Pharma.

Khara motioned to the top page and leaned back in her chair.

"By all accounts, we are a business dealing in medical psychology research. We couldn't physically take our criminal subjects out of prison. People would question what happened. So we intercept them, make them disappear before they are officially put into the system.

"For our initial tests, we used violent criminals. All but one of those experiments failed. VOS-treatment, as we found out later, brought out the subconscious voice we repress, the voice that we hear at night, the voice that is our "true self." External values of good and evil… what we thought we created, was not effective, or even safe."

Khara rubbed her arms. "These violent criminals were uncontrollable, their minds too tainted.

"We moved to nonviolent criminals who had a record. But those also failed. For a brief period, we tried juvenile delinquents, alcoholics, and drug abusers, but they all had too many subconscious inconsistencies. None of them reacted well to the treatment."

"And then Streye happened."

"Yes. Before I met him, I didn't even consider using suicide attempters. But looking back, it was the best decision we could have made."

"Except he already had schizophrenia."

"Yes. Because of that, we only implanted three basic AEX codes. Successfully. We could have given him the complete seven, but we didn't want to risk it."

"And you discovered that suicide attempters were the best subjects."

"That's why the Vice President started his campaign against suicide. Contrary to what the religious right publicly stated, it didn't originate with his religious beliefs. It merely made it easier for him to convince the people that the Suicide Prevention bills were needed. It made suicide reportable as a crime, we gained access to those who failed, and then we either recruit them or put them in prison."

"You jail the ones who don't agree? How barbaric!"

"Yes, on paper it does sound terrible, but we needed leverage to… persuade them to participate. The ones who are not compatible are sent to a rehabilitation center. It's treatment-oriented."

Khara crossed her legs. "We are still not completely sure why the process works, albeit extremely selectively, with suicide attempters. Our current hypothesis is that suicide victims hold the same negative thoughts about the world that violent criminals have. However, because their subconscious is less external-focused on hating and wanting to hurt the world, and more internal-focused, hating oneself or the lack of control, their subconscious is more adaptable to our code of only doing enough evil when good is the final result."

"How reliable is the process? Are we certain they will be controllable?"

"Psychotechnology is a new science. We're still trying to find patterns and trends. Because we have no data, experiments are dangerous and subjects hard to come by. As of now, suicide attempters have been more or less controllable. Reliability… we don't even have enough subjects to make a claim."

Eve pushed the papers away from her. "What do you need me to do?"

"Because of the delicate nature of neuromodulation, we need you to track the emotional, mental, and psychological progress or regression of our agents and recruits."

"I'm a psychologist, not an experimenter."

"That's exactly it. You will be their psychologist, psychiatrist, therapist, friend, whatever they need. There's only so much that data can measure. You will bring the qualitative aspects of psychotechnology to our research."

The older woman shook her head. "This kind of research is beyond me."

"Your methods are stable, traditional, effective. You will be someone they go to for support. Someone to listen to them. Someone to tell them they are not monsters."

Khara

Conference Room
9th Floor, K-Pharma   (Three years ago)

A 90-inch flat-screen television hung on the far wall of a conference room, its width reaching the corners of the room. On the opposite side of the rectangular room stood a window overlooking large expanses of greenery, buffered by an anti-glare screen.

Along the two walls perpendicular to the television and window, there hung three large black-and-white photographs: one with medical instruments, one of a human brain, and one featuring a medieval dragon.

Underneath those photos were three words:

PROGRESS. INFORMATION. POSSIBILITY.

A black oval conference table sat in the middle of the room, surrounded by six black leather chairs with silver armrests. Three chairs were occupied by men, two by women, and one was empty.

Khara, sitting at the head of the table, crossed her fingers in front of her mouth. Her violet eyes caught the light from the window.

"Ladies and gentlemen, we have all gathered here, in this room because of one reason. Because we believe in a better world. Because we believe in the power of science and human achievement. Because we know that waiting for the government to make the right choice will never happen.

"Crime is detrimental to our nation. Increasing the amount of people in jails is detrimental. Paying for criminal's crimes, crimes that are preventable and criminals who are curable, is not going to make us great again. We must remove the root of the problem, whether by psychological manipulation or direct removal. That is the basis for AEX, Alternative Experimentation."

She looked around the room.

"Randolph and I hand-picked each one of you because we want the same thing: to turn our immoral, welfare state into something better, where there are no crimes because people no longer desire to commit them."

"What, like Phase Two? Congress has already vetoed it." A ruddy-faced man sitting with his back to the window was the first to speak.

"If society always obeyed the government, we'd all be dead, with no progress, no evolution." She set her hands down flat on the table. "AEX does not need government approval. In fact, it relies on no one knowing it exists."

A woman in a uniform thumbed through the papers in front of her. "You talk a big game. So what is AEX? What does it do?

"We are going to eliminate criminals by controlling other criminals' sense of right and wrong."

Someone coughed.

Khara continued. "With AEX, I'm going to take out two birds with one stone: reduce the criminal population and procure important scientific data on the psychology of morality. We will be taking those not in the system, untracked by the U.S. government, and alter their minds just enough to do our bidding to kill criminals who have too long and too often evaded the law."

"How are you going to alter their minds?"

"You don't need to worry about that. Just know that AEX will take care of it."

"So how will this even be accomplished? This is big enough to draw prying eyes."

"You all have very important jobs. You will do all that it takes to prevent news, information, or names from being leaked out to the public. That goes for television stations," she looked at the first man who spoke, "inmate containment facilities," another look, "emergency fleets and police efforts," another look, "and public health groups."

"This is all so... convoluted. Why not just kill criminals outright without the whole mind control aspect?"

Khara suppressed a sigh. "That is not progress. Progress is evolution, harnessing the power of the human brain to better humanity. Merely killing them is not sustainable in the long run. People will still have the urge to commit crimes."

"But aren't you going to be killing them anyway?"

"Yes, to test out the mind manipulating aspect of AEX. Our ultimate goal is to change the thoughts and behaviors of criminals, so we have to put them in situations where we can see if their VOS, the second voice, is changing their actions."

"By only putting them in situations of killing others?"

"Assassins are only a subset of our agents."

Before anyone else could speak, the door opened. A silence hung over the five people in the room until the man sat down in the empty chair.

"Mr. Vice President, you're okay with this? Experimenting on people?"

"Progress cannot be made without certain...dangers. They have already committed crimes and are in no way innocent in any sense of the law, or in the eyes of God."

He paused. "We are giving them a chance for redemption. Their choices are to give their minds and bodies to AEX, or suffer in the penal system. Either way, they will be paying for their crimes."

"What is the incentive for picking AEX? It seems to me that a limited time in even a labor prison – excuse me – commune, is much better than a completely brand new science that fucks with my head."

Randolph looked at Khara. "They get to live a normal life outside of their missions. Isn't that what suicide attempters are all looking for? A way to feel normal?"

"A political leader, man of religion, allowing this…"

"Sacrifices must be made from the greater good. Rules, religious or not, once they become hindrances to society, must be revised." Randolph looked at the black screen of the television. "The hard part is keeping it hidden."

The other woman leaned back in her chair. "Keeping civilians in the dark is easy. But the Feds?"

"I'll handle them." Randolph checked the watch on his wrist.

Khara nodded. "There will be an AEX sector in K-Pharma. But you will not have access to it unless I or Randolph are present."

She ran her hands through her hair. "Once you agree, you will all become traitors to the U.S. government. There is no going back."

AEX
Introduction

Memo: Findings, weekly update [C]
From: Rita
To: staff, K
Date: October 25, 2014

Before reading, note <u>confidential</u>.

❖ VOS does not work with present or latent schizophrenia.

❖ Treatments are more effective for recruits over age 20.

❖ VOS can only work if it has a point of trauma, an event to bond
   to.
   o "Clean" recruits reject VOS completely. Recruits who forget
      their trauma reject VOS.

❖ To protect memory of that event, VOS retreatment is effective.

o Pain is an essential part of VOS bonding. Subjects must maintain
   a medium-level pain.

o The higher the trauma, the more successful the VOS treatment.
   [Attached is data chart showing correlation of trauma, memory
   retention, success rates, and levels of VOS treatment]

o   Newest research topic: (trauma and VOS) looking at emotional trauma of specific event and its effects on VOS effectiveness

The finalized codes:

1.   Do not disobey instructions or orders of AEX's leadership and handlers.
2.   Never speak of AEX to an outsider or reveal those in AEX.

3.   Report back after missions within the hour.

4.   Eliminate all witnesses. All other civilians are not to be harmed.

5.   Do not fraternize with other agents.

6.   Do not interact with anyone from your past.

7.   Never start an interaction with outsiders unless for the mission specifically.

AEX

Observation Room
10th Floor, K-Pharma   (Three years ago)

Patrick had to maintain his posture.

He sat as straight as he possibly could, keeping his shoulders back. His neck arched slightly as he sucked in his stomach and kept his gaze directly in front of him. His abdominal muscles ached.

But he had to keep trying. After all, *she* would hurt him if he stopped sitting perfectly.

His eyes darted frantically to the place where she stood, where she always stood. She was standing there now, her condescending gaze piercing him to the mattress. At the moment, she wasn't talking, wasn't screaming, wasn't making any noise or doing anything except staring at him.

Sometimes it occurred to Patrick that this was all silly, since she never moved from that spot, no matter how much she threatened him with physical harm. But then the fear took over, and he had to stay on this bed, completely still, had to make everything perfect. She could beat him, hurt him, make him regret ever existing, if he so much as wavered slightly from her instructions.

She never made promises she couldn't keep, even if it was hours, days, weeks from now. She would always make him regret what he did.

He winced as pain shot through his back along his spine. It felt like lightning striking his every nerve, and his entire body went numb.

Just as suddenly, it was gone.

It never dawned on Patrick that every shock lasted longer or that his control over his body was almost nonexistent. All he sought was the sweet emptiness when it left his body.

He relaxed his back, reveling in the feeling of no pain.

"What do you think you're doing, you little shithead?" The woman's lips were still, almost as if she hadn't said anything at all. But Patrick knew. And he knew what was coming.

He straightened his spine. "I-I-"

"SHUT YOUR MOUTH! WHAT DID I TELL YOU ABOUT KEEPING THAT BACK STRAIGHT! YOU'RE GOING TO BE JUST LIKE YOUR PIECE OF SHIT FATHER, END UP IN JAIL, BE RAPED, AND KILL YOURSELF!"

The woman's eyes seemed to bulge out from her face, her voice echoing in the small square room. Even though the air remained still, her hair began to lift, swirling around her head, as if it had a mind of its own.

Patrick's face twitched and shifted away from her slightly. But he made sure to keep his back straight.

She pulled down her blue suit jacket, straightening the dress shirt underneath and patted her matching blue pants.

"I should have killed you when you were born. Once I saw your face, I knew you would bring this family shame. You're a dumb piece of trash, worth less than the clothes I bought for you." She had calmed down slightly, but her hair was still weaving in the air.

"When you were three, you stole $10 from me, YOUR OWN MOTHER, in order to buy candy. Me, who had given you life and everything you needed. You stole. I wish your grandmother hadn't called at the very moment I forced your head underwater. I wish I drowned you then, and I wish I drowned you now. WHY WHY WHY didn't I kill you."

Patrick pinched his lips together, and kept looking ahead.

"You knew I had a reputation to uphold. You knew how society saw us, me a single mother, you a degenerate. And yet you chose to get a girl pregnant when you were 16! 16!"

She sighed. "I always wondered what it would be like if you had a father figure. Maybe have him beat sense into you. But seeing as how you were always a faggot, you probably would have fucked him too and turned him into a shit."

Patrick's face twitched again.

"See, I can't even tell you to sit like a proper gentleman. Always had to move, always had to do things wrong. Disgrace. Just like your own son. I hear he's retarded, probably got some disease from your slut. Who knows, maybe he'll turn out just like you."

Patrick put his hands to his ears, rocking back and forth. "Stop, stop, stop, STOP, my dad did not have sex with me!"

"There you go again, denying something that was clearly true. Why do you think he left? Why? We were so happy, and then you seduced him and he left me!"

"NO, NO, NO that is not what happened. STOP!"

From behind the one-way glass, a man and two women observed him. The man, a tall African-American man with sharp glasses and a gray suit, was holding a clipboard. His badge read Dr. Marcus.

"We've learned the most from this man." He set the pen in the clipboard. "Patrick Harding. Thirty-five years old, tried to commit suicide two years ago by disembowelment. Third test subject, absolute failure. Only after we gave him the VOS did the CPS check come through."

A young Hispanic woman in a white robe. Badge: Dr. Faye. "What happened?"

"His mother was extremely abusive, and family members suspect she tried to kill him on multiple occasions. Her torture lives in both his conscious and subconscious mind."

Khara tapped her fingertips against the boot she had propped up on her knee.

"Isn't the AEX code supposed to filter out certain thoughts and memories? Isn't that the secondary purpose of VOS?"

Dr. Marcus nodded. "The code doesn't alter one's definition, only enhance it. Because in his subconscious mind his mother was still "good" despite everything she did, VOS merely expanded control and gave her prominence."

"And that nullifies the present-past mental barrier we aim to install." Dr. Faye sank down in the chair next to Khara.

"Right."

All three looked back at the man sitting on the bed.

"We have to narrow our recruitment process. We can't use subjects whose subconscious can no longer distinguish between objective right and wrong."

They looked at each other.

Khara was the first to speak. "How do we do that?"

"More research."

"Which means more recruits, and more failures."

"More money."

Outside AEX
Introduction

The Globe Report
"Psychotechnology: braining a better future?"
By: Pria Parre
January 10, 2013

Advancements in technology have changed our world, some say for the better, fewer say for the worse. Computer technology has connected people and ideas around the world. Biotechnology has improved the lives of those who would otherwise suffer. And now... Psychotechnology?

A United States-based pharmaceutical research and mass production giant K-Pharma, creator and distributor of the "happiness" pill series, recently announced its interest in behavioral rehabilitation of violent and non-violent criminals.

Kharavera Terraza, CEO and founder of K-Pharma, announced that she would prioritize and respect patient consent and personal boundaries. "K-Pharma was created to cure the world's ailments. We have had worldwide successes with completely curing AIDS, asthma, and diabetes, each containing certain genetic and biological components. With Phase Two, we hope to cure and remove the biological component of crime."

While Congress and the President have stayed silent, proponents of psychotechnology have discussed the universal benefit of this research. Criminals who have biological tendencies toward crime would have more control over their actions. Families of those imprisoned have less fear of another crime creating instability within the home. Children of those imprisoned would have positive and constant adult presence at home, preventing the creation of future criminals. The general public would be less fearful of ex-convicts who are back on the street. Reducing the amount of people in prisons would save the country billions of dollars, money that would go towards education and public health.

Human rights activists have spoken out against this new field of study. Even the politicians most intent on increasing criminal punishment are concerned about the rights of those prisoners, and whether or not experimentation on their brains violates man's most basic rights.

There has been no attempt by Ms. Terraza to detail the process required for behavioral modification, what machines and drugs will be utilized, and the casualty and fatality rates of test subjects. There are no current regulations on technology designed to manipulate and influence the mind.

Comments or questions should be directed to P. Parre at pparre@globereport.com.

AEX

Office of Evelyn Wells
9th Floor, K-Pharma   (Two years ago)

Evelyn was fifty-five, and thought she had seen everything. If someone told her years ago that she would be a psychiatrist for assassins with controlled schizophrenia, she would have laughed at them. It was a ridiculous concept, almost oxymoronic, that a mental illness could be controlled.

But she had long stopped laughing.

Eve checked the time on her watch, and glanced at the DVD before putting it into the computer slot.

The video started out in an empty room, each white wall dominated by a large dark mirror with grainy texture. The camera was situated in the corner facing the entrance. To the left was a metal table and three chairs, one on the side of the camera, and two on the side closer to the door.

One of the interview rooms where recruits are taken after recovery.

Footsteps drew closer to the open door. The wooden plank swayed, and a man in a gray suit entered. He had a scar running from his eyebrow to his right temple, dark brown hair, and wore a pair of spectacled glasses.

Dr. Stewart.

The first psychologist that Khara recruited. An intense but cold man with questionable morals and scientific impartiality. Eve wasn't fond of him.

But then again, he wasn't the only one.

Eve often found herself at odds with most of the staff. The entire leadership was aggressively progressive, and she was traditional, focusing on the patient instead of the scientific potential.

Her attention turned back to the video.

A pale hand grasped the door frame, and a tall, sickly girl limped in, her face the color of sour milk. Her left arm was wrapped in bandages and pressed against her side. Her hair was damp, strands plastered against her face. The black roots stood out from the dark red dye.

Thorn.

"We could just bring the wheelchair in here." He motioned towards the darkness outside of the door. "You have barely-"

The girl shook her head weakly. The long silver gown hung around her, swaying with each step she took.

The path from the door to the table was only about six feet, but her face had developed a layer of sweat by the time she reached the table. She shuffled the last few steps, arm clutched to her chest.

The hand that wasn't bandaged grasped the table so tightly that the flesh around the hold was white.

Her feet slipped.

Eve gasped.

Thorn held up her hand as a sign that she was okay, and crawled up to finally sit at the table. She closed her eyes briefly, breathing through her mouth. When she opened them, her breathing had slowed. The doctor nodded to somebody stationed outside, and they closed the door.

He sat down across the table from the girl. Eve wasn't sure if she had blinked even once.

"You said you had a proposition." Her voice was the only part about her that was Thorn. Firm, quiet.

The doctor rubbed the bridge of his nose. "You know that suicide is a crime."

"I don't see how that's related, but okay. Yes."

"And that the punishment for suicide is labor in prison."

"Yes."

"Do you want to go there?"

The girl laughed softly, but then stopped. Her face was pinched in pain.

"What if I told you didn't have to?"

"You're going to help me finish the job?"

He shook his head, and the glow faded from her face. "There's a project I'd like your help on."

She kept her eyes on him.

"Do you believe that your subconscious has a voice?"

She hesitated. "I don't know. Why?"

"What if I told you that there was a way to make it audible? You would have your conscious thought, the one you have now, and then another voice that gives you with a second opinion, of sorts."

Thorn stared at him blankly.

"Technically it will be a hallucination. But it's you, just a different you." He leaned back into the chair. "It will bring out your alternative self. One that we would like to help you enhance."

"Why?"

"You get the ability to control your emotions, the ability to enjoy your thoughts, the ability to live."

She leaned back dubiously. "A voice can do that?"

"A person's subconscious is extremely powerful. We often don't hear it because our mind can only have one dominant presence, since any conflict with the main conscious would mentally destabilize the person. But our process is designed to equalize the power dynamic so that neither voice controls. It's the ultimate self-control and management tool."

"So why was I chosen?"

"You have all the qualifications that we are looking for."

Thorn was silent. "And what do I have to do in exchange?"

AEX

Office of Evelyn Wells
9th Floor, K-Pharma   (Two years ago)

Evelyn sat on her ottoman and stretched, stifling a yawn.

An alert beeped on her iPad. It was ten minutes before her next appointment, and she was ready for some coffee. Probably not a great idea, since it was almost four in the afternoon, but she was going to need it. She rose from the couch and grabbed her coffee cup from her desk.

Glancing at her watch, she was satisfied that she still had seven minutes left, and twisted the door knob.

Thorn glanced up from reading a hardcover copy of *The Prince*, and smiled at Eve. Eve smiled back, but had to hide a disappointing sigh. So much for coffee. She motioned for her to come in, but Thorn waved a hand.

"Go get your coffee. There's no hurry."

Throwing the other woman a grateful smile, Eve walked to the kitchen area of the office, and poured herself a cup of lukewarm coffee. She added two packets of sugar, sipped it, and then added a dollop of half and half.

Thorn was still standing in the same spot, one leg perpendicular to the floor, the other propped on the wall behind her. She was dressed in black jeans and a red t-shirt that said "smile or I'll murder your whole family," matched with black sneakers and a sleek silver bracelet on her left wrist. There were two distinct bulges on her hips.

Grasping her coffee with one hand, Eve opened the door to her office with the other. Thorn nodded and followed her.

Eve sat down on her recliner, Thorn on the long couch. This was only their second meeting, but the girl had gotten comfortable with her faster than other recruits had.

Eve took another sip of her coffee as Thorn stared at the painting of a three-headed dog on the opposing wall.

"Are you supposed to have those kind of paintings in here? Aren't you worried that it'll make some of us crazy?"

Eve turned her head to look at the painting. "No. It's my job to provoke you as much as possible within the confines of this room."

Thorn's dark brown eyes met Eve's green ones. The gaze held.

Thorn mumbled an apology and looked away.

"Why did you apologize?" Eve set her coffee down.

"I know my stare can be pretty intimidating." She looked at the ceiling. "Making the shrink uncomfortable is probably not a good idea."

"This is about you. I am your sounding board." Eve interlocked her fingers on her knee. "How is your VOS? The last time, you mentioned that she was mostly silent."

Thorn crossed her legs and her eyes looked past Eve's shoulder. "I hear her more regularly now. But recently, she's appeared in my dreams."

Eve jotted down some notes. Thorn's eyes flicked to the paper but continued to talk.

"She's reorganizing my thoughts, and I'm aware throughout the whole process. I wake up not knowing what exactly she did, but I'm more efficient. When I read mission logistics, I feel attention directed to what is most important, tactics whispered to me, a focus I would not have otherwise. I could stare at ML for thirty seconds, and be able to incorporate all the information. She strengthens my memory."

"What about missions?"

"I've only been on three missions since the last time we talked, but it has gotten much better. I'm faster, more confident in my pre-mission, and we connect more when she's taking over my body for fights."

Eve nodded, and put her notepad down. The question that she'd been waiting to ask. "How do you feel?"

What she wanted to ask was, do you still feel the urge to commit suicide?

Thorn pushed her lips together. "I'm okay, I guess. Neutral is perhaps the best term for it. I don't feel angry, or sad, or as you want to hear it, suicidal."

"What about positive feelings?"

"Just neutral."

Outside AEX

The Westin
Downtown Los Angeles   (Two years ago)

Army veteran and mercenary Eli "Pound" Rodriguez stood in front
of the fake wooden door, hands crossed in front of his hips. He'd
fought in brushfire conflicts and dusty wars and killed so many
people in so many different countries, but this was by far the most
interesting job he's had.

The body count was the lowest. He only got physical once – a moron
who had come too close to the Vice President – but Eli enjoyed every
single day of it. Maybe it was the prestige, maybe it was the pay, but
it was definitely the loose women who saw his title – Commanding
Officer of VP Security – and gave him so much ass that he was
literally drowning in it.

He nodded to his second-in-command Harvey "Balls" Basker,
standing diagonally across the hallway. Taking one more look at the
empty hallway, he took out his phone.

Six new notifications from four numbers. Olga, Janelle, Germania,
and Yvette.

To all but Yvette, he responded vaguely to their queries as to his
plans for the night. To her, he wrote the most graphic response
detailing exactly what he wanted to do to her tonight. Where he was
going to take her, which part of her to kiss first...

He was salivating just thinking about it. Long golden hair, piercing dark brown eyes, skin smooth as butter. All sitting on a pair of thick and muscular toned legs.

And the things she could do with those hands.

"I see experience doesn't exactly equate to quality, as always."

Eli glanced up slowly. At this point, he shouldn't be shocked at all by Khara's silent appearance. This woman seemed to hover above the ground, her movements inhumanly quiet.

He put the phone back into his pocket and refrained from speaking. The first and only time he retorted, not only did she put him in his place, but it also earned him a verbal reprimand from his actual boss. The one who paid him.

She raised her left eyebrow at him and motioned for him to open the door.

Eli followed orders. He was great at it, so great he spent twenty years selling his life for the government.

But when she disrespected him like this, all Eli wanted to do was choke her, just to prove exactly how weak she was. To see her gasping for breath, face turning red, then purple, her hands slapping weakly against his arm.

But he couldn't. Not yet.

His hand latched onto the door handle and gripped it so hard he was surprised the metal didn't crumble in his hand.

The door, now fully open, allowed her to step into the room. She turned to face him, their eyes only a foot or two away from each other.

She stared directly into him, violet eyes flashing. "I do suggest that if you try to be intimidating, do it without your dick sticking out of your pants."

Her heels clicked over the threshold.

Eli hadn't even noticed she was wearing heels. He rubbed his hand into his eye socket as he shut the door behind her, making sure he didn't push the steel-core door too hard.

Balls came over and patted him on the shoulder. "Sorry man. No bitches should be talking to us like that. Someone ought to put her in her place."

Eli opened his mouth to respond but he knew better. This *was* her place.

Kharavera oozed power. Eli suspected that even the VP, as capable and charismatic as he was, felt diminished in her presence.

It might be the tightness with which she held her posture, the purposeful gait with which she walked, or the almost manipulative way she talked, but she made him question exactly how much was bark and how much was bite.

Eli suspected most was the latter.

While he didn't know shit about politics, he knew enough to know that she was dangerous.

Then again, whatever it was his boss was involved in, wasn't his problem. He gets paid millions for his brawn, not his brains.

So he nodded along to whatever Harvey was saying, and retrieved the phone from his pocket.

AEX

Office of Evelyn Wells
9th Floor, K-Pharma   (Two years ago)

Eve sat down at her chair and clicked on the video, fast forwarding to the part where she left off.

Dr. Stewart was conversing with someone standing behind the camera, and he was drawing a graph on his paper.

"VOS picks up on the subtlest clues, actions, indicators, or inklings of thought, and can sense beyond the traditional five senses. Nothing escapes the "gaze" of one's subconscious, just like no childhood experience escapes the memory of the unconscious.

"That is why even highly-trained professionals cannot compete against a regular civilian with VOS. The conscious mind can only do so much, even an extremely intelligent one."

"So it's not actually part of the subconscious."

"No, it's an external filter, you can call it. The advantage of VOS is that it doesn't control the mind. It's a bug that detects and analyzes information to provide the conscious mind with advice."

He paused. "What that also means is that we don't have full control or access to it. Once it exists as a separate entity… we can only wait and see to see what it will do."

Anthony
Introduction

Fresno, California

When Anthony was 10
(Ten years ago)

His dad was always popular. At parent-teacher conferences, at the store, on the street, he was always the center of attention, female and male.

Anthony didn't care, really. He reaped the benefits. Good grades, free food… all of his classmates were jealous. After all, he didn't have curfew, his dad let him do whatever he wanted whenever, and gave him the freedom no other ten-year-old boy had.

Anthony knew he should feel happy or grateful. But he didn't feel anything. Not happy, not sadness.

But that was also nothing new.

Doctors told his parents that he had a very distinct form of congenital hyper-analgesia, where he didn't feel physical pain or most emotions. His mom tried desperately to teach him to feel, to empathize.

But Anthony just didn't have the capacity to understand.

After a particular incident with the can opener, his mom left. His dad became obsessed with "fixing" Anthony, doing anything he could to help him "feel," even though doctors said that it would never happen.

It didn't matter though. No matter what his dad did, nothing would change his diagnosis.

On this particular day, his dad told him to go to the skate park. After an hour and falling countless times, Anthony got bored. Bored of scraped knees and elbows, bored of people, bored bored bored. Everything was so boring.

So he decided to head home, maybe make himself some dinner.

But when he opened the door, something felt wrong.

The muffled groans. Slaps.

He rushed to the bedroom. Part of him wished he had reacted to actual fear instead of years of conditioning. His pulse was steady.

Anthony's hand was about to push the door open completely when he saw them.

Mrs. Girden, his science teacher, tied up on a hook in the middle of the room, naked except for leather straps wrapped around her body. His father was walking around her, using what looked like a flyswatter, to slap her. Muffled screaming.

Was that a gag in her mouth?

Anthony wanted to close the door completely, go outside, escape the burning in his cheeks. His face… he felt it burn.

He felt it.

His eyes remained peeled to the scene. His mouth was dry. Wasn't Mrs. Girden married – a slap of the swatter. He leaned too far on the door.

It creaked.

His father's eyes met his son's. The older man's eyes widened, but he didn't say anything.

Anthony's father turned Mrs. Girden to face the doorway, and hoisted her up so that only the tips of her feet touched the ground. He spread her legs open, while his eyes bore into his son's.

"Come here."

Anthony shook his head.

What was this feeling that he was feeling? Was it disgust? Was it shame? He couldn't be sure.

"Son, get in here. It's okay, she can't see or hear you." Anthony hadn't noticed the blindfold or earplugs, but he shook his head again.

His father didn't say anything for a few seconds. "You're feeling something, aren't you? You feel something and you don't know what it is. That's why you're still standing there."

Anthony pressed himself into the wall, staying completely still.

But his eyes watched his father run his hand from the inside of her calf, to her thighs, up her slightly rounded stomach, pausing only slightly to pinch her side. That same hand massaged her breast, slapping, and slid up her chest, to grip her throat.

Anthony finally found the strength to move.

He was going to walk away, go to his room, maybe to the library, maybe to the park. He was going to escape this…strange and confusing situation.

He was going to disobey his father's one command.

But as he pushed himself away from the wall, he found his legs walking in the wrong direction.

Towards the room, towards his father and the woman who graded his homework and ate lunch with him, towards his father's smile.

His hand was numb as he closed the door behind him.

Anthony

Broken Finger Peak
Sierra National Forest

August 17, 2018
12:15 p.m.

"Anthony, what are you doing?"

The blond man balanced on a rock ledge so fragile it looked like it would crumble if he moved. He lay down on the path behind him, legs dangling over the side of the mountain, thousands of feet above the valley. His shoulders were wedged between two rocks on the wall.

He squinted into the sky. "I'm enjoying it here."

He spread his hands out to both sides, reaching as far as he could. The tips of the fingers on his left hand brushed against the face of the other man.

Wrapped in rope, the upper half of the other man's body was on the ledge, while the bound lower half from the waist down was supported by nothing. His eyes, rimmed with dark circles, were wide and panicked, and his dry white lips crinkled as he tried to scream.

The wind silenced his muted shouts.

"You're not on vacation." The keyboard clacked on the other end. "You have until the end of today to get back to AEX."

He looked at the Bulova watch on his wrist. "It's already noon."

Listen to her.

"You're not in the business of interrogation. You're a killer. Do your job."

He rolled his green eyes. "Yes, yes. You keep telling me that." He tilted his head so the earring phone wouldn't scratch the ground.

Don't you want to have more fun with other people?

"And you keep ignoring it." She sighed. "I'm your handler, not your mother. I don't want to see you get the T-treatment for disobedience again."

Anthony poked at the man's head with his hand. "Fine."

Anthony was a good agent. He hadn't failed any missions they gave him, never caught unawares or unprepared. His voice always told him what to do, when, how.

They were a beautiful team.

But... AEX was impatient and demanding. They wanted efficiency... He wanted to have fun. Fun with his targets, fun with his weapons, fun with himself. Focusing on the end result was boring.

So sometimes he took a little longer, did more than he needed to.

But it wasn't like there was anything wrong with that. His targets were all going to die anyway. He didn't see why it had to be quick.

His nose twitched.

His preference for making them suffer was the only reason they preferred Thorn. He was better than her in every way, smarter, faster, stronger... But they liked her because she followed their directions like a good little girl, a little-

She's none of your concern. Let's finish the job here.

"Good." The phone clicked off. Anthony lay there for a few more moments, savoring the icy wind slashing at his face, the chill of the snowy mountains burrowing deep into his skin and his bones, the crispness of the air in his lungs.

It had to be at least ten below, and he was only in shorts and a long-sleeve shirt. He didn't feel the cold, so he didn't mind it.

The disposal was annoying, though. Anthony hadn't intended for the assignment to be so long or disposal so difficult.

If only the French diplomat's man wasn't so quick to notice his disappearance. Quicker than AEX had predicted, the assistant alerted all law enforcement and security agencies, forcing Anthony to come up with a new disposal method. He couldn't use the cleanup crew, his regular dump sites, or be seen on camera.

So, he had to solve this problem himself. Where was the best place to kill and dispose of a body, a place where no one would come looking?

Snow, rocks, and blinding whiteness.

The Sierra Nevada mountains.

As he lifted his hand, he watched the movement and texture of his skin, his joints, his nails. The hyper-analgesia destroyed most of the sensory receptors in his body, and muted his body's responses to any type of extreme change, whether it be temperature, pressure, or cuts.

He felt almost nothing. Vision was the only way he could "feel," by watching his body's reactions.

His thoughts drifted to his father. The man who thought he could help a son when doctors couldn't.

Anthony almost chuckled.

His father didn't know that maybe Anthony was made this way on purpose, that his senses were deadened to protect the people around him.

Once the impressionable, unfeeling child found that hurting others made him feel... there was no going back.

The day before his nineteenth birthday, Anthony had stabbed his father, just to see what it was like. His hand jammed the blade into his dad's body over and over, and enjoyed every moment of it.

Then he wondered what it'd be like to stab himself.

The twelve stab wounds he gave himself, to his chest, arms, legs, stomach... Didn't kill him. He would have continued to stab, but neighbors called the police.

They had to pry the knife out of his clenched hand. When he awoke, he found himself in AEX, full of questions but no remorse.

He liked to touch the scars to remind himself. Of who he was. Of what he could do.

His eyes burned as he looked at the sun's reflection off of the white snow. Turning his head, his eyes fell on the French dictator, cocooned in rope.

Anthony enjoyed this. Enjoyed torturing the torturer, hurting those who hurt others, reminding people that there was still someone crueler out there.

He sat up quickly, reveling in the dizziness.

He was aware that the blood rushing from his head made him see double, triple, throwing off his balance, but he enjoyed the risk. One wrong move, and he could end up at the bottom of the valley, unfound, buried in snow, broken and dying.

He loved that thrill. And he made sure his target saw the look of pleasure that flickered across his face.

Anthony stood up on the ledge, and then crouched on his heels next to the man. He reached toward the man, and was pleased to see Pierre flinch as he removed the cloth gag from his mouth. The man moved his mouth and licked his lips, but didn't say anything. Defiance was mostly gone from his dark eyes. But not completely.

"Any last words?"

The man pinched his lips. "My men will find me. They will hunt you down and murder you like the worm you are. God protects those who do his bidding."

"Murder and terrorism is doing His bidding?"

The man narrowed his eyes at him, not at all intimidating.

Anthony frowned. "I do hate it when you don't beg. It really takes away some of the fun." He nudged the shoulder of the cocoon with his hand, pushing it a few inches closer to the edge.

"No matter what-" The pitch of the man's voice increased threefold.

"Your men won't find you. You won't survive the fall, although you may survive long enough to die from your injuries. Broken bones, ruptured organs, bleeding out... You'll live just long enough to realize that this is where your story ends. You will not be avenged."

This time, Anthony nudged the cocoon a few inches closer to the edge with his foot, watching the color drain from the man's face.

"You-" The man's eyes widened as his waist hit the edge of the cliff.

Anthony stood up. From his pocket, he took a piece of glass he retrieved from the man's house. Slowly cutting his finger with the edge of the glass, Anthony watched the blood slide onto his palm. Before it could drip, Anthony jammed the glass into the base of the man's neck.

He closed his eyes in pleasure as the man's scream echoed in the valley. Taking a long look at the jagged peaks around them, he slid his foot towards the edge, sweeping the man and his screaming over the edge.

It was a long and beautiful twenty seconds.

AEX

Office of Evelyn Wells
9th Floor, K-Pharma   (Six months ago)

Thorn sat down on the couch, sporting a large bruise on the right side of her face.

Eve took up her pen. "How has this week been?"

"It's been fine. She's been pretty quiet lately."

"Pretty quiet?"

Thorn waved her left hand. "I haven't talked to her for two days."

"And she hasn't come out once?"

Strange. Eve made a mental note of that.

"She mostly speaks to me on missions."

"What about when you are off?"

Thorn looked towards the ceiling. "Not really. If I'm not on a mission, she usually doesn't come out."

Again, strange. VOS of other recruits come out randomly, no matter what they were doing.

"What about moods?"

"I've been feeling fine. She's still there, but I haven't needed her."

"Needed her?"

"She...neutralizes me. When I feel pain."

Eve leaned forward, her hands on her knees. "What pain?"

"Headaches. They make it impossible to think."

"Do the pills not work?"

Thorn shook her head. "I don't take the pills."

Every agent and recruit took pills. Every single subject, starting from the day they received the treatment. The pain during and after bonding was supposed to be excruciating and permanent.

"They didn't offer it?"

"They did. But I don't need them."

"You just spoke of the pain."

"Yes. But it's controllable. On a mission, that pain is gone."

Eve paused. The pills maintained the bridge between conscious and subconscious. Without the pill... Could it affect the VOS bonding? sHow is her subconscious functioning with the added burden of pain?

"You are the only one who can withstand the pain."

"Am I?" Thorn glanced at Eve's face, hands, and posture.

"You are definitely the most well-adjusted."

"You say that like it's a curse."

"I just don't know what you're capable of. At any moment, you could lose your conscious mind..." Eve let her words fade, but her message was clear.

Thorn wasn't offended or mad. "Yes, I could turn into Trent or Anthony or be turned into another experiment. But if I keep worrying about that, what will be the point? I want to live as normally as I can. Wasn't that the whole point in agreeing to AEX?"

Eve looked at her. Despite the thoughts running through her head, she could only nod.

AEX

Nursing Station   August 20, 2018
10th Floor, K-Pharma   1:25 p.m.

Two nurses stood side by side in the white hallway. Thick and thin black wires ran along the edges of the ceilings, snaking into the rooms, winding along the walls.

A security guard stood along the wall every four doors, feet splayed, arms together, face masked. Guards had two handguns at their hips and an assault rifle on their backs.

"Doesn't feel too much like a lab." The brown-haired girl in the blue outfit, with a square name tag that read "Taylor" looked both left and right down both hallways, and edged closer to the taller, black-haired woman whose age was inscrutable.

Her name tag said Rita. "What does it feel like?"

"A hospital." Taylor slid her hands down the front of her scrubs. "More like an institution."

Rita smiled. "When we recruited you, you said that you had experience in a lab, and experience with mentally challenged individuals."

"Yes, but I thought I would be running experiments. I don't really have any medical expertise."

The nurse glanced at the clipboard standing on a ledge right outside a white metal door marked I-4. "Actually, we're going to need some of your expertise. You'll be advising Dr. Stewart."

Taylor's confusion showed on her face. "Advising?"

"Don't worry. He'll explain it all. But most of this will be learning on the job. There's no handbook, just the contract you signed when you came in last week."

"The fifty-page one?"

"That's the one. Pay close attention to the Confidentiality section."

Taylor had so many questions running through her head, but the older woman looked so sure and calm that she decided to wait to ask.

Rita took the clipboard out of the ledge and handed it to Taylor. "Tell me about this person."

"Uh…"

"As I said, learning on the job. We're getting a running start."

Taylor took the clipboard and quickly scanned the first page. "Female, age 20, normal height and weight, suicide attempt eleven months ago, now undergoing…isolation?"

Rita nodded. "Go on to the second page."

Taylor gave her a look before flipping the page. "Recruited on 9/12/2017, passed initial background check and requirements," she traced her fingers on the page to keep track of where she was looking, "suffers from extreme paranoia and delusions post-injection... Self-harm attempted, restraints required."

She lowered the clipboard enough to peer into the room. Through the window panel she saw a toilet in the middle of the room, sink to the right, small table near the door, and a flat queen-sized bed, on which a black-haired girl was tied, spread-eagle, a gag in her mouth. She was struggling against the cloth and Velcro restraints, her hair tangled with sweat. Her wrists and ankles were bruised but not bloody.

"You mentioned that we don't look like a lab. And you would be right, to a certain degree. We run AEX, which is both a lab and an institution." She patted Taylor's shoulder.

"What is… AEX? Nowhere on the contract did it mention it."

"AEX is the program that will eliminate crime and criminals by altering consciousness."

"How? Is this…"

"No, we are not sanctioned by the U.S. government."

Taylor kept staring at her.

"But we hope to find a way to alter the human consciousness without doing damage to the rest of the brain. To be able to install a better, more moral version of ourselves without losing our free will. We're creating the science of selective schizophrenia, to alter our subconscious to create a better 'us'."

"But… why would you want to create schizophrenia? Isn't it more important to find a cure?"

"How do we find a cure for something we can't fully understand?" Rita shook her head. "By creating a separate identity, using the power from the subconscious, we are able to create VOS, the voice of subconscious, that bonds the beliefs and codes of AEX with the recruit's own mind.

"Their minds are supplemented by the "planted" code, but they are able to think freely. Since we know exactly what we are creating, we can better isolate and focus on the actual process of the illness, its origins, and its weaknesses."

"But… no one would volunteer. Who would?" The words seemed to be forced out of her mouth.

"Yeah, that was a big downside to the project. We can't take anyone who would be missed. They couldn't have close family or be watched by the government. We also can't recruit publicly."

Taylor leaned her side on the wall beside the door.

"We couldn't take innocents from the street. Plus, what would be our leverage? What's stopping them from saying no and leaving, taking knowledge of our research with them? So we decided to go with criminals not yet caught, thus not yet in the system.

"We found out the hard way that common criminals did not have the willpower, strength, or common sense to persevere through the VOS process and harsh training. Surprisingly, a lot of them did not have the guts to kill someone in cold blood.

"The VOS process also did not work with violent criminals. Many became uncontrollable, their subconscious unable to coexist with the AEX codes.

"We later discovered that suicide attempters are most fit to be VOS hosts. At that point, committing suicide was technically illegal in the eyes of the law, but no lawmaker enforced it. Until we decided that it was the only way to get our recruits."

"That's why we had those crackdowns."

Rita sighed. "Yes. We created hotlines and teams to retrieve them, before the government could reach them."

"But what can they do like that?" Taylor's eyes drifted back to the girl.

"What you're seeing here is a failure of that process. When successful, they can remember, process, sense, analyze, and plan at maximum efficiency, because there are two entities: conscious dealing with the present, VOS dealing with the details."

"Why did she fail?"

"Our procedure is not fail proof. We only have trial and error." She twisted her neck. "She was one of our earliest: our background checks weren't exactly the most thorough, our injection process was brand new, and we didn't have as much support staff."

Rita wet her upper lip. "Nothing was wrong until two weeks after her initial treatment." She shook her head. "And then something just snapped. We're still trying to figure out what happened to make her this way."

"But why is she gagged and tied?"

"If we do not, they will die trying to commit suicide. Failed VOS encourages negative thoughts instead of blocking them."

She set the clipboard back on the ledge.

"And that's where you come in."

"Me?"

"Yes. You're going to have an active part in redesigning the process. We've only had six successful... ones. We need new eyes on VOS. Dr. Stewart and Dr. Faye were very impressed with your work on schizophrenia at John Hopkins."

"But... What does that mean?"

A brown-haired man wearing a white coat stepped out from room I-6, closing it quickly before the yelling could be heard in the hallway. "Oh, Rita, is that our new researcher?"

"Yes, Doctor." She turned to Taylor. "This is Dr. Stewart. He is in charge of the VOS process and the recruits." She turned to the doctor. "This is Taylor."

"Ah, yes! You're just what we need right now." He examined her from head to toe and motioned for her to follow him. "Let me acquaint you with the work that you'll be doing here."

AEX

Office of Johann Stewart   August 20, 2018
10th Floor, K-Pharma   1:50 p.m.

He saw the look on her face.

"I see Rita's given you some things to think about." Before Taylor could mumble a response, he waved his hand. "No worries. I think you'll feel a lot better once we get more scientific."

Dr. Stewart led Taylor into his office, a sparse and dark rectangle-shaped room. He pulled out a chair, and pushed the loose papers on the floor and set the two books on the table.

He patted the back of the chair for her, as he grabbed the rolling executive chair from the other side of the desk.

"Tell me about your previous work in schizophrenia. Your research was extremely interesting."

Taylor set a hand on the arm chair. "I looked at neurochemicals that can buffer experiences or symptoms of schizophrenia. We were working with older patients primarily, and had just recently tested and observed a younger group of thirty-year olds. I was only an assistant."

"Yes. That's the kind of flexibility and thinking we need here. Our research intends to delve deeper into the way our conscious mind gathers information and processes thoughts… and by including the subconscious, we hope to create a higher form of thinking."

"By installing that AEX code."

"Right. Our ultimate goal is not just to increase the brain's capacity, but to create a separate consciousness, fueled by the connection with the subconscious."

"Why?"

"Some people need to listen to the voice that is too often silenced. Criminals, for instance. With VOS, they can become better versions of themselves. Our voices become something different, something tangible."

He flipped to a picture of a cloud-like mass, divided into three chunks. The biggest was labeled "unconscious", the medium-sized one was labeled "subconscious", and smallest, taking up about 1/7 of the mass, was labeled "conscious".

"The conscious is perhaps the weakest part of our psychopresent mind. It generates the thoughts and processes we need to exist. The conscious is fueled by the subconscious, and after that, mostly by the unconscious. By utilizing the subconscious, our minds can do so much more.

"But we also cannot overload the subconscious. That would be disastrous. That is why we limit the actual rules we implant into the mind. By limiting our codes to seven principles, we create the VOS but offer the already present mind a certain degree of free will."

"Why seven?"

Dr. Stewart flipped a thick stack of papers in front of him, looking for something. After a few moments, he shook his head and turned back to her. "We've found that anything more than seven is counterproductive. Too much interference with their natural process nullifies the entire procedure. The subjects become uncontrollable, unable to distinguish their active voices from passive voices. Too much to handle by just the subconscious, and an overload to the conscious."

"You're talking about schizophrenia-induced insanity. Is that what happened with the girl?"

"Sadly, yes. We gave her too much for her mind to process."

Taylor took a deep breath, the first real breath she's taken since this morning. Something pricked at her mind.

"So those with VOS just exist as experiments? That seems to be a waste of mental capability."

Dr. Stewart didn't respond.

Anthony

Ubezi Residence   August 24, 2018
Santa Monica, California   8:30 p.m.

Blood. So much blood.

Anthony closed his eyes as he inhaled the coppery scent, rubbing the red stickiness between his fingers. He felt a rush of adrenaline enter his bloodstream.

Blood was so raw, so pure, so earthen... the only constant he could rely on in this world. Something he could actually feel.

The muffled, high-pitched whine of the middle-aged woman strapped to the coffee table broke him from his reverie. He opened his eyes, and spread his arms as wide as they could go, releasing a loud bellow from his chest.

He looked down into her eyes. His grin widened as he saw her gaze flit from his face to the scalpel in his hand. He felt himself get hard.

What are you waiting for? She didn't hesitate to take advantage of those young girls, selling their uteruses for the highest bidder.

"I know. How do people do that to the ones who trust them? That's sick."

We need to make her pay.

"Yes."

For each girl she destroyed, cut her twice.

Anthony nodded to himself. It only made sense.

He pointed to his head as he waved the scalpel in front of her face. "My voice loves to play games. He comes up with the best ones... Games I'm sure you play with your female patients. Isn't that right?" She screamed into the already bloody gag, squeezing her eyes shut. "Except they didn't do anything except trust the wrong doctor."

He slid the blade along her cheek, down the side of her neck, along her exposed collarbone, pausing at her bicep.

"Closing your eyes isn't going to do you much good, Doctor Ubezi."

You should get some salt water to clean her off with. The first round is making it very difficult to see where the fresh skin is.

Anthony paused. VOS was right. There was too much fresh and dark blood clinging to her skin, preventing him from seeing which places his scalpel hadn't touched.

He squatted down so that his face was next to the doctor's. "Karma is a bitch, isn't she? Are you feeling what they were feeling when you cut out parts of their body for a couple of bucks?"

He patted the side of her head. "It's okay to be afraid." He set the scalpel on the side table, close enough that she could see it.

"Do you think your friends who now own those uteruses would come save you?" Her eyes were still shut as she moaned into the gag.

He shook his head. "Yeah, I didn't think so either."

Anthony had a desire to blindfold her, have her completely at his mercy, but he also wanted her to see everything.

A blindfold would be too nice.

He stood back up, went to the kitchen, and took a red bucket from under the sink. After dumping the contents out, he washed it thoroughly with dish soap and hot water, the plastic steaming under the faucet.

Make sure you put plenty of salt in that water. It'll keep the wounds from getting infected, and it'll give her a nice little sting.

Anthony and his VOS were always in sync. Despite the agonizing pain of the treatment, he realized later that it was well worth it.

He now had a partner, someone who believed in him and knew him like no one ever had. With it came some new values and rules, something they installed for discipline. Maybe AEX put it there, maybe it was pulled out of his subconscious. It didn't bother him.

He was too busy learning to feel.

Rummaging through her spices shelf, he found a carton of salt that was three-quarters full. He dumped half of the contents into the bucket, looked at the bucket, and then poured the rest of the salt in. He set the water to lukewarm and began to fill up the bucket, enjoying the light musty scent that wafted to his nose. When the bucket was almost full, he took it out of the sink.

As he set the bucket of water on the ground next to the coffee table, he realized he forgot a cloth.

The bathroom. She must have some soft cloths in there.

Anthony prowled through the house, until he found the bathroom. Clutching a cloth in his hand, he ambled back to the living room.

"Rachel, come on now. Open your eyes." Anthony kept his eyes on the scalpel as he dropped the cloth into the water and soaked it. A few seconds in, he took it and wrung it out. "This will hurt some."

He placed the cloth on her right shoulder, draping it on her skin for maximum coverage.

Her hoarse voice screamed into the gag.

He dipped the cloth back into the bucket, and cleaned her left side. Her screams were now pleas and cries, and her whole body quivered and shifted, trying to get away from the pain.

As he dipped the cloth into the water for a third and fourth time, he noticed that it was turning a dark pink, and then a light red.

He almost couldn't hear her over the sound of his pounding heartbeat.

Now you see, there are so many areas to play with.

Anthony gave himself a small squeeze as he rose from his squatting position and took his blade from the corner of the side table.

Looking down at her wriggling, pained form, those long painted toes, those long fingers, he realized that his skin was flushed.

"Now," he twirled the scalpel between his fingers, "those are some beautiful breasts."

Outside AEX

Frank Residence   August 26, 2018
Thousand Oaks, California   7:00 p.m.

Tonight was going to be the night. Gabriel Frank, mayor of Los Angeles, father to three kids, husband to a homemaker trophy wife, was going to have the best night of his life.

Well, second best night. Seven days ago he met the sexiest, most intriguing woman at a pointless work function. Beautiful eyes, amazing ass, and the kind of confidence and rolling hips that only women who were good in bed had. She wanted a favor, and he wanted her. That was the main reason why he delayed accepting her bribe until she agreed to go on a date with him.

At Chateau l' Eau, his favorite spot to take... clients.

He smirked to himself. Usually he had to go on the hunt, but she had come to him. No one knew about his fetish. His weakness. Not his wife, not his supporters, not his advisors. He was not picky. Maids, waitresses, rich girls, matrons, women on the street... As long as he got his fix, he didn't really care where they came from or where they were headed.

It wasn't as if they were going to go anywhere after he was done with them.

His security detail was called off for the night. There was no need to have more witnesses than was necessary. He could very well handle himself. And whatever he couldn't, Victor would do it for him.

He was looking forward to tonight though...

He'd had his fill of so many low-class peasants, women who didn't know their way around class and conversation. This was going to be different.

Like all the other ones, she wouldn't know, couldn't know, who he really was... a monster. Gabriel tightened his tie and admired himself in the mirror.

Yes, his gray suit always worked wonders with the ladies, no matter the width of his waist.

His sausage-like fingers grasped the lapels, sliding over the buttons, tucking into his pockets briefly. He patted the front, where the buttons of his shirt and suit were a little tight.

He may not be a handsome man, but he had power. And that was more attractive than a six pack or toned biceps could ever be.

The bell to his room rang. "Sir, your limousine is ready. The other one has been sent to the address you specified."

Gabriel turned to the door. "Victor, your services are on time, as always. Excellent job. Where are my wife and kids?"

"Your wife is at a charity function. Molly and Michael are at a youth camp for the weekend and David is at his friend's house."

"When my wife comes home, please inform her that I have a late night at the office." He was sure that she suspected his infidelity, with all his late nights and private meetings, but in the same quiet dignity she handled childbirth, she completely ignored his indiscretions.

Gabriel did good in picking a woman more interested in her comfort than the integrity of their marriage vows.

"Yes, sir."

"That is all. You may have the evening off. I will call you in the morning."

"Thank you, sir." Fading footsteps from the door signaled Victor's leave.

Gabriel really liked Victor. He did his job perfectly, was always on time, listened well and never asked any questions.

That reminded him: he needed to give him a raise next month.

Gabriel opened his bedroom door and made his way to the circular staircase. Taking special care not to step in his new lambskin leather dress shoes wrong, he made his way down to the first floor of his ten-million-dollar mansion.

Yes, public service was worth it. So much for his dad's warning that it would get him either in the poorhouse or in the grave. Dumb businessman to the end – his father couldn't understand how to play.

Yeah, he showed that old fucker. He thought of that bastard every time he fucked, every time he finished, and every time he *finished*.

The front door with the automatic sensors beeped quietly as it opened.

Yes, it was good to be powerful.

Good to be king.

Thorn

Chateau l' Eau
Los Angeles, California

August 26, 2018
8:00 p.m.

Thorn forced another enthusiastic smile as the target droned on, interspersed with the occasional "accidental" grope.

He leaned in to whisper something in her ear, but it was just a ploy to crush her breasts against his chest. She smiled and muttered something encouraging.

Thorn, do your job. If you cannot distract him, you cannot complete the mission.

Thorn pushed the indifference and disgust into the back of her mind. With her hand, she tried to adjust her dress. It was too tight and constricting, cutting into her each time she moved. She needed to get him alone to a place without witnesses.

Unintentionally, her hand brushed the side of his leg. Taking that as an invitation, he set his hand on her knee. Without meaning to, she slid her knee away and brushed off his hand, only realizing what she did after his body tensed.

She put on her most flirtatious smile but remained silent.

"You're different from the rest," he whispered, eyes blazing. His face was flushed from the five cocktails he had chugged in succession. The hand resting on the back of the booth seat slid closer to her, and he ran a few strands of her hair through his fingers.

"How so?" Thorn needed to keep him talking. He was both smart and sexist, which presented an interesting conundrum. He would see through her playing dumb, but if she became too opinionated, he would doubt her femininity.

"Well," he mused, unaware of her internal conversation, "you're beautiful but not overly so."

She didn't react.

"What I mean is," He motioned with his right hand as his left touched her back in an effort to comfort her supposed hurt feelings. "I've had stunners and supermodels, and all of them have shown me more interest." *You mean, in exchange for favors.* "Yet you, you've made every effort not to touch me."

Thorn nodded, not sure what to say. She couldn't keep going at his pace. It was taking too long. She needed to close this mission, soon. But the thought of physical contact, even if it meant a fleeting touch, sent bile up her throat.

He waved the waiter over for a bottle of champagne. After the mousey man departed, he turned back to her. "But if you weren't interested, why did you agree to dinner? Why did you wear this dress? Why make it seem like a date?"

Because this is the only time you don't have your guards.

He set his chin between his thumb and forefinger and peered at a spot beyond the booth.

Get him angry. Make him chase you out of the restaurant. Head north towards the residential area.

Thorn picked up her glass of pinot grigio. "Why does it have to be straightforward? Can a woman not be both interested and hesitant, beautiful and reserved?"

"I never thought about that." He twisted the ring on his finger, unconsciously.

"If you enjoy easy, then we have nothing more to say here. My money is a reflection of me - if you can't play, then you can't win." She gathered her purse and set two hundred-dollar bills on the table. "That should cover my bill. Give me a call when you're ready."

She pushed back her chair. Just as she rose, his bulky stature rose on the other side, so suddenly he hit the table. "Wait."

She paused, but did not turn back around.

"I... May have been hasty..."

"You shower me with your praise, throw in a few insults to bring down my self-esteem, and all the while act like you don't know what you're doing. Please."

His face got even redder and he plopped down. "Wow... I never..."

She held up her index finger. "Call me when you're ready. Or not."

Her heart raced as she walked out of the restaurant. Thorn didn't even notice the stares of the other patrons, now on the mayor, who was following her.

She had barely gone around the corner when she felt his hand envelop hers. With a sharp twist of his wrist, he flipped her back around to face him. His face was red, breath uneven, chest heaving.

She recognized that look. She would recognize it anywhere.

"You slut. How dare you embarrass me back there."

Thorn wished she was a little more shocked that he could so easily switch personas, but then again, he was a psychopathic murderer. Her eyes flicked from his face to his hand, to the flickering light three hundred feet away, to the shadows that covered the corner of the building and their bodies, to the clenched fist on his other hand.

Thorn brought her eyes to his and gave him a smile. "Thanks for making this easy on me."

She twisted out of the hold on her wrist, elbowed his arm, earning a grunt from him, and pulled away to stand a few feet away from him. "I was betting that your pride wouldn't allow you to let me leave."

His forehead furrowed, eyes narrowing on her face. He held his arm gingerly at his side.

"You're going to regret that. Get off of your high horse, bitch. I didn't come out here to fuck your pretty brains out." His voice trembled with anger. Both of his hands turned into fists, and he shrugged out of his jacket, leaving it on a bench next to them.

Her smile didn't waver. "I didn't say you did."

She withdrew her knife from the center of her chest, from the sheath attached to the middle of her bra. She ripped the bottom part of the dress off to reveal tight pants underneath. "Although I *am* surprised that you're not as cautious about people finding out your secret hobby in the open street."

His eyes widened slightly as he paused. His eyes skimmed over her face, her smile, her clothing, the knife in her hand. "What-"

Before he finished his statement, she slammed the side of her palm on his neck, pushing his face into the brick wall. Before he could react and push back upright, she situated herself directly behind him, kneed him at the apex of his legs, and using her hands at the back of his neck, slammed his forehead into the wall. He fell on his back.

Crush him with your legs.

Thorn set her legs on either side of his torso and pushed on his shoulders back towards the ground so that his scrunched face was looking into the sky.

Leaning forward so that her face was a few inches from his, she tucked the knife back in her bra.

His gaze followed her hand, confused. Using a weapon for distraction didn't usually work on targets used to fighting. But Gabriel wasn't a fighter; he picked and murdered those significantly weaker.

And that was his weakness.

She leveraged up his torso upwards with her thighs so that there was enough space under him for her legs, and she slid her calves underneath his hefty bulk. The back of her thighs pressed against the biceps and forearms still grabbing onto his crotch.

And then she started to squeeze.

And squeeze.

Her hands pressed on his esophagus just hard enough to prevent him from screaming. As her legs cut off movement and oxygen, he began to feel his lungs, his heart, and his chest being crushed by the same legs that had caught his eye.

And squeeze.

She tightened her thigh muscles incrementally. Until the last breath left his body, eyes bulging out from their sockets, tongue rolling to the back of his throat, face turning a distinct shade of red and then blue and then purple.

Until she was sure that he wasn't going to get back up.

Well done. Time to report it in.

Thorn

Residential Area   August 26, 2018
Los Angeles, California   9:15 p.m.

Someone saw it. And they were following her.

Thorn knew she was being followed the moment she left the shadows behind the restaurant. Despite his agility, which was impressive for a civilian, Thorn knew where he was, how far away he was, and how long it would take to trap and kill him. But he hadn't made a move or seemed to be any threat, until now.

He was moving faster, almost speed-walking, towards her.

Don't attack. I don't sense ill will.

He was still a witness. She had to take care of it.

When he was four feet away, he rushed at her.

Don't attack. Thorn had to restrain herself from plunging the knife into the man's face.

The man grabbed onto her jacket with a shocking amount of strength. Thorn ripped her arm from his grasp. Everything in her demanded blood.

Calm. Thorn felt VOS regulate her emotions, bringing them down to a manageable level.

The man dropped to his knees and held onto her leg, lightly, rocking back and forth. Thorn looked around, making sure no one else was around to witness this murder.

Listen to him. He's no threat.

She found her hands in the vicinity of his neck. He was muttering something, jumbled words and phrases. She leaned down to hear what he was saying. He suddenly turned his face towards her, their noses mere inches apart.

"Thank you, thank you, thank you, thank you," came out in a garbled pattern.

He had tears streaming down his face, the liquid turning from clear to brown as it ran down his face. His hands were still touching her clothing, although not as tightly.

Thorn wasn't sure if this was a trick, but she's seen enough manipulators to determine that he wasn't one.

She couldn't help herself.

She knelt down next to him, her hands still within millimeter reach to her weapons. "Why are you thanking me?"

"You killed him. You killed him. You killed him," he kept saying the phrase over and over, swaying back and forth. There was no accusation in his words.

"Who are you talking about?" Thorn wasn't about to assume, even if she was entirely sure this was about Gabriel.

"That man, that dirty, evil killer. I saw you with him tonight." He swayed back and forth with tears running down his cheeks but a smile lighting up his face.

"I don't know what you're talking about." Damn meddlers.

"No, no you don't. And even if you did, I wouldn't tell anyone. That man deserved to die. Deserved to be stabbed in the face and neck and heart and arms and legs and eyes..." He made stabbing motions with his hand, as the other supported his weight on the ground.

"You shouldn't go around saying that. You'll get in trouble."

"I don't give a damn. He raped and murdered my wife, and from what I've heard, dozens of women. Because of his money and connections, nothing is ever done. The DA doesn't accept the case because there's no evidence. There's no one pursuing that case because most of the women are married, undocumented, or immigrants, so no one wants to step in to fight for you. We have no power. My wife believed in justice. But now she is dead."

Thorn didn't know whether to pat him on the shoulder, say something, or leave. So she just waited.

He looked up at her. "Thank you. Thank you for avenging my wife, my neighbors' wives, the daughters and mothers and sisters of those who are living ghosts... If you hadn't done it, I could never have lived with myself until I did."

"How did you know I was going to be there?"

"I didn't. Since the day I found my wife in the garbage, I've been waiting outside his window, following him, watching him, hoping to find anything to help me destroy him. I eat, drink, and sleep from a distance where I can see everything going on in that house, every woman he brings over, every friend he knows, every drink he has... When he leaves, I know where he is and when he's coming home. If only I had the arsenic my father gave me." After a brief reverie, he shook his head and nodded at her.

"I will take this secret to my grave. My wife is finally at peace. And I, along with her."

Come, time to go.

AEX requires no witnesses. Thorn thumbed her dagger. It would be quick.

You cannot. Don't worry – he won't be our issue.

Thorn pried herself from his grasp. His arms dropped limply in front of him.

The hand on the other side produced a gun and he lifted it to point at the side of his head.

Thorn turned away, having no desire to be a voyeur in the last moments of this man's life.

The shot echoed, a short eulogy for the death of a man who didn't seem to matter, and a metaphor for the impact of his death.

Let's go.

Alden
Introduction

Obituary
San Diego Journal
05-26-2008

Local hero and police chief Henry McKenna passed away this past Saturday. An arsonist set fire to his home while he and his seventeen-year-old son, Alden McKenna, were sleeping. Reports estimate the fire started at 2 a.m. on Saturday, May 24th. SDPD was alerted to the blaze by a resident and arrived on the scene at 3:30 a.m. The San Diego Fire Department put out the flames by 4 a.m.

Henry McKenna experienced severe third-degree burns and was rushed to the ER. He passed away at 7:43 a.m. His son, Alden, received burns on his face, neck and shoulders but doctors predict a full physical recovery. He is scheduled for surgery on May 29. Due to the trauma, he is suffering from short-term memory loss. The family requests privacy.

An unidentified charred body, what police believe to be the arsonist, was also found at the scene.

Alden

Police Department   September 1, 2018
Los Angeles, California   6:50 a.m.

Bulletproof vests and blue uniforms shifted restlessly in the small conference room. Half of the officers had coffee cups clutched in their hands. Others were munching on breakfast sandwiches. A few were chewing on protein bars.

This is weird.

Alden stepped into the room, wary. None of these police officers, from one of the most dangerous cities in America, had bags under their eyes or anxiety in their bodies.

These men were content.

This didn't exist except in utopian novels.

Alden stepped into the room and took a seat in the very back row. He felt a hand clap him on the shoulder.

Instinctively he reached for his weapon and turned to the assailant, ready. But he found himself looking into the startled, apologetic eyes of an older, salt-and-pepper haired, fatherly looking officer. The man raised his hands, palms forward.

"Hey, hey. We're all good here."

The young man relaxed, clipping the gun back into its holster.

"No need to do that! We're all friends here, aren't we?" A loud cheer went up in the room, and then all but a few went back to their original conversations. "I'm Ulrich. You're the new guy."

The young man narrowed his eyes at the other man. Surprisingly, the older man laughed and patted him on the shoulder.

"That wasn't meant as an insult, kid. We know this is year eight for you. But everyone new to L.A. is a rookie, even if they're twenty-eight like you, or fifty-one, like Charlie over there." A white-blonde man sitting in the second row waved back at them.

The rookie nodded slowly. "I'm Alden."

Ulrich stuck out his hand. "It's nice to meet you. I've heard a lot about what both you and your father have done, and let me tell you, I am impressed." The front door opened and a small, wiry woman walked to the table podium at the front of the room.

"Okay, ladies and gentlemen, let's get down to business."

All of the conversation in the room trickled down and then stopped.

"Before we get down to business, I'd like to welcome our newest member to the LAPD, Alden McKenna, who comes to us from Phoenix, and prior to that, Newark. He has a record of nine hundred and eighty arrests and an outstanding track record of dealing with criminals on the street, and lawyers and families at the station. Let's give him a warm welcome!" The thunderous wave of applause deafened him.

Thankfully, the chief moved along with the agenda.

"I assume you've all heard of Kamden's unfortunate demise. I needn't remind you that the family wants privacy at a time like this. Keep an eye on reporters and rabble-rousers. No matter what happens to members of our community, we need to give families what they need. And right now they need silence and time for mourning."

Heads bobbed up and down.

"Crime rates, especially in the downtown area, have been steadily going down. We had a 60% drop in drug and nonviolent crimes, and a 40% drop in violent offenses. Since this is the beginning of a new month, I'll be randomly assigning you different sectors of the city."

Cops were assigned to different areas? Familiarity with an area guaranteed precautions, knowledge of the community, and improved communication. How was switching that up in any way beneficial?

"The rest of you get to practice your office skills." A few guffaws.

The woman sitting next to him leaned over and whispered. "That's where you get to sit in the office, process complaints and walk-ins, and talk to family of those being held on bail."

Alden nodded his thanks. She smiled.

He turned back around to the front.

"...continue the good work!" As the chief began listing off pairs of officers and their assignments, the woman leaned over.

"I've heard a lot about you. Is it true that you busted an entire sect of Triads in Jersey?"

Alden shrugged. "I had a good partner. We followed our instincts."

"And the weapons bust?"

"We borrowed some identities. Got pretty lucky." He gave her a small lopsided smile.

She leaned closer. "What about those burn marks?"

Her hand reached over to touch his hand. He jerked his arm away.

"Those are from a past I'd rather forget."

Khara

Office of Kharavera Terraza   September 5, 2018
9th Floor, K-Pharma   4:15 p.m.

The day could not end soon enough.

The cleanup crew's reports on Anthony's missions was startling. And concerning.

Khara still had to go talk to Faye about agents in production for Germany. But first: a memo that Penny sent her labeled 'urgent'.

She clicked on the link, and the television screen on the far wall brightened. An older teenager stood in front of an old house covered in graffiti. His head and torso were covered by a faded blue hoodie, and he wore a pair of jeans that looked like it's never been washed.

"...I woke up in the middle of the night. Heard something in the front yard. I grabbed my bat and walked 'round back. So I could look out in the driveway. It was my brother."

He took a deep breath. "He committed suicide three years ago."

The camera turned to the reporter, who looked confused.

The boy shook his head. "He disappeared one night. We received pictures of him at the hospital after his suicide attempt and then they sent him directly to prison. We couldn't even see him."

He wrung his hands. "And then last night he was here. He was talking to himself, like "I'm home," "No, shut up, what are you doing? They are going to kill us," "I need to see my family," "No, you're just a weak punk who can't handle the real world," "axe isn't the real world," and..."

Upon hearing that mispronounced word, Khara picked up the phone and pressed one number. "I need both of you in my office, now."

"...called to him, and he turned to look at me. He recognized me. He even said my name. The next second he told me to stay away, that I was going to die if I came any closer."

"Did your brother have a mental illness?"

"NO! He wasn't crazy. Whatever happened to him in prison, that turned him crazy!"

Khara turned the sound off.

There was a quiet tap on the door and two men walked in, locking the door behind them. One was stocky and muscular with blue-black hair, and the other was a tall and lanky blonde, with a scar running vertically from his jaw to the base of his neck. They were wearing the black and blue suits of the cleanup teams.

Khara motioned towards the television. It was now showing the chief correspondent of the White House. "Did you hear about this?"

Their heads turned towards the screen simultaneously.

The tall one turned back. "Not until this moment. But we will get this resolved."

"You know why I can't involve another agent."

"Yes, ma'am."

"Bring him back alive." Her eyes turned back to the screen, where they were showing a picture of Trent from two years ago.

She nodded to them. They left as quickly and silently as they came.

Khara pressed a button on the keyboard. Within moments the screen changed from the news to the face of the Vice President.

"Is there a reason why Stephen failed to keep this Trent thing under wraps? Not only that, but somehow the White House is interested in this too."

"The White House is so bored they want their hands in everything. I have a meeting with Langston tomorrow. I'll try to find out as much as I can. As for the media, we can't have our hand in every cookie jar, for goodness sakes."

"Did you know that he was going to show this?"

Silence.

"Randolph…"

"No. But you don't need to overreact."

 "Overreact? Keeping news like this off the air is his job. I'm going to talk to him."

"You're making a big deal out of this. It's not like this is going to tie anything to anyone."

"Sure, you're not so concerned because it's only AEX's name out there now. But you know what people are capable of. Once something leaks, it's a matter of time before all involved parties are exposed."

"Are you threatening me?"

"I literally don't give a dog shit about you. Find out why the White House is involved, Randolph."

Another couple clicks on the keyboard, and the screen went dark.

Randolph
Introduction

Elegrant Penitentiary
Three Rivers, California   (Five years ago)

"Alright, Sherman, it's time." The guard rapped on the door to the cell. He was arms-length from the barred door. "State your last request."

"You know exactly what I want. It's been my request for the past twenty years."

The man in the small cell was shriveled, like a date left out to dry. His white hair stood up and across as if winds had blown through each strand. His hands, while large, was prune-like and calloused. "I want to watch the video."

Unlike federal or state prisons, the privately owned and operated Elegrant maximum security prison had many of its own rules. Instead of a last meal, prisoners were given a last request, and if reasonable, the warden would grant it.

Upon entry, microchips were inserted into each prisoner to induce electric shocks if they happened to get out of line. Security guards at Elegrant had to undergo a long selection and training process, usually involving a hand-to-hand and firearms exam.

While the location was not as isolated as other maximum security prisons, Elegrant boasts only one escape and zero rescue attempts, mostly due in part to the "blood contract."

Any attempt to escape could result in the immediate death of his or her closest family members. Neither the families nor the public knew about the contract but Elegrant drummed it into the minds of the prisoners. And since there was no visitation and life sentences, that information would never get out.

The sole inmate who had attempted escape… was captured and had to live knowing that he caused the "gas leak" killing his daughter and grandson.

The government didn't seem to know about the contract, and if they did, they turned a blind eye. After all, Elegrant was so effective that even individuals deemed the "most dangerous" and treasonous to the United States were kept there.

Sherman Duarte was the ex-Secretary of Defense. He was incarcerated after it was revealed that he condoned hundreds of under-wraps experiments at military sites. He had decided that any man who required military confinement was someone not worthy of human rights. They signed over their life as soon as they betrayed the United States or fought against it.

Certain activist groups found admissible evidence against him, and he later confessed in court. Sherman regretted nothing; he would rather rot in prison than be considered a coward for protecting his land. Prison was never a big deal to him; he went in knowing what he did was right and that he fought for what he believed in.

"Yeah, I figured. Apparently you've been asking for that since the very first day. Come on, then."

The guard unlocked the gate with a retinal scanner and key. The electronic gate memorized the turning motions and timing mechanics of his hand, so escape was almost impossible even if someone stole the eyes and keys.

As he clipped the handcuffs onto the old man, the guard gave him a measured look. "Seems like your family finally decided to put you behind them."

Most surprising was the "exit process" for Elegrant. Due to the political climate, maximum security prisons no longer executed criminals (except for the CIA, but no one knew what they did anyway) and even the ones who committed high crimes and treasons were given life sentences.

Criminals with shorter sentences were kept in "communes," where they worked throughout their imprisonment, balancing out the costs of keeping them housed and fed.

However, because Elegrant is private maximum security, they created a caveat to that rule. If families and legal guardians of those with multiple life sentences with no chance of parole signed away their life and agreed to complete secrecy, then they were allowed to put people to death.

The government, of course, does not "know" about this.

Unlike many whose families gave up on them, Sherman wasn't offended or even perturbed by the guard's comment. After all, he'd been waiting for this day.

"Yes, I no longer want my mistakes to hold my family back."

The guard nodded to himself. Old Sherman wasn't friendly, his crimes unforgivable, but at least he recognized when he was wrong.

The guard walked behind Sherman, hand on his arm, and led him to a small room with a laptop sitting on the desk. Cuffing him to the magnetic setup, he sat him down. After double-checking the restraints, he pressed play on the computer.

The screen was dark for a few seconds. As it brightened, it cut to a homemade video. An eight-year old boy with light brown hair and a huge smile was laughing. Behind him stood a woman, her golden hair sweeping in the breeze as she spun him on the merry-go-round.

The camera was turned to the recorder, a younger version of Sherman, with a square jaw, military haircut, and an Army uniform.

"That's my boy! Look at him go!" His voice was full of laughter.

The older, imprisoned Sherman smiled a little, but grew somber immediately after his face twisted in a way it was no longer used to.

"Daddy, daddy!" The boy pushed himself off the metal contraption. The video dropped and shook as the man embraced the boy, who had run into his arms.

"I'm so glad you're home, daddy! Mommy and I missed you!" The boy kept hugging, and the woman came up to join the embrace.

"I knew I'd find you both here."

"Sherm, I've missed you so much." The woman's voice was low and husky.

The video scratched. A different image appeared.

A funeral.

Sherman was in the foreground, his face marred with deep wrinkles and his hair white. Beside him stood his son, now as tall as his father, but gangly where Sherman was broad.

A woman walked up, weeping, and Sherman gave her a perfunctory hug. A couple came and went, and Sherman nodded his head. His son didn't seem to register the guests at all.

Suddenly, a hush fell over the crowd, as a man in a suit walked near the grave. He was followed by six men. Sherman's eyes narrowed but he didn't hesitate to reach out when the man stuck out his hand.

"Mr. President, you didn't have to."

The boy's face turned towards the newcomer, his face contorted in fury.

"Nonsense. I need to be where I can support my men and their families."

"Is that why you pardoned my mom's murderer?" The son's voice was low, almost a growl. The crowd, already quiet, went completely silent.

The President turned towards him. He moved to stand in front of the boy. "Randolph, the world is full of evil, some we can prevent, some we cannot. I'm so very sorry for your loss, and my part in it. I pardoned him for a crime he did not commit. I could never have predicted he would do this." The president set his hands on both of the boy's arms. "I'm very, truly sorry."

The boy shrugged out of his hold, and left the gathering, pushing aside several of the bodyguards.

The video fizzed again. This time it was a family meal, Sherman and Randolph sitting in a mostly empty room. As utensils scratched china plates, neither of them spoke.

"Congratulations on the priesthood," Sherman mused, looking at his son.

"Thanks." Randolph glanced at the camera. "Can we turn that off? I don't know why we are filming this."

"Your mother bought me that for our first anniversary." His voice cracked. "I want her to be here, as much as she can. It's a celebratory day after all."

They both continued eating. Neither of them looked at the camera.

"Randolph, I want you to know that I love you very much. No matter what you hear, make sure you always stay true to yourself. Do what is right for you, for this world we live in. Do not be swayed by others, because they will never know what you know."

Randolph looked at his father for a long time. "Yes, dad."

"Your mom would be very proud of you."

They both continued eating. The video faded to black.

Sherman felt liquid drip on his hands. Only then did he notice he'd been crying.

Yet even as tears rolled down his cheeks, he felt a lightness inside. He'd remained true to his word, his country, his wife, his son. He had no regrets, and now he's finally made peace with himself.

He raised his eyes and nodded to the guard stationed behind the one-way mirror.

The man strode back in, closed the laptop screen, and started unchaining him. They were silent as he led him from the room to a chamber at the end of the hallway.

As he entered the chamber, he saw Randolph, now the Vice President of the United States. His son, his legacy.

Sherman almost didn't recognize Randolph, after twenty years of only seeing him in his memories.

But he recognized the fire in those eyes.

Randolph gave him a short nod.

To those watching, it looked snobbish, almost disdainful. Exactly what he wanted it to look like. But Sherman knew.

Sherman knew that his son will make the tough choices the United States needed to become a better and stronger nation. A nation that required something more than ideals. More than laws.

And as he took his last breath, before the gas entered and spread throughout his body, he smiled, knowing that he had left this world in better hands.

It was worth it.

All of it.

Randolph

White House   September 10, 2018
Washington, D.C.   11:30 a.m.

This was unlike any other meeting he'd ever had with the President. The man never sought him out, and when he did, it was always quick and terse. Five to ten minutes of Randolph talking while Langston looked over papers.

The younger man had never sat down with Randolph in the Oval Office, nor had Randolph ever wanted to. But sitting on the couch, faced with the portraits of great men, he couldn't help but be in awe.

"Randolph, is there anything you need to tell me?"

The President of the United States, seated beside his Secretary of Defense, had his legs crossed and an arm draped on the backrest. However, the intensity of his eyes belied his physical signs of relaxation.

The six years have not been kind to him. Crow's feet at his temples, wide streaks of white in his hair, permanent hardening around his mouth. But those features only enhanced his distinguished look. One well-placed glance, and he could instill fear even in the most arrogant of world leaders.

Langston presented himself as an educated and passionate man, working for the people as more of a delegate than a trustee. He never liked galas, speeches, or awards, but he did enjoy a nice suit. And as he sat there in his pinstriped three piece (the jacket was tossed onto the armrest) with the top two buttons of the white shirt unbuttoned and cuffs loosened, Randolph realized that this was the most intimate conversation they've had.

"What do you mean?"

"Let me rephrase the question. Have you been keeping anything from me?"

Randolph knew this day was coming. Before he could say anything, though, he needed to see how much the President actually knew.

"If you're talking about my discussion with the Chinese about their invasion of India-"

"Something within our borders. Takes advantage of the public's trust of the system, while condoning acts of violence against our own citizens."

"I handled that police brutality case without you because I thought we both agreed that immediate removal of those officers was the best course of action."

Best course of action, my ass. They're all just foolish bleeding hearts.

Langston rubbed the bridge of his nose. "Hannah..." He turned to the Secretary of Defense.

Randolph had never interacted with her, but always admired her work ethic. She observed everything her troops did, interacted directly with the soldiers on the ground, and could play the politics of D.C. like it was a Monopoly game. The fact that she was young and Muslim, taking over the position right after the twenty-year conflict in the Middle East, was direct evidence of her capabilities.

"Any action against residents and citizens of the United States is considered hostile and treasonous. A leader who directly participates in and encourages this type of activity would be considered a traitor. You know what that means." Her dark brown eyes flashed.

"What are you getting at?" Randolph splayed his hands outward, in a submissive gesture. "I'm sorry if I've caused trouble with the civil rights groups. I thought we agreed on the police issue."

"Randolph..."

The president hesitated and glanced at Hannah, who nodded almost imperceptibly.

"We've come into contact with someone who claims there is a company with government sanction producing mentally unstable assassins."

Faking a laugh, the Vice President looked both of them in the eye. "What?"

Apparently his ruse was convincing enough, because Hannah shrugged. "We thought the same thing you did. But the source was extremely detailed, and despite his... instability, he sounded like he was telling the truth."

"Now when you say source..."

Hannah leaned in. "An armed gunman ambushed the President and took him hostage. During this time, the man informed Langston that such an organization existed with the support of higher ups in the administration."

"Does this have something to do with the fellow who attacked his brother?"

"It was him."

So that's why the White House was involved. "There was nothing about you on the news."

"We can't trust anybody. The less people know, the less panic we cause." *Yeah, preaching to the choir.* "We also don't want other nations hearing about this."

Randolph sat back on the couch, trying to keep a mental transcript of the meeting. "So who was this guy? Are you sure he wasn't just crazy?"

"That's the strange part." Langston reentered the conversation, having made a decision that he could talk to a treason suspect. "He *was* crazy. During the talk, let's call it, he kept talking to himself. Had a full-on conversation! Then he sat down, stared me straight in the eye, and told me about this program that took people off the street, gave them hallucinations, and made them kill for the government."

Not exactly accurate, but Randolph wasn't about to correct him. "What is this so-called group called?"

"He was going to tell me, but the voice convinced him not to. It was so strange, like it prevented him from doing so."

The President rubbed the back of his neck. "I wouldn't be taking him so seriously if he didn't name off certain individuals who had died or went missing in subsequent order, and described every detail, to the location, time of death and manner of death."

"That's fishy. Where did he get that information?"

"He said he killed all of them."

The silence that hung in the room was thick. "How many?"

"Seven. And he said that there were many others like him out there."

"What about evidence? There's got to be something."

"He said the group removed all of the bodies." Langston looked at his hands. "A part of me suspects that my son, Hunter... if this organization exists, maybe his death was connected to it."

Randolph rubbed his forehead, in both real and feigned worry. "Where is this man now? We should question him for more information, and see what the hell is going on."

Hannah nodded. "We would if we knew where he was."

"You mean the fifteen Secret Service members couldn't take him down? Why are we even paying them?" *At least subjects retain their abilities even after going against code.*

"Calm down, Randolph. Don't blame them." The President seemed very taken with his passionate outburst.

Randolph smirked inwardly. *Sometimes I amaze myself.*

Langston sighed. "He was a shadow. We never saw it coming. He did everything without hurting anyone, and then he left. No threats, no bullets."

"What is being done? Have you told anyone else?"

Hannah shook her head. "You were our first suspect." She didn't look sheepish or try to explain.

"Any particular reason why?"

The President spread his hands in front of him. "Come on, you know why. We were never friends to begin with so you wouldn't have run this by me. You enjoy the concept of absolute power, and your sense of right and wrong lay somewhere between Hitler and Mao. But... you don't care for the scientific community, and this has the stench of research all over it."

The Vice President nodded. "I respect that, and the fact that you came to me personally." He leaned forward, legs on knees, over the table. "Let me help you."

"Hm."

"You say we were never friends. That's true. But that doesn't mean I don't want what's best for this country."

The President opened his mouth and nodded. "I'll think about it."

Khara

Research Laboratory   September 11, 2018
11th floor, K-Pharma   5:05 p.m.

"We cannot produce that many in such limited time." Dr. Faye took the papers from Khara's outstretched hand. "You know what happened when we rushed the batch after Thorn."

Lynette Faye was young, the youngest on the team, but she was ambitious. After earning a triple bachelor's degree and an M.D. from Harvard, she specialized in both psychiatry and neurosurgery. Despite her drive, hospitals and research facilities were hesitant to hire her, due to her tactless communication style and inability to follow orders.

In that time, Khara found her.

Khara appreciated the woman's candor because she knew that Lynette had results in mind. "I know. But we don't have a choice. Germany wants them within the year."

Lynette shook her head. "Push the date back."

"I've already delayed her."

"Ten agents within one year? We've been doing this for four years and only have six viable agents. What were you thinking selling her what we can't make?"

She was the only one allowed to talk to Khara like that.

Still, it stung.

"That's too slow. We should be picking up speed at this point in our research."

The doctor, dressed in casual jeans and a t-shirt, set the papers on the desk. "Should, yes. But we're not there yet. We can't hurry this process." She paused, and then added, "No matter how much money we need from investors."

"I know you want each agent to be exactly right, perfectly researched and thought out. But we need results, any results."

"You want quantity, but you need quality. These are humans. Their brains are permanently altered by the treatment. If we don't use the right subjects, use too much or too little VOS treatment, not give the subconscious enough time to bond... you're letting potential threats out onto the street and within AEX."

"I know you're right. But we have to find some way." Khara tapped the papers. "This is what I'm looking at. I just want you to understand."

Picking up the papers from the desk, Lynette's eyes skimmed over them, pausing briefly on the end cells of the numbers document. The minutes that passed were silent.

She turned it back to the first page, and handed it to Khara. "I see."

"It's not that I don't want us to perfect it. It's that we have to keep AEX alive for long enough to do so. Research on the failures is not giving us any results, and keeping them is expensive."

"What is Randolph doing? Isn't he supposed to help fund us?" The arch in Lynette's tone understated the disdain she had for the man.

"He's doing what he can."

"Is he now."

"Preservation."

Lynette arched an eyebrow. "For himself."

Khara smiled at the woman, whose brown hair and hazel eyes stood out from her tanned, angular face. "You know how politicians are. As parties shift, alliances dissolve, and the state of the nation is like it is now, he has very few strings he can pull. But we need him. For now."

Lynette sighed. "We'll try to speed up research."

Khara took out a picture of Thorn from the files. In the picture, Thorn was asleep on a hospital bed, her skin a dull white and eyes clenched shut. "We need more of her."

The doctor gave her a long look. "You know that she can't be replicated."

"Not yet."

"There are too many extraneous variables that determine the VOS, the subject's reaction." She crossed her arms. "The fact that we created a fully bonded VOS is a miracle all in itself."

"I didn't think you believed in luck, Lyn."

"I don't. But the fact is, we didn't know what we were doing, and Thorn's VOS just happened to be effective, without the side effects that Val, Anthony, or Aaron experienced."

"But it's possible."

"Yes. Just don't expect it to happen."

Thorn

Thorn's Apartment
Los Angeles, California

September 16, 2018
7:30 p.m.

Thorn stood in the doorway of her one-bedroom apartment and scanned the room.

Nothing appeared disturbed. It was pitch black and silent, exactly what she needed after that mission. As her eyes did another once-over, she sniffed the air.

No strange scents.

If someone had been here, her heightened senses would know and VOS would alert her. She stepped inside the living room and shut the door gently, engaged the deadbolts, and leaned her back against the wood.

It was a pain to always be on edge even as she approached her home, but she trusted her body more than any security system or machine. You can bypass code, but not VOS.

Rolling her shoulders, she took off her pleated black leather jacket and hung it on the coat rack next to the door. At the same time, she tilted her heels up, and pulled down her left boot with her right foot, and then vice versa. Kicking them off, she moved into the living room and turned on the light to its dimmest setting.

The walls were painted a purple-beige, warmed even more by the yellow lightbulbs. Burgundy rugs sat on waxed wooden floors. Mahogany tables, frames, and stands stood around the room, carrying their burdens of flowers, pictures, mirrors, and keys.

Releasing her hair from its tight bun, Thorn rubbed her fingers along her scalp.

She checked her hips for the Glocks and bra for the knives. Satisfied that they were where she expected, she walked to the kitchen and took a bowl of leftover pasta from the fridge.

A memory appeared in her mind. Her mother leaving, the house silent, and her being alone, heating up leftovers.

Don't go down that route, Thorn.

I haven't heard from you in a while.

You didn't seem to need me. You know I only come when there's a relapse in the air, or you need me to get you out of something.

I thought the treatments were wearing off.

You know that's not the case. I'm always going to be here.

But what am I doing here? What's my reason? The woman I just killed… she had a life purpose, something she was striving for, something she thought was right. But I… I just exist.

You're here because the world needs you. You need to eliminate the drain on society and heal whoever and whatever we have left.

But why?

Because you don't have anything else to care about.

What do you mean?

The voice was quiet.

Anthony
Inside his mind

The same nightmare, after every mission. Every single mission.

Anthony was sitting in a room filled with skulls. Animal skulls and human skulls, alien skulls and bones of all kinds. Skulls with soulless eyes and grinning teeth. Thousands on thousands of pale bone under the red light of a blood moon.

There was no earth and no sky, just endless death surrounded by red.

Something held him to the chair, preventing him from running. He almost didn't turn to see what it was, but he did. Because in his nightmares, he always did.

It was the chest of a dead body, its ribs so crushed that he was actually sitting on mashed organs.

He always told himself he wasn't scared, never had been. It was uncomfortable, sure, like staying awake for a surgery, but never frightening.

Making sure his hands didn't touch anything, Anthony turned back around. The skulls, the blood, the bones, they were all still there. But now, directly in front of him, only a few feet away, was a large primate skull, its jaw opening and closing while maintaining a smile.

Its mouth opened.

"This is what you wished for, Anthony. Endless death so you can feel. To avenge your emptiness, your sorrow, you turned everything in you to rage." It turned its massive head side to side, keeping its black eyes on Anthony.

Anthony had been through this so many times that he was only slightly paralyzed. "I never asked for this."

He wasn't sure why he couldn't move or why his mouth was dry, because the skulls never touched or hurt him. They surrounded him, tried to terrorize him, but none had ever taken any steps towards harming him. They seemed content just to torture him from afar.

The skull stared at him, the jaw rotating in its hinge. "How does it feel to be dead inside?"

The waves climbed higher with each crest, until they were at the height of Anthony's knees. Skulls crashed against each other, bones flowed out into the tide. The wind picked up, spreading the stink of dead flesh and fermenting blood.

Anthony still couldn't move his body. He could feel the coldness and at the same time, warmness, of the red liquid, felt it seep into his pants, his shoes, his skin.

He watched as the blood surrounded him, absorbed him.

The skull moved to the side as two figures emerged from the hellish swirl. Two familiar body shapes, smiles, eyes, hair color, standing in the center of the lake. Momentary silence. Until the figures started screaming, writhing as flesh melted off their bodies and fell into the lake, until all that was left were two skulls and skeletons, standing in the water, reaching out for Anthony, slowly making their way towards him.

He shied away.

"You can pretend like we're not here, but we are. Just waiting, for the day you let us out."

Thorn

Thorn's Apartment
Los Angeles, California

September 17, 2018
2:23 a.m.

Thorn... This is no longer who you are...

Thorn found herself tangled in her bedsheets, sweat on her brow, entire body shaking.

Her left hand had torn the pillow, and her right hand was wrapped around her knife. The blade was already released.

You are no longer that girl.

Fold that knife and put it back on the nightstand.

Thorn, half asleep, paused for a second before doing what VOS said.

You are safe. Take a deep breath and slowly exhale.

Thorn took the breath, and released it. She took another deep breath.

The voice soothed her. If a person, someone else, had told her what to do, she would never have listened.

But VOS... She trusted her completely.

That is because I am you, and you are me.

Khara

Office of Stephen Libbe
23rd Floor, Libbe Media
Downtown Los Angeles

September 18, 2018
8:00 a.m.

"When we first started the program, it had vision. It was a plan to clean our cities, our states, our great nation, all without risking the lives of innocents."

The elderly man sitting with his hands perched on his knees stared intently at Khara, sitting across from him. They were separated by a gilded mahogany desk.

"It was simple. We take those who have died once and come back," he motioned with both hands to the pile of papers on the left, "and make them our weapons."

Khara, dressed in an elegant red dress suit, arched an eyebrow at the old man.

"You agreed with AEX's mission. You agreed to keep the public in the dark. You even called it a hush-hush revolution."

"And it has turned into something monstrous, something gross, unholy!" The man, agitated, stood up and slammed his hands on the table. "You have to correct this.... This thing! Or else-"

"Sit your ass down." Khara's voice didn't rise above a whisper, but the threat behind it was clear.

His eyes flicked to the door, but even knowing that the guards were outside was less comforting than he'd thought. Her violet, almost-metallic eyes followed his every move, but she didn't budge.

"Don't talk to me that way."

"Don't scream at me like a child." She knotted her fingers in front of her crossed legs. "I am doing what I need to do. AEX is progressing as we predicted it would. What is there to correct?"

He frantically motioned around. "As we predicted? We didn't imagine creating psychopaths who murdered for fun. We didn't imagine the President breathing down our necks, and don't forget his cabinet. How were we to imagine the cost-"

"You believed in this."

He looked down.

"I'm concerned that this path is diverting from the one we initially planned. I'm scared that we will be thrown into a pit so dark the CIA won't be able to find us. I'm scared that we are creating more monsters than we are taking out. I'm scared that we bit off more than we can chew, and that this whole program will become uncontrollable." His voice faded. "I have things to lose. My family, my life."

"Did your vision for the future die so easily?" She sat straighter, leaned forward. "Don't you want your life to have purpose?"

The man seemed to shrink in size. "M-my children are my purpose. I want them to live long and well. Libbe Media, that is my legacy for them."

"And they will have it. The children is who we're fighting for. We're eliminating those who would cause harm to them. Criminals. We're taking them down."

"By creating worse ones."

"Right now it seems like that. But it's part of the process. You don't hear about the successes from our education subset."

The conversation lulled from there. He no longer seemed as impassioned to leave the project, but he also wasn't convinced.

As Khara left that office, she knew he was going to be a problem, now or later.

Stephen, who owns and manages the largest media conglomerate, who has single-handedly redirected the attention of the American public, was getting cold feet.

The back of her eyes ached.

Her fingers typed in Randolph's number. He was going to have to put a stop to this.

Alden

Police Department
Los Angeles, California

September 20, 2018
5:30 p.m.

Two men had disappeared the past month: the corrupt mayor who ruled the underworld of Los Angeles, and the prime minister of France, a man he suspected was more than just his gaudy rings and blinding smile. They both vanished without a trace.

Two powerful and well-guarded men, and no one knows what happened.

Gabriel Frank had been at dinner with a woman at Chateau l' Eau. Witnesses say she provoked him and he stormed out. His car was still on the street, but there was no sign of him anywhere. He had not gone home, to work, to his kids' camp, or his wife's fundraiser. Even his weasel-like butler seemed genuinely surprised and distraught.

Pierre Jutney, the diplomat, had been taken from his office by a blond man, in broad daylight. No trace of either one of them.

Alden was mostly shocked by the nonchalance of the police department. Everyone was acting like nothing big happened, that two famous men in this town had not just up and disappeared, or been done in by foul play.

He didn't know these people in uniform. They weren't even acting like law enforcement.

But it wasn't just the police. The media seemed to have completely ignored the deaths as well. Not one news channel covered the disappearances, and despite questions from concerned citizens, the news had brushed off the two cases. These were big-name men, men whose deaths should be reported, looked into, questioned.

His eyes landed on the police chief, who was standing at the podium at the front of the room, laughing with Ulrich.

He raised his hand. Her attention was drawn to him immediately. "Alden?"

"What about the two disappearances?" The room became silent.

Her smile wavered a little. "There are higher authorities dealing with that right now. We've been told to stay out of their way."

"But we should be doing something. This is our jurisdiction."

She put a hand up. "I understand your frustration, Alden. While that may be true in other precincts, we have different rules to play by. Our Investigations team is working with the FBI to provide as much information and assistance as needed and requested."

Before Alden could respond with another question, the chief moved on to cover the next order of business. She needed uniforms to be a heavy presence at the annual black pride parade, their organizers and leaders already receiving threats.

"Alden, since you're so eager to get some real police work done, you're going to be monitoring the corner of Ridge and Main. I need to go down there and establish relationships with the business owners and familiarize yourself with the people." She rattled off a few more names along with the locations of where they are responsible for, but his brain didn't process any of that.

Something was very wrong here.

Khara

Office of Kharavera Terraza
9th Floor, K-Pharma

September 27, 2018
3:48 p.m.

Khara lifted Trent's head up with her index finger. "He put up a fight, did he?" There were multiple facial bruises, a swollen left eye, and cuts on his lips. "You subdued him with the injection."

"Yes, ma'am." The two men stood on either side of the agent, holding him up for her inspection. "We also took care of the tracks he left and the people he spoke to."

"No witnesses."

The man with the scar nodded.

"Did he say anything?

"As far as we can tell, his code still prevents him from speaking about AEX. But…" They looked at each other. "We can't talk any sense into him."

Trent groaned. His eyelids fluttered open.

Within a few seconds of realizing where he was, he began struggling. Both men holding him grunted with the effort of keeping his arms restrained.

"Hello, Trent."

He clenched his teeth together.

"Do you know what you have done?"

He looked to the left, refusing to meet her eyes.

She grabbed his chin in her hand and forced it forward.

"I gave you a second chance, giving you VOS when you would have died. And this is how you repay me?"

He still refused to speak.

"That's fine. Where you're going, you don't need to speak." She motioned towards the door with her hand. "Take him to Dr. Stewart's lab. Tell him we have our first VOS removal subject."

They turned to leave. Before they were completely out the door, Khara knocked on her table. "Whatever you do, don't let him escape."

Khara

Office of Kharavera Terraza   September 27, 2018
9th Floor, K-Pharma   4:00 p.m.

Nikolas Pretorius, prime minister of South Africa, father to two dead children and husband to a ghost of a woman, took Khara's hand. He was self-conscious about his wrinkled suit, but she didn't even give his jacket a glance.

"Nikolas, welcome. I hope your flight wasn't too long."

An older woman with her pale blond hair in a bun came in, her hands holding a tray with water, tea, and finger cakes.

The man enveloped her hands in his. "Khara, wonderful to meet you."

Khara motioned for him to sit, and only did so after he did.

"Tea?" She motioned towards the serving tray.

"Yes, please." As she set about pouring the tea, he interlaced his fingers in front of him on the desk. "You must keep this meeting between us. As the leader of my country, I cannot permit my soldiers, my people, to realize I am cavorting with an enemy."

She set the tea in front of him and nodded. "You can be assured that I take confidentiality very seriously." She took a bite of cake.

He sipped his tea. "How exactly is your business alive? America is quite stringent towards domestic violations." He poked at the cake she put on his plate.

She smiled at him again. "We have our ways."

He gave a knowing nod. "I see." He leaned back in his chair, giving her more space. "So, AEX. I've read the documents you sent me. A voice of the subconscious... How do you make sure it's just one?"

"We use monotone treatments so it's less likely that multiple sounds will corrupt the subconscious." She took another bite of the cake. "However, very rarely does psychotechnology work the exact way we want, and it does happen that more than one develop. That's why we have layers of emergency measures.

"Currently we are working on a VOS removal procedure. It might be used as an eraser, of sorts, for the voice."

His discomfort was evident on his face. Khara stopped talking and waited for him to speak.

"The reason I am here," he sighed, "is that I am not strong enough to protect my family and my loved ones from the evil in this world. My daughters were brutally murdered because my enemies wanted to send me a message. My wife was savagely raped but kept alive to show me their power."

His voice slowly faded. He cleared his throat.

"I am in a precarious position, not just with our neighboring countries, but also within my own. How will I know these agents won't run back here? Or that their past will catch up to them?"

"Our priority when creating agents is to protect AEX and our partners. Like we said before, the VOS has a code of regulations it operates by. Recruits cannot speak of this or approach anyone from their past, or else their VOS will break down, rendering them catatonic and ineffective.

"Since complete memory erasure is dangerous, we cannot just remove memories permanently. That would destroy the person. We use memory blocking and emotional triggering, to prevent memories from affecting their work."

Khara set down her plate. "We mostly remember the feelings associated with people and events, not the actual objects. If we remove that feeling, that memory is dampened and they will not recall it voluntarily. Memory blocking does that by taking away the emotional connection."

Penny appeared in the doorway. Khara waved her away.

"The triggers serve as a backup. On the off chance that a memory is revived, we attach strong negative emotions to those people and events. When they think of it, the agents feel fear, revulsion, anger, or nausea. That prevents them from further discovery.

"Luckily, most recruits form that invisible memory block quickly, almost automatically, and very rarely are the triggers even necessary."

"The whole memory part of it is so uncertain. And not reassuring at all."

"That's a risk you're going to have to take, if you believe this is your only choice to stay in power."

The sudden chill in her tone startled Nikolas. "So what *do* you know for certain?"

"That they will change the world."

Anthony

Fisherman's Wharf
San Francisco, CA

September 28, 2018
9:25 a.m.

Anthony saw that head again, the skull from his nightmares. But this time it was in the middle of San Francisco. This was reality.

And yet it was here.

The skull had followed him from the moment he'd left Rachel Ubezi. VOS made sure he knew exactly where it was, even though he couldn't see it.

It had followed him through Los Angeles. It appeared at his destination when he drove. It trailed a distance behind him when he walked.

Initially, Anthony didn't feel the urge to run. The skull would disappear, just like it did in his dreams. It hadn't even spoken.

But now Anthony was beginning to feel more and more claustrophobic, knowing, realizing, that the head wasn't going anywhere.

He couldn't tell AEX about it. They would retreat him, or worse, deactivate his active agent status. Then he could never carry out missions again. The only joy he had in life.

So he cut off all communication with AEX.

The skull stared at him, smiling, silent, hovering three feet above the ground. Those eyes...

Anthony shivered.

He pulled up his collar and readjusted his hoodie, hoping that it was just a fluke of his imagination that the skull got closer to him with each passing day.

But it wasn't imagined. It followed him, now just five car-lengths away. Still a distance, but its progression was unnerving.

He felt a chill crawl up his spine. No, he couldn't feel. That was just his imagination.

Where was VOS? It disappeared yesterday, after telling him to stay in public. For what reason he didn't know.

Anthony felt... alone. Scared.

VOS was the only thing that understood him, more than AEX, more than himself. It told him things, whispered secrets into his ears.

It ached for killing, just like him, and it was going to take him to a new level of being, a new kind of living. With the voice, he no longer felt trapped. He became powerful, stronger than he could have ever imagined.

It had guided him here, far away from Los Angeles, where he wouldn't draw attention to AEX, but still hadn't said anything about the skull. He needed its help to figure out what was happening. Why the memories he thought he forgot were becoming more vivid, why his nightmares were becoming reality, why he could *feel* things.

VOS had to appear.

It had to come out and tell him to do something, anything to rid his mind of this thing. He wasn't even sure if he was hallucinating anymore. Even people walking in the street avoided it, walked around it.

They were. They didn't look at it, but they walked around it. That meant it was real. How did it get out into the real world?

"I... told you... we existed..."

For the first time since it started following him a month ago, it spoke.

Anthony's hand grasped the knife in his pocket, seeking comfort in its familiarity.

VOS, where are you?

"I'm afraid he's gone. From here on out, it'll just be me and you." The voice was getting stronger, clearer.

"VOS! Come out!" Calling to it inside his head wasn't working. Maybe out loud it will. "Come out! What are you doing?"

A few passersby looked at him. Before he could meet their eyes, they ducked their heads and walked away. Some began typing on their phones.

The skull didn't respond.

He spun around in a circle. He stared intently at a woman nearby talking on the phone.

"...he just suddenly appeared at my computer, like-"

Anthony ran at the woman and jerked the phone out of her hand. She took one look at him and sprinted towards the other side of the wharf.

"VOS? Is that you? Come back." He couldn't hear what the other person on the line was saying, but if it wasn't VOS, it doesn't matter.

He needed it. It was the only thing that could help him now.

"He told me this was going to happen." The Skull neared him, now two-and-a-half feet away. "He needs you to prove that you really want him back."

"How do I do that? How do I prove I'm worthy?"

"You need to kill ten people right now."

A part of Anthony still doubted. "How does killing ten people-"

"Either do it or don't. Either way I'll be here. But there's only one way you're going to get your precious VOS back."

Anthony looked around him, at the couples, families, and groups of tourists huddled together. People drinking coffee, people eating, people laughing and singing.

His hand tightened around the blade in his pocket. His other hand touched the gun. But he didn't want to use it.

"This will bring VOS back?"

The skull didn't speak.

Anthony couldn't bear another moment without it. It was his friend, his partner, his lover. It was everything to him.

He picked his targets as his eyes searched the crowd.

One. Her blood was watery.

Two. A little meaty.

Three. Fingers were sticky from a lollipop.

Four.

The police arrived.

Five. Six. They were a little more difficult with their vests and guns. But no matter.

Seven. The skull was still silent.

Eight.

Nine. His arm was getting tired.

Ten. No, that one didn't count. She was too old.

Eleven.

There. That has to have fulfilled VOS's requirement.

"Good. Now you must run."

"What?"

"In serving your VOS, you have gone against AEX. To achieve your full potential, you must stay out of their reach."

"What should I do?"

"Run. Hide. Become one with your prey."

Yes… that sounds like something VOS would say.

The skull hovered over the fifth body, a lurid grin on its face.

Thorn

Baldwin Village   September 28, 2018
Los Angeles, California   11:00 p.m.

"Man, that ass was somethin' else!"

Two men sauntered down the street, their button-down shirts open at the neck, fitted jeans sitting low on their hips. They didn't attempt to hide their faces because they didn't need to - everyone recognized and feared them. Even the cops stayed out of this neighborhood.

"Shit, she could really put it down." The one many know as Clamps swiveled his hips in a grinding motion as his tongue lolled out of his mouth and touched his bottom lip in a suggestive manner. "Guess Ol' Nate really couldn't handle it." He smiled lewdly.

Blade cracked a smile, but his eyes kept scanning their surroundings. "That serves him right – thinks he's better than us now."

"His wife doesn't think so!" The two men stared at each other for a few moments, and then whooped with laughter.

Thorn watched and waited. *Well, they definitely didn't make it hard to find them.*

Twisted Saints, an informally-run drug and human trafficking ring, the most powerful and only one not controlled by a traditional gang. Their two-man leadership style made them quick, and their reputation made them ruthless.

Thorn stayed with the shadows, keeping pace with the two men, who were now discussing the positions they managed to get the man's wife in, and what they were going to do to her and her daughter next time.

No matter how much Thorn dealt with lowest of the low, she never ceased to be surprised by their disregard for human life.

But then again, who was she to judge?

You are doing this for a greater good, Thorn. It's always harder for the right person to do the right thing than for the wrong person to do the wrong thing.

"Yeah, yeah." She muttered only as far as her ears could hear, but the distaste was only half-hearted.

She jogged lightly on the balls of her feet through the grass of a neighbor's front yard, and leaped over a short fern hedge.

Thorn arrived at the junction of two streets to stand behind the wall of a garage with a full view of the concrete sidewalk path.

This was the spot.

She had to finish the job quick and clean. The neighborhood was so densely packed that if even one person saw, the entire block would be in an uproar. Every single one of them would be a witness.

And AEX code for witnesses was no witnesses.

Wait just beyond the edge of the lights. Go for Clamps first because he's the louder of the two. Blade will attempt to shoot you, but make sure you get to him before he draws. You don't need the attention of a gunshot.

VOS continued to talk to her, but Thorn knew that it was mostly for her comfort. When the time comes, VOS would take over her body.

Her body started moving as soon as they stepped into the shadows.

Thorn
Memory

Office of Duke Marcus
9th Floor, K-Pharma   (One year ago)

"Amazing. The VOS has gone silent, you remember nothing, and yet you are processing at perfect capacity." He put the different colored balls, cards, and notepad back into his bag.

"I don't understand what that has to do with anything."

"We're still not sure the amount of control your VOS has over you and your thoughts. So we want to test memory, analysis, and calculations. Do you remember how you did it?"

Thorn paused to think. "No."

"We're going to see if it's your conscious mind that's blocking out the memories or if your VOS is actually preventing your conscious brain from getting to it."

Thorn leaned back on the sofa.

"You're going to be listening to a chant. It's designed to help you regain control over your VOS. A repellent, in a way."

Van, her handler, came in and put headphones on her head. The chant was calming, and she felt herself becoming pleasantly distracted.

Dr. Marcus held a knife in front of her face, close enough that her nose tingled. He pulled it back so her eyes could focus on it. He began to swing it in front of her, holding it by a blue ribbon.

"You will watch the sharp edge of the blade, keep watching," he murmured, his voice inflecting higher with each syllable. "Watch and notice the smoothness sliding through air like butter..."

* * * * * *

Thorn opened her eyes.

Dr. Marcus and Van were leaning over her.

The chanting was gone from her headphones.

Dr. Marcus touched a hand to her forehead.

"Her vitals are fine."

"Did something happen?" Thorn pushed herself up, feeling strangely weak.

"Or not happen."

"What do you mean?"

Van removed the headphones from her head. "Can you tell me what you remember?"

"I remember you waving that knife telling me something about gliding through air like butter... And then the two of you standing over me."

Thorn brushed the back of her right hand against her forehead. It was dry, but her mouth tasted coppery.

They glanced at each other. Van was the first one to lean back and sat himself down on the chair across from the sofa. "You don't remember."

"No."

They were both sitting now, elbows resting on knees. Dr. Marcus rubbed his chin. "You didn't respond at all."

"What do you mean?"

"I asked questions, about the mission, about you, about the VOS, about thoughts running through your head. You didn't respond to any of them."

"I don't-"

"Dr. Marcus programmed the VOS to respond to the questions when paired with the chant."

"So, how could I not respond?"

"That's what we're trying to figure out." Van looked at the headphones. "Either the chant hypnosis didn't work, or your VOS controls a lot more of your brain than we thought."

"Is that good or bad?" Thorn unconsciously touched her palm to the side of her head. "I feel like I'm myself."

"We're not sure."

Khara

Office of Kharavera Terraza   September 29, 2018
9th Floor, K-Pharma   9:15 a.m.

Khara sat behind the antique desk in her executive leather chair, and tapped her pen on the back of her hand as she leaned towards Eve.

The white-haired older woman looked worried. "There are signs that Thorn's VOS is changing. Evolving."

"That's not necessarily bad news."

This might be the break we need for the research department.

Khara rotated her chair around the other side. "Is she still controllable?"

"Yes, but-"

"Make sure she keeps her appointments. Keep me updated on each one."

Eve didn't say anything.

Khara put her pen on the desk. "We're in new territory here, Eve. When I say each one, I mean everything. Got it?"

Eve gave two sharp nods. "If-"

The cellphone sitting on the notepad rang. Khara looked at the caller ID and ignored the call. She directed her attention back to Eve. "Go on."

"If her VOS can evolve, that could mean the code we implanted is self-aware, that her subconscious could actually reject certain-"

"I think we're getting ahead of ourselves." *Lynette needs to hear about this.* "We don't know what her VOS is capable of, if it's actually evolving, or if it's just a different version of the codes we've created."

If we could change Thorn's environment… see if her VOS could adjust to a completely different life. That would prove psychoevolution possible.

Khara could barely keep the excitement from appearing on her face as she read her notes on the computer. T*he possibilities…*

"I suggest we take her off of missions for a while." Eve crossed her legs. "We have to see what she's capable of, or if we can keep her as an active agent."

Khara shook her head. "We can't take her off missions. She's too valuable. Her expertise is beyond any of the others, aside from Anthony, who's got his own problems."

"Speaking of Anthony, where has he been?"

"That mission with the French diplomat seemed to crack his psyche more than usual. His VOS reacted very poorly. Lynette thinks his disposal method brought up memories of his past."

"That's not good."

"His handler is trying to locate him so we can put him under retreatment. But as of now, he seems to have isolated himself."

"He's dangerous. Should we let him be alone?"

"I'm sending a team to retrieve him."

"Did he break a code?"

"It doesn't seem so."

They both paused.

Eve uncrossed her legs. "What if we reduce the number of missions we send Thorn on, give her a lighter role, something that we need done, but usually by another subsect of agents?"

"Well, we need her specifically for the high-kill missions. She's just too good." Khara flipped through her notebook. "But we can give her a more immersive role, more real-life, to balance out her VOS."

"How?"

"I have a perfect position in mind. One of the agents in E-Division is going to need time off for the baby. Thorn will take over for her."

"Baby?"

Khara smiled. "Remember, agents who kill are only a small portion of our research. We're trying to examine the influence of VOS in all different lifestyles."

"But…"

"I want to see how her VOS would deal in a completely new environment. We need to get her in an emotional and high-stress situation with human interaction, where she's forced to change from her current detached and high violence situation with almost no human interaction."

"Why?"

"To create an environment where the VOS can actually become something other than what we created. We don't want her VOS to only perfect itself into a killing monster."

Randolph

Lobby
4th Floor, Libbe Media
Downtown Los Angeles

October 1, 2018
2:45 p.m.

"Mr. Vice President, Mr. Libbe really appreciated the time you took to grace our station with your presence. He said he would be remiss if he did not invite you to his office for a drink."

Randolph checked his watch. Finally. The man did not keep to a timely schedule. "Where is he?"

"On the twenty-third floor. I will escort you."

Randolph rose from his seat. His bodyguards followed them.

The boy pressed the up button for the elevators. "There's a," he looked around, "rumor going around."

Randolph nodded for him to continue.

"There's a rumor that some government official is trying to create robots to thin out the human race." The intern glanced at Randolph's face, hoping to find confirmation.

Randolph gave a measured laugh. "Robots? Everyone's making robots nowadays."

"No, like experiments to make them, to kill humans. I overheard the secretaries talk about how Mr. Libbe was part of this huge conspiracy to keep the corporation from being found out, and that he has close ties to some politician."

Randolph's head was reeling, but nothing showed on his face. That damn loose-lipped idiot. "That's interesting. Did they mention who was involved?"

The boy waited for a second longer, and shrugged. "No, just someone powerful. Like you."

Randolph was thankful that the elevator came when it did.

They entered the elevator, and the intern pressed the button for the twenty-third floor.

"That is a strange rumor, indeed. Thank you for bringing it to my attention."

The intern lifted his shoulders to his ears and dropped them, embarrassed. "Please don't tell Mr. Libbe. He hates it when we ask questions. But I'm really curious."

"Maybe there is some truth to it." Randolph patted his shoulder. "I won't tell him a thing."

And that was perhaps the most honest thing he's said all day.

Randolph

Office of Stephen Libbe
23rd Floor, Libbe Media
Downtown Los Angeles

October 1, 2018
3:30 p.m.

The man behind the desk was not the man Randolph knew. The man he had joked, drank, and debated with, the man whose fury had driven Randolph himself, was gone, leaving behind an empty shell.

Stephen was wizened and withered. His hair was white and brittle, his face pale, his posture... It was as if the past year had sucked the life out of him.

Randolph burst in, expecting the ruddy-faced, blustering man who had so eagerly supported the idea of AEX, declaring his loyalty come hell or high water. The warrior willing to hide the truth so America could be great once more.

Randolph practiced what he was going to say, multiple times. His lecture was to be angry and loud and demanding, instilling fear and loyalty in this man.

But the frail old man behind the desk shocked Randolph. Stephen was already wrecked by fear, with nothing else to gain. Or lose.

The practiced words eager to jump off his tongue were thrown back into his throat.

The media mogul looked up at him. "Randolph." He tiredly lifted his hand. "Sit, please."

Randolph sat. "Stephen, what is going on?"

Stephen sighed. "I'm sorry, Randy." He rubbed a shrunken hand across his face, the loose skin sliding on his visible bones. "I can't do this anymore."

Randolph had to search for the words. "Do what? The AEX project? Stephen, you can't just-"

"Please. Let me explain." He leaned back in his chair. "When we started the project, I was extremely naive. I believed that the world deserved a better quality of life, better quality of citizens, than what we had. I felt that we needed to be the ones to do something, because the government wouldn't. To a certain degree, that is still true." He swallowed. "But all this lying, this nonchalant attitude towards human life, people who've suffered already, this experimentation…"

"You knew about all of this going in."

He nodded. "I did. At least I thought I did. I didn't realize the impact that media, or more like, the lack thereof, on these incidents, would affect me so much. No matter how much we want to change the world, we still live in a democracy.

"I don't like what we've done, Randolph. We lied to the people, we lied to the President, we lied to ourselves." He shook his head. "I can't."

Randolph wanted to yell at the man who was bringing his and his father's dreams to a screeching halt. But he couldn't garner the energy to even move his arms from the chair.

Randolph slammed a fist against the arm of the chair. "You are going to keep it going. You are going to because you cannot throw us under the bus."

Stephen put his hands up, palms forward. "No, you are right. Just because I've become weak doesn't mean I should destroy everything we've worked for. But I also couldn't let loyalty destroy my conscience."

Randolph stilled. "Stephen."

Silence.

"What did you do?"

"Nothing."

"Stephen, don't goddamn lie to me."

"For a man of God, you sure take his name lightly."

The silence in the room spread so thick their breathing sounded as loud as bellows.

"I'm not going to come right out and tell the public that we created assassins with induced schizrenia to kill criminals. There would be a revolution. Our heads would be rolling across the Senate floor."

"Fine. So then. What. Did. You. Do."

Randolph's blood pounded in his ears, and his eyes were so focused on Stephen that everything else seemed to fade from sight. "Did you leak it?"

"No... not in the way you think."

"What?"

"The people will understand. Some people. It's-"

"THE PEOPLE WILL UNDERSTAND?" Randolph never shouted, never raised his voice. It was action, not volume, that inspired fear. But he was so close to strangling the man in front of him, so close, he could feel his pulse in his fingers. "How can you be so stupid?" His fingernails crushed the seams of the chair.

"You give them too little credit-"

"After all this time as a billionaire, media owner, politician in the shadows... After all of that, you can still say that the people will understand? That all of them will see the truth behind our project? That our assassins actually do benefit society? That widespread knowledge will bring, what, peace? Unity?"

He snarled upon seeing the look on the man's face. "Pardon. Forgiveness. That is why you are doing this. Why you are selling out everything we've worked so hard for."

Stephen narrowed his eyes. "I have the most to lose! You didn't put your life and your wealth on the line! I'm not going to reveal everything! Just-"

"Enough? Was that what you were going to say?"

"It's... it'll be fine..."

"Stephen, we've been friends for... how long? Eight years?"

"Yes." The older man looked confused.

"Based on that, I'll forgive this transgression. If you take care of the leak. But. If this gets out in public at all. I hope you're ready."

The look in his eyes speared Stephen to the seat.

Sputtering, Stephen pointed around the room. "You can't do anything to me."

Randolph stood up, narrowed eyes cutting through the man's soft words. "I am not doing anything. You will be paying for your sins soon enough." He turned on his heel and stormed out, waving roughly at his three bodyguards to come and follow him.

As he got in the elevator, he dialed Khara's number.

"Yeah, we have a problem."

Khara

Observation Room   October 4, 2018
10th Floor, K-Pharma   10:45 p.m.

Khara stood behind the one-way mirror, leaning her forehead against her arm on the glass. She was dressed in a long black armless gown and comfortable black flats, a loose gold bangle dangling on her wrist.

Her eyes drifted back to the treatment room. Two doctors and a nurse were standing to the right as a third doctor attended to the man sitting precariously on the hospital bed in the middle of the room.

The black-haired, blue-eyed man was in his mid- to late-twenties, with narrow shoulders and long deer-like legs. He had healed cuts and burns along his arms and legs, and dark bags under his eyes. Tremors ran throughout his thin frame. Even as he sat still, his limbs couldn't stop moving.

The doctor lifted his head to shine a light into his left eye. The man's head continued to bob, and his shoulders slouched. The doctor spoke aloud during the examination, as the nurse wrote down his observations.

He lifted the man's left arm, dropped it down, lifted the right arm, and then swung it in a circle. As soon as he let go, the leg resumed its violent shaking.

Even through the glass Khara could hear the sound of metal clanging with each shake of his leg.

The door behind her slid open. She turned to see Randolph breeze through, having enough sense to leave his guard dogs outside of the door. He was in such a rush that he shut the door before Eli could even give her his traditional nasty look.

"What's going on?"

"This is the fourth recruit that has shown symptoms of rapid-onset Parkinson's after treatment. There's only six more to go before we have to start at zero again."

Her fingers were silently tapping on the windowsill, a nervous tic left over from her childhood. She didn't even notice it until he raised his eyebrows at her.

He turned his attention back to the room. "Do they know why this is happening?"

"Their brains adjusted to the elevated levels of dopamine we injected into the gray matter. The "normal" amount to maintain their neurostability is no longer enough, and now they can't rid them of the shakiness, slow movement, and stiffness."

He released his breath. "What does that mean?"

Khara pressed her lips together. "They're useless. They can't stand independently or hold a cup without dropping it, and are in no way, shape, or form going to be able to carry out missions."

Outside AEX

White House   October 5, 2018
Washington, D.C.   10:20 a.m.

The door thudded against the wall as Langston barged into the room. "Randolph, we have a tip as to where-"

Randolph's secretary recovered from the door slam. "Mr. President."

He smiled at her. "When the Vice President comes back from lunch, can you tell him to see me?"

"He's not at lunch, sir."

"Well, then, where is he?"

"I'm not sure, sir. He took off two days ago. Said it was an emergency."

"Did he say where he was going?"

Langston set his hands on his hips.

"Do you have his schedule?"

"He did not, sir. But I have his schedule here."

She handed him a paper booklet.

"Do you mind if I take it?"

"No, sir. I have another copy."

As he left the room, he motioned for his assistant.

"I need you to locate Randolph. He's like a ghost around here. I can't have my VP running around the country when I need him here."

Alden

Linger Motel   October 8, 2018
Downtown Los Angeles   7:30 a.m.

God, the stench.

Alden had been to his fair share of horrifying crime scenes. But this one... He definitely hadn't expected this.

It was overpowering. The pungent flavor of blood, acidic sharpness of vomit, and reek of vodka punched through his nose and eyes.

Alden stabilized himself against the wall, and took the next five seconds to compose himself before stepping foot in the door.

The landlord followed closely behind him, occasionally peering over his shoulder. The middle-aged Middle Eastern man had owned this motel for several decades, seen fires, shootings, murders, and political scandals, but never any suicides.

This was a lovers' hotel, after all. Who would come here to kill themselves?

When Alden arrived and met with Ahmed, the soft-spoken man told him that the neighbors reported the smell. The girl who rented it had paid him a thousand for two nights, which now was nothing compared to his losses, having had to relocate several couples and one party.

Ahmed had pounded on the door and yelled angrily, but there was no answer. He unlocked the door and was looking around the room when he saw her reflection in the mirror. That was when he turned and called the police.

Ahmed was smart enough to bring a rag doused in fragrance, holding it up to his nose.

Keeping his hand on the firearm on his hip, Alden edged closer to the door. He motioned for the older man to go around him and unlock the door. Ahmed slid the key into both locks, and turned in opposite directions. The door clicked, Ahmed withdrew the keys, and went to stand behind Alden.

Alden unholstered his standard issue, and lifted it up in front of him as his boot tip touched the door, slowly pushing it open. The gun barrel was the first in the door, and then his arms, and then his body and face...

But the scent...

His stomach heaved, and he was glad he didn't eat or drink anything that morning. He had a strong feeling that if he had, he'd be retching in the hallway, like Ahmed.

The room was clean, with no sign of forced entry or conflict.

In fact, everything was too clean. Nothing was out of place. Even the bed was still made.

He did a thorough scan of the living room and bedroom, trying to breathe from his mouth. He took in a deep one before stepping in view of the bathroom, its door wide open.

He first saw the thin layer of pink water on the tiles.

"Oh..."

He lowered his gun a few inches, holding it with one hand while the other wiped his forehead. His boot-clad feet stood at the edge of the tinted water. After checking the bathroom and making sure there was no one else, he took a step into the water. It squeaked and the water splashed.

He didn't look down. His attention was caught by the figure soaking in a tub so full that red water was spilling out of the sides. Sitting by the tub was a half-empty handle of vodka, soaked in black vomit, and a small bottle of pills, tipped over into the murky goo.

The woman in the tub with her back to the door had twisted her light brown-blond hair on top of her head. Tendrils were plastered to the side of her face, which was as pale as the marble washed walls.

"Ma'am?"

No answer. Protocol called for it, but he hadn't expected her to respond. He holstered his gun at the same time his right hand came out and touched the base of her jaw.

There was a pulse. Turning to Ahmed, he yelled,

"She's still alive!"

Was that even possible?

The smell was from late last night, which meant she had to have been bleeding out for the past eight hours. Combine that with the vodka and the pills... She should be completely cold. And dead.

"I'll call the hotline!"

"Wait." Alden held up his hand. "I'll take her. It'll be quicker than waiting."

Ahmed had an unsure look on his face. "But... suicide hotline is mandatory."

"If they give you trouble, just tell them I told you not to call."

Ahmed still had the look on his face, but he made no effort to get his phone.

Alden motioned towards the girl. "Do you have robes? To cover her up when I take her out."

Ahmed rummaged through the closet and took a robe from its hanger. He walked to the edge of the bathroom but made sure his shoes did not touch the liquid on the bathroom floor. He set the robe on top of the toilet.

Alden unstopped the tub. "Do you have any mats I can use to dry my boots on?"

Ahmed shook his head and pointed towards the towels hanging on the wall. "I'm going to have to destroy everything in the bathroom anyway, just use those towels." He wandered back into the bedroom, pressing his hand to his face. "More costs! And I just redid the living room in 203C..." His muttering faded away as he moved farther and farther from the bathroom.

Alden glanced at the towel rack, on top of which perched two fluffy pearl-white towels. He tried ignoring the squelching as he retrieved the towels.

The bathtub gurgled as the last of the mixture went down the drain. Alden used one of the towels to wipe down as much of her body as he could, and lifted her onto the toilet.

She was light. Too light for her frame.

He covered her body with the robe, and knotted the fabric at the front. Alden threw both of the towels on the inclined doorstep.

Picking her up in his arms, he made his way to the door, watching as the boots left bloody prints and black grime on the towels.

AEX

Cappuccino Café   October 8, 2018
Santa Monica, California   11:20 a.m.

Aaron flicked the pen between his fingers, looking at the ten words written on the page.

LOWER CRIME RATES AND HIGHER HAPPINESS RATINGS SUGGEST THAT AMERICANS

It's been 3 hours since he picked up the pen and notepad.

He ripped his gaze from the handle of the pen and stared at his phone, expecting her to call at any second. And his answer would still be the same.

Nope, not done.

It was an easy mission. A slow one. But the position as a journalist was only to keep an eye on the media and report suspicions back to Khara. There was no killing involved, even though he was specifically trained for elimination.

He hated writing.

Did they not read his psych evaluation? He had to 'work' with his hands.

It's your duty. You wouldn't be here otherwise.

He fully immersed himself in the reporting world, so deep that sometimes he forgot his original purpose. He created a second life that he often mistook for his first. A stable job, a beautiful girlfriend, an intimate group of friends...

But no matter how much fun he had, how invested he was, the voice never allowed him to forget. Reminding him why he was there, to whom did he owe his life, and that he really wasn't ready for a normal life.

His eyes glanced around the café as he picked up the steaming cup of green tea and sipped. His eyes fell back to the words on the notepad, wishing that the thin blue lines on the page could give him inspiration for the article he was (supposed to be) writing.

His cell phone rang, jarring him out of his wishful thinking. Without looking at the caller ID - no one else called him on this phone anyway - he clicked it open.

"No, I'm not done yet."

Khara's voice was unamused. "How is your VOS allowing this lackluster performance?"

"Because I hate this."

"That does not answer my question."

He tapped the pen against the paper, a little more aggressively than was necessary. "Give me something hands-on. You know I'm good."

He had asked, pleaded, begged for something else, something that involved him breaking some bones. Khara hadn't even let up once. Something about him being too valuable to risk it.

"That's actually why I'm calling you today."

"Not to goad me?" Aaron began to sketch an outline of a gun on the notepad.

"Don't push your luck. I didn't think I needed to."

"Fine. I'm terrible at my job. Happy?"

"You will be. Happy, that is. You're already terrible at your job."

"Har, har."

"We have a leak."

Finally. His VOS sounded more relieved than he did. "What do you want me to do?"

"Stephen Libbe leaked to someone. Someone he trusts. I need you to find out who the reporter is. And eliminate him."

"Stephen? Really?"

"Yeah. He surprised us too."

"And there's only one?"

"As far as we know. But there might be more. And if there are…" She trailed off. He knew exactly what she meant.

"I have authority to terminate?"

"Yes. This is of utmost importance."

Yessss. He nodded his head slightly before realizing she couldn't see him through the phone. "Got it."

He set the phone back on the desk and stared at the words some more.

Nope.

Guess this was his lucky day. No more writing.

Thorn

Vaughn High School   October 10, 2018
Los Angeles, California   2:10 p.m.

"Miiiiiiiiiiss, why are we still doing work?" The whine came from the back of the room. "Why can't we just watch a movie and relax?"

The curly-haired girl huffed and laid her head on her crossed arms. The worksheet remained empty on the desk next to her.

Thorn's eyes wandered to the clock, and ignored the girl's whine.

How was substituting at a high school supposed to help my missions?

She looked at the notes their teacher left for her. "Before our next class, I want you to finish this chapter and have your discussion questions ready."

Do other teachers sound as confident when they have no idea what's going on?

"The 20 questions on the back, or just the discussion questions?" A bright-eyed black girl was avidly writing the directions onto her notebook, and flipped the page when she reached the bottom. Her energetic demeanor contrasted with the disinterested mood of the rest of the class.

"Just the discussion questions."

The bell rang. Papers were shoved into folders, pens and pencils dropped into pouches, and the mad dash for the door began.

Thorn gathered up the papers on the front desk and sat back down on her chair. The scholar sitting at the front of the class packing up, and with one backpack strap on her shoulder, walked over to the desk and handed her some papers.

"Ms. V, here is my work for the next week. Sorry I won't be in class, but I'm going to visit some colleges I'm thinking of attending."

"Alie, don't even worry about it." Taking the papers, she set it into a basket and sat down in her chair. "Have fun on the trip."

"Thanks, Ms. V. You're the best!"

As soon as the door closed behind the girl, Thorn heaved a huge sigh, and leaned back. She glanced around the room, beautifully decorated by a woman whose upcoming birth was the only barrier between her and the kids she so clearly adored. Everything in the room was cut, stapled, and placed just right, each inch of the classroom covered with college memorabilia, posters, and assignments.

Thorn wasn't sure why Khara gave her this mission. How was teaching the Constitution to almost-adults in any way helping the world be rid of criminals? Did they have an undercover assignment? Was she supposed to get close to the other teachers? Administration? She still had no definitive answer.

She rubbed her temples. There it was, the constant headache, her only friend.

How could they trust her to enrich young minds? She could barely keep herself afloat.

Interacting with people, with children, was exhausting. Combined with her headaches and the constant nightmares that plagued her dreams, it was becoming hard to distinguish pretend from reality.

At least on actual missions the headaches went away and she could forget about everything around her, if only briefly.

You may not feel it, but you are growing. Developing your relationship skills.

Her left leg vibrated. Alertness immediately replaced exhaustion, and she sat up.

"How's it coming along?" The voice was deep, and ever so familiar.

Pressing the phone to her ear, Thorn reached into the side drawer which contained a safe. She input a ten-digit key code and the door to the safe unlocked with a soft click.

Touching her guns made her feel infinitely better.

"Great."

"It can't be that bad."

Thorn was silent for a full ten seconds. "Why am I on this job, Van?" She took a notepad from the interior of the safe, as well as a black engraved pen, and set them both on her desk. "I could be doing anything else, and it'd have a bigger impact on crime."

Van's voice hesitated on the other line. "I don't know, Thorn. I know as much about this mission as I've told you."

Thorn sighed. "Can you give me any more details? Why this school? Why this subject? Do I keep doing this until the end of the school year? I really can't, Van. I might actually kill some of them."

She heard laughter on the other end. "Your VOS won't let you do that."

"What, kill children?"

"No, kill someone who's not a target."

They both fell silent.

"Could you find out more for me?"

A mock hurt sound came from the other end of the line. "You flatter me so. As if they trust me that much."

Her hand unconsciously rubbed her left arm. "Please just try. Do you at least know how long I'll be here?"

"No, sorry. I was just told to give you the ML for this and check in with you every day."

"That's it?

"I'm telling you all I know."

Thorn rolled her shoulders against the back of the chair and glanced at the clock. "Yeah. Okay. I have to get some work done, then."

"Look, Thorn, I'll try to ask and see. But you know how it is. And I can't guarantee you any answers."

"Thanks, Van."

AEX

Security Room   October 10, 2018
10th Floor, K-Pharma   2:30 p.m.

"I need Thorn to pick up a subject from Central Hospital in a few days."

Van turned from his computer.

"As the CEO, I'm surprised you attend check ins."

"I like to keep track of my agents. They are my business, after all."

"You hardly did for missions before this. But you've been here every day since she started this new one."

Khara ignored him. "Subject attempted suicide a few days ago, and instead of calling in on the hotline, some hotshot officer took her to the hospital. Pickup teams would attract too much attention. Thorn needs to get her out quietly."

He unhooked the page that said "Mission Logistics" and wrote in her instructions.

"Do you have any more details about this particular mission that Thorn could know? That I could know?"

"No. What is on the ML is on the ML."

"This is out of both of our depths. She has no idea what to do."

Khara gave him a look. "She knows far more about it than you think. VOS will guide her. After all, what do you think the pre-mission treatment was for?"

"I see."

"Think about it this way: when it was a normal targeted mission, do we tell you the reasoning?"

Van thought about it. "Not always."

She nodded. "This mission is no different."

He shrugged and turned back to the screen, following the dot indicating Thorn's position.

Van took a sip of the coffee on his desk and grimaced at the cold bitterness. When he turned back to make a comment about Thorn's route of choice, Khara was gone.

Khara

Observation Room   October 15, 2018
10th Floor, K-Pharma   2:45 p.m.

"Streye, we have a problem with Anthony."

He cracked his neck. "Anthony is just a little weird, you know how kids are."

Streye remembered the last time he saw the boy. Mangy hair, baby face, quick with his hands. A loner. Even during observation, he didn't speak to anyone unless he was required to.

Streye appreciated that. He didn't like people either. In fact, he wasn't sure who in AEX actually did.

Khara gave him a disparaging look. "When have I ever been spooked by a little weirdness?" She looked around again. "No. He's been murdering civilians."

That got Streye's attention. "What happened?"

She took out a picture from her coat pocket.

"This is what I mean." Khara pointed to the picture. "He never called the cleanup crew. He doesn't respond to phone calls or alerts in his system. We don't know what his VOS is doing." She pursed her lips. "It took them more than three hours to get the whole place

150

spotless."

"I thought you handled this after the wharf incident."

"We sent a team. But... they were unsuccessful."

"They brought in Trent."

"Trent's VOS was malfunctioning, which was why they found enough clues to track him. Anthony's is fully active and making sure he covers his tracks."

He looked at her and then back at the picture. "This is…"

He trailed off, not sure of even what to say.

"It's torture."

Streye gave the picture back to her. "What does this mean?"

"Not sure. But whatever it is, we need to contain him. We can't have him creating more issues for us right now."

"You need another VOS to track him down."

She nodded.

"Do you know his location?"

"He was in San Francisco about a week ago. We haven't been able to track his more recent movements."

"Are his targets related?"

"No. None of his recent kills have been actual missions. After the wharf, he's been going after low-level criminals. And civilians."

"Damn it all." Streye sighed. "This is not good."

"As you said, he's always been a weird kid. No one knew when the weirdness ended and the craziness started."

Thorn

Vaughn High School   October 16, 2018
Los Angeles, California   2:50 p.m.

Thorn looked at the stack of papers sitting in the box, and slid the one at the top towards her.

What are we doing?

You're a teacher, aren't you? We grade papers.

"The nation is no longer divided by class or race or color - we have evolved beyond that. Now we are divided by religion and non-religion." Thorn tapped her red pen against the side of the paper, not surprised that Alie wrote the essay.

"The establishment clause in the first Amendment is still valid, untouched by a neutral House. It is unspoken that non-religious folks have the same inherent rights as that of church-goers, but state governments have begun limiting access to certain public areas."

Thorn let VOS take over. She circled the word "folks" and wrote "citizens?".

"Our President is non-religious, representing the slowly disappearing minority, but they are either unaware or uncertain of these new laws. Churches, select cemetaries, parks, restaurants... It is beginning to look a lot like the segramation of the blacks and other minorites."

Thorn corrected the misspellings.

"I do not understand how it is possible to maintain separation of church and state when our own government is divided by religion and non-religion." Thorn crossed out the first person reference and wrote in the margin that Alie should not deviate from third person.

"I come from a religious family," Thorn had to circle the "I," "so it is considered rude of me to bring up this topic. Treating people differently no matter their set of beliefs is a wrongness of the Equal Protection Clause." Thorn circled wrongness and wrote in "violation." She drew an arrow from the comment about the third person, down to this section.

Alie did not make many references in her paper, which was required for an A, but she made excellent arguments.

She wrote "B+, add in references and turn back in," and set it aside.

The ringing of her cell phone interrupted her train of thought.

"I need you to go check on a potential recruit at Central Hospital."

"Why not send a pickup team?"

"Would draw too much attention."

"I-"

"Assigned mission."

Thorn sighed and hung up, unlocking the safe under her desk.

Khara

Office of Kharavera Terraza
9th Floor, K-Pharma

October 16, 2018
3:00 p.m.

"Are you sure Thorn is cut out for this? She's a killer. We molded her VOS to be that. Why would we want her to change? We're just asking for trouble to happen."

"Eve, our research needs to take more risks. We don't have the time or the resources to wait around for another agent's VOS. We need to know how her VOS is evolving and if we can harness that."

"It-"

"I know you're concerned. But AEX needs this research. If we don't get more effective agents in production, then everything here is wasted. The recruits, the research, the agents, the money... you remember why we're doing this, right?"

Eve sighed. "Yeah. To create a better, safer world through psychotechnology."

Khara gave her one short nod. "I understand your relationship is closest to the agents, but they're nothing without more. They're just test subjects."

"Means to an end."

"Don't sound so bitter. All of them would be dead without us in the first place."

Khara took a bite out of her cucumber sandwich. She chewed it for a few moments before setting her gaze back on Eve. "Has she spoken of any differences in her VOS? What can you tell from her behavior?"

Eve glanced at the notes on her lap. "She's in exactly the high-stress situation you wanted to put her in. She doesn't know what's going on, but is doing what the instructions and her VOS is telling her."

"What about her VOS? Has it… changed?"

"She hasn't noticed, aside from helping her get through the day, with what to do and what to say."

"Brain scans?"

"Scans show activated prefrontal areas, and bloodwork indicates high dopamine levels in the bonding areas of the brain."

"Interesting. Do you think she's bonding more?"

"Since we didn't do a base level test, I can't be sure."

"Has she said anything about the children?"

"Aside from the added stress of dealing with teens, her trauma during her teenage years is probably what's causing the most difficulty."

Eve paused. "Why? Is there someone she should be paying attention to?"

"No." Khara took another bite of her sandwich. "Curious, that's all."

Thorn

Intensive Care Unit
Central Hospital
Los Angeles, California

October 16, 2018
4:00 p.m.

Thorn stepped into the hospital, her uncertainty about this pickup increasing with each step.

AEX has a plan. Don't overthink. A wave of calm spread across her brain.

The automatic doors slid shut behind her.

Left.

Her feet took her to a corner room in the unit, a 20x20 room divided into six sections by poles and linens.

She immediately spotted the girl, who looked nothing like the reference photo. No smile on her face as she slept, no devilish sparkle in her eyes, no flowing curly hair.

Thorn called Van back, tapping her earring phone. "I'm here. What do you want me to do?"

"How does she look?"

"Tubes sticking in and out of her body, eyes covered by gauze, half of her head wrapped and lying on a donut pillow. Barely breathing, just how AEX likes their recruits."

"I am aware of her vitals. I need your subjective opinion on her progress."

"Progress?" She took a glance at the girl's battered face.

"She's improved 100% since two days ago."

"Well," her eyes scanned the parts of the girl's face and shoulders that were visible. "She doesn't seem to have sustained too much damage. Her breathing is regular, twitching fingers means connected nerves and sensitivity. Nothing some time won't improve."

"Will she be VOS-ready in three weeks?"

"No." She felt VOS. *Bodily stress increased the chances that VOS treatment will bond effectively. The subconscious becomes more susceptible to external pressures during physical pain.* "Probably."

"What does your VOS say? We need her extra senses."

"That's what she said."

"Will she be able to move?"

"I'm not a doctor. But I think so." As Thorn ended her sentence, she saw the girl's eyelids flutter.

"I need you to bring her back to AEX."

"She's stuck on a hospital bed. Every little thing could jeopardize her life."

"That's why this is your mission. Your VOS can help you figure it out. Bring her in by 4 p.m. tomorrow."

She hung up the phone.

We're going to need a gurney.

Alden

Lobby
Central Hospital
Los Angeles, California

October 18, 2018
1:00 p.m.

"Good afternoon. Last week I brought in a young woman to the emergency room. I'm checking in to see how she's doing."

The male nurse spared him a quick glance. "Day and time."

"October eighth. I dropped her off at about eight, eight-fifteen."

Keyboard keys clacked. "Hmm, says here she's been discharged."

"When?"

"Doesn't say."

"Do you know where she went?"

The man offered him an exasperated look.

"Officer…" He checked Alden's badge. "McKenna. Taxpayer money should go to people who want to be saved, not those who try to end their lives. When she left, she did the rest of the patients here a favor."

Alden

Palazzo Pizzeria   October 18, 2018
Los Angeles, California   12:15 p.m.

Alden parked his car by the curb next to his favorite pizza place. But he had no stomach for food, not after what the nurse said.

As he got out of his car, a reflection caught his eye.

A woman, walking on the other side of the street, favoring her left arm. Her face was half covered by the hoodie, but from what he could see of her face, she was young, in her twenties or thirties.

Her eyes were in shadow, but her entire body was focused on the sidewalk. Too focused.

She felt… off.

Alden turned to get back into the car, but stopped. It would be too suspicious, following a girl with a sedan. At least he was in plain clothes.

As the woman passed him on the other side of the street, their eyes met.

He shivered.

Empty.

Without hurrying, he made his way across the street.

He kept his eyes on her back, memorizing her features, her stride.

Not once did she look directly back at him. She didn't make any move to run or escape. Her pace only matched his, keeping the same distance between them.

The woman turned into a closed alleyway. If she was trying to escape, she wasn't doing a very good job of it. He was about to –

She wasn't there.

He stood, mouth slightly agape, at the mouth of the alley. There were no outlets and no doors, except for where he was standing.

Yet there was no sign of her.

He looked to the left: dark brown stained bricks and black from ash and soot.

He looked up: it was a blue-gray sky framed by the walls that shot up 9 feet. Definitely not jumping distance.

He looked to the right: more stained bricks and some broken down cardboard boxes, no doors.

He looked down: no sewer grates.

What the hell?

It was as if she melted into thin air.

Alden

Police Department   October 18, 2018
Los Angeles, California   2:30 p.m.

As soon as Alden got back to the station, he started typing.

He entered the description of the girl from the motel.

Nothing.

He replaced adjectives with synonyms.

Still nothing.

He leaned back in his chair and rubbed his face.

Why did she leave? Did someone take her?

An image of the mystery woman he followed flashed before his eyes.

Were the two related? No, they couldn't be.

He leaned forward and typed her description into the search bar.

Nothing.

No, that would be too easy.

He was going to have to start from the basics. Crime statistics. The connection has to be hiding in plain sight.

Missing persons reports, deaths. 82 missing persons in the past year. Homicide deaths: 238. Too many to filter out.

What about accidental death? Did they have a category for that?

No, they don't.

His eyes fell on the newspaper clipping on his desk. The story of the fire next to a picture of Henry McKenna. It reminded him of his past, of what he was capable of.

"I won't let you down. I'll find out what's going on."

Alden's hand rubbed the center of his chest. The tattoo throbbed.

He was going to get to the bottom of this. Even if this was only a hunch, there was no solid evidence to go on, and he had limited access to people and records.

Something was wrong, and this was the place to start.

The Chief definitely wouldn't be on his side for this. Neither would the other officers. He asked too many questions. They no longer trusted him.

It didn't matter to Alden that they didn't like him. He was no stranger to that. But their wariness cost him the relationships he needed to get things done.

The high profile deaths, the media blackout, the woman. They were all connected. Somehow.

They had to be.

From his chats with Ulrich, he knew that crime went down dramatically in the past two years. That's where he'll start. All deaths, missing persons, or homicides.

He'll look up news and reports for all cases from the past two years. Something will add up.

Nothing leaves no trail.

He narrowed his search filters to encompass what he wanted.

1,526 results.

His mouse hovered over the first link. But just before Alden clicked, he stopped himself.

He couldn't use his actual login credentials.

The department was watching him too closely. He had already overstepped his boundaries, when he questioned the chief about the disappearance of those two men.

He couldn't risk getting caught working on something unassigned.

He needed to create alternating logins.

A new ghost identity that used other officers' information in rotation.

Outside AEX

Cafeteria   October 23, 2018
Elegrant Penitentiary   1:10 p.m.

Every eye in the cafeteria was focused on the two flat-screen
televisions. Prisoners were sitting down, standing up, leaning, and
squatting, but there was no talking. Even the security guards were
entranced.

"Recent evidence suggests that the four gruesome murders are
connected. The signs of capture and torture point towards a single
killer."

The picture changed to blurred-out images of four bodies. Even
though the images were altered to make it television-friendly, nearly
everyone in the room grimaced.

"Jesus." One of the oldest prisoners in the compound, Earl, a black
man who had conspired to kill the last president, shook his head.
"Kids nowadays have no respect for the human body."

Trevor rubbed the loose skin on his face. He couldn't help but notice
that the way the cuts were made, the healing scars that appeared on
the skin, the lack of bruising or broken bones...

"Earl, look at it. The killer made those with love. Twisted love, but
love nonetheless."

"We would like to extend our gratitude to the anonymous individual who gave us a lead into this absolutely horrifying case. We welcome any assistance that you, the public, can provide for us-"

Earl curled his lip at Trevor. "Guess you see the similarities because he's one of your kind, eh?"

"-do not have any suspects. Whoever this murderer is, he or she is on the loose and extremely dangerous-"

Trevor stood up. "What-"

Both Trevor and Earl began to seize violently, eyes rolling to the backs of their heads. They fell to the ground, bodies still twitching.

One of the security guards closest to Earl touched the headset on his ear. "Yes, warden, everything is fine here."

He motioned for the two other security guards to lift the men's limp bodies up onto the nearest tables. The two prisoners, still experiencing the aftershocks of the electricity, continued to seize.

A few prisoners stared at the security guards, but most of them lost interest in the interaction as soon as the microchips began to do their work.

It was nothing new; everyone experienced it at least once. Those who were smart never got shocked again. Those who weren't as smart…

That source of entertainment gone, they turned their attention back to the televisions.

"The informant stated that these killings may not actually be the work of a deranged individual, but of a private organization that utilizes these people to carry out special tasks. Whoever has more information will be rewarded handsomely."

Khara

Office of Kharavera Terraza   October 23, 2018
9th Floor, K-Pharma   2:00 p.m.

Khara tapped her fingers against her desk as she waited for Streye to pick up the phone.

"Yeah." His voice was as it always was: unhurried, firm.

"Are you close at all?"

He waited a second longer to respond. "Getting there. He's a tricky bastard."

The phone scraped against something.

"Well, hurry. Another set of victims just appeared on television."

Streye made a sound that could be a chuckle. "He's more productive than we ever were."

"This isn't a joke, Streye."

"Sure. He's a hard man to track down."

Khara took a breath, anxiety crawling over her skin. "I believe you. Just… do it before he gets any more media."

Alden

Police Department
Los Angeles, California

October 24, 2018
3:30 p.m.

Alden rubbed his temples as the phone rang.

Its shrill, high-pitched whining made him want to pitch it through the dirty, opaque window.

He almost crushed the phone handle. Why did the police department still have phones made in the 1990's?

"Good morning, you've reached the Los Angeles Police Department. This is Officer McKenna."

"Thank God. I thought I would never reach you." The man's voice was frantic, short of breath, as if he had been running.

Great, not another one.

"What can I help you with today, sir?" Alden reached for the list of prepared responses he had on his desk.

"Please, Officer, I don't have much time. I know you're going to think I'm crazy, but I'm not. I don't know how much influence they have over police, but definitely the chief."

"Sir, please slow down. What exactly is your concern?" He was about to start reading off the list of mental health hotlines, but something in the man's voice made him pause.

Maybe all the old man needed was to be heard. Plus, it wasn't like hearing him out would waste more of his time any more than answering phones already was.

"They know I told the police. THEY KNOW." The man's breathing sounded like he was going to hyperventilate. "I couldn't let them keep going. A lot of people were killed, more will be if I didn't reveal them."

"Sir, who is they?"

"I can't tell you. If I do, they will murder my wife and children. I love them. I can't not do anything, but I feel so useless, unable to say everything. They are powerful, they have so many connections. I couldn't stand it anymore. The killings are getting out of hand – they can't control it anymore. I couldn't let them do that, it was wrong."

"Sir, please slow-"

"But now it's too late – they know. They're going to get rid of me. I knew I was a dead man during my meeting with *her*, that look she gives, I knew right then that I was going to die, it was just a matter of when and where. I disappointed her and I disappointed him, and I've ruined my family too.

"The least I could do is let my children live in blissful ignorance – another reason why I can't tell you anything more – but know that there is an organization that is eliminating people, criminals."

"Sir-"

"I know my time is coming. Don't give me whatever spiel or line you were going to, probably think I'm crazy."

Alden glanced at the paper in front of him.

"My name is Stephen Libbe, look for my name or my body, and know that I was telling the truth. I don't know if they have this line bugged, but it doesn't matter. I've already spoken to a reporter, a well-trusted one. They can't stop it now!"

"Sir, I need you to tell me your address."

"What? Why?"

"I'm coming to you." Even though he was pretty certain the man needed psychiatric help, he wanted to make sure. His gut told him he should pay the man a visit.

And he never ignored his gut feeling.

"Why?"

Even if it turns out that the man was insane, at least Alden can make sure he wasn't being abused or mistreated at home. "I want to speak with you in person."

The man told him the address.

Alden hung up, making Stephen promise not to go anywhere.

Thorn

Libbe Residence   October 24, 2018
Glendale, California   3:50 p.m.

"You're too late!" Stephen leaned forward in his velvet chair, shoulders bowed, eyes narrowed.

The silver barrel of the gun in his hand gleamed.

He has six rounds. It looks more threatening than it actually is. You know everything you need to take him.

Use the books on the ground as barriers.

VOS, as always, was calm.

"How can you work for such a group? Sure they fucked with your brain, but you still have a human part of you in there, don't you?"

Thorn didn't respond.

He suddenly looked older. "I couldn't. I tried. How do you get your hands dirty and not feel a conscience? Do you regret what you do? Ever think that those lives weren't for you to take?"

"You helped create me. Shouldn't you be asking yourself?"

Take his gun.

"I never killed anybody! But… you do… and continue to. How do you live with yourself?"

Thorn shrugged. "Guess they made me the right way. Could you imagine creating assassins who felt bad about what they did?"

She took a step towards him. He didn't seem to notice, and she kept talking to distract him.

"What, now that you see the results from your little project, you don't like it? I'm this way because AEX created me. I don't feel anything because I shouldn't be able to."

She took another small step. "You asked me how I live with myself? I couldn't. I didn't. I was going to die. But they recruited me. And now here I am, dead in all senses except the fact that I'm breathing."

His face crumbled.

She stood there, waiting, eyes on the gun.

Just a few more moments.

"You monsters are all the same." The hand clutching the gun twitched. "I've seen the news."

Thorn let her body relax. "Put the gun down, Mr. Libbe. I'll make it quick for you. But if you wound me, I can make no promises."

They faced each other silently.

"I could." He looked at the gun. "But maybe I'll take you with me!"

He pulled the trigger.

Thorn ducked behind the closest stack of books.

He just had to do it the hard way.

Thorn

Libbe Residence
Glendale, California

October 24, 2018
4:05 p.m.

Thorn wiped her hands on Stephen's jacket and pants. She was unable to get the gun, at least when it still had bullets, so she had to resort to a more hands-on resolution.

Usually it wouldn't have been an issue, but something about the whole mission felt different... from her other missions.

Was she missing something?

He was a target, yes, but she felt... dirty.

Thorn had an urge to vomit all over the stained wooden floor, but managed to think about something other than the coppery, sticky mess on her fingers.

This wasn't her normal adrenaline rush.

Remember to take his phone and documents.

At least VOS still remembered what she had to do. Records of his calls, the reporter's contact information, and a complete copy of the files he received at the beginning of his partnership with AEX.

Poor bastard never should have gone back on his word.

With one last wipe on his pants, she stood up.

She shuffled through the books and papers on the desk.

Her eyes flicked from paper to paper, looking for anything that would hint at where he kept the materials. Her hands left a pink streak on any material they touched.

She looked at her palms. Why was she shaking?

She usually enjoyed combat. She was good at it, even if it ended up messy. Guns were cleaner, but also more unpredictable.

Right there. Her hand had barely touched a pair of scissors when VOS directed her attention to the pile of paper in the trash bin under his desk.

Did he try to cut up the documents? Without a shredder?

Just as she tucked the papers into her pack, she heard someone open the side entrance to the house.

She scooted to the nearest wall, took the second, clean blade out from her bra. She snapped the blade open.

That feeling in the pit of her stomach rose again.

This is the mission. Don't forget.

Why did VOS have to keep repeating that? She knew this was her mission.

Keep your focus.

"Hello? Stephen?"

Thorn hoped it was the reporter. It would save everyone the trouble.

Heels clicked on the floor as the door shut behind the intruder.

Heels prevent her sharp turns or sprints. You know what to do otherwise.

"Stephen, you left your phone at my place. I figured your wife wouldn't-"

She almost tripped over Stephen's corpse.

The woman turned to run, mouth open to scream, when Thorn's arm came across the front of her face, and the blade plunged into the side of her throat.

Thorn held the woman, tightening her grip as the woman struggled to break free. Within seconds, her body became limp.

When you take out the knife, drop her head so the splatter will be easier to clean up.

The woman's purse hit the floor first, and the contents spilled out.

Thorn slowly dropped to her knees, letting the woman's body slide from her grasp.

She pulled the blade out with her right hand as her left pushed the head forward. The weight of the head collapsed the wound on her neck, spurting blood down, not out.

Only when the body was completely prone on the floor did Thorn rifle through the objects in the purse.

Lipstick and hand lotion.

Car keys. Pink phone.

Black phone.

Thorn retrieved the key from the floor, and turned on her heel.

As she put the phones in the bag, her fingers hovered over the pile of papers there, wanting to tape them together to reveal the secrets of AEX. But she couldn't.

VOS prevented her from breaking those codes.

Report back in.

Thorn tapped the earring. "Van, it's me. It's-."

"You need to get out."

She caressed the papers again. "What?"

"There's a police cruiser coming your way. Leave."

She withdrew her hand and zipped up the bag. "Yeah."

"There's another mission for you."

Another pause, and there was a muffled conversation, as if he was listening to someone else. Khara, probably.

"I will message you the address. The target is connected to the Twisted Saints. He's been causing a lot of trouble since their deaths."

"I have to grade for class tomorrow." She looked at the blood on her body. "And I also need to change."

"I'll call you in two hours. It has to be done within the week. Bodies are dropping."

"What about Libbe's materials?"

"Keep them safe until you get back here. Just don't be seen."

AEX

Aaron's Apartment
Los Angeles, California

October 25, 2018
8:25 p.m.

Aaron sighed.

It's been more than two weeks and he still hadn't discovered the leak. No one knew who Stephen had spoken to, even those closest to him. He still had a few days left before Khara could send him the phone numbers from Stephen's phone.

Had he gotten lax? Back in the day, he could squeeze the information out of a rock.

"Aaron, I'm home!" A petite woman with dark brown hair kicked the door closed, her arms carrying a jacket and a heavy plastic bag. She set her keys on the key holder next to the door, adjusted her purse, and walked into the dining area, dropping the bag off at the table and setting her coat on the back of the chair.

Aaron was so busy he forgot Pria's trip ended today. That woman loved to stay busy. His woman.

He smiled to himself. "Welcome back!"

He bounded down the stairs and jumped down onto the first level. Walking briskly to the woman, he gave her a kiss and a hug. "Welcome home. How was your trip?"

She gave him a wide grin. "Long. A month away from you is too much." She turned to put her scarf on the coat rack. "Can you believe we're about to be married in less than five months?"

"No. I keep thinking I'm in a dream. Also, wondering if you've been on drugs this entire time."

They laughed, and he kissed her again.

Aaron set the plates and the forks on the table, and opened the plastic bag to set the takeout containers on the table.

Pria took a seat. "How did your writing go today? Last we talked, you were in another slump."

"Better after you called. I had so much inspiration after you told me about your crazy interaction with the delivery guy."

"Ha, I'm glad my catastrophes are serving you well." She took the box with the pad thai.

He gave her the curry. "We're symbiotic. You give me ideas, I give you good lovin'."

He winked at her. She clawed playfully at him. "Oh stop! We don't want the food to get cold like last time you distracted us!"

She took a small sip of the curry before pouring it over the rice on her plate. "Oh, that's just right." She poked her fork around in the plastic tub before spearing a large piece of chicken.

After they were both done divvying up the food, they held hands and said a short prayer.

"So. I was going to wait until it was published. But, I just can't!" She was almost vibrating in her seat. "A week ago I found out something that might actually change the world."

"The last time you were this excited you won $5 in lottery tickets."

"They're performing psychological experimentation on people."

She leaned forward, her hair almost falling into her food.

"That new corporation that we've been hearing about with those medical advancements? They're taking criminals and putting them into this process called V-O-S, and they install a second personality and voice inside their head."

No wonder you couldn't find out who the reporter was.

"But why?" Aaron's hand twirled the noodles on his plate. "That seems like a waste."

"No, that's where it gets good." She took a bite of her roll. "Apparently there's a sort of secret commission where some criminals are reprogrammed to become assassins." She paused over her food. "Others are made to become doctors, lawyers, educators, lawmakers, inserting themselves into every corner of our society."

"What?"

"Yes, and the best part? It's sanctioned by the Vice President."

"Duarte? There's no way."

She leaned back in her chair. "Yep. They're making killers who are legitimately crazy, so a group of people – I'm going to find out who – can use them against enemies of the state. No need for us to get angry at the police, when it's someone else doing the killing, hiding and politicking."

He pretended to be deep in thought. "Are you sure? I mean, how much can you trust your source?"

If you're trying to save her, you can't. She already knows too much.

She waved a hand in front of her face impatiently. "I trust him completely. He would never lie to me."

"And you're going to tell the public?"

She scoffed. "Of course I am. This will change everything!"

You have your mission.

He looked at her excited quavering form. "You think that's a good idea? I don't want you putting yourself in danger."

She has to disappear no matter what you say.

She frowned at him. "This might be the article that elevates me to the L.A. Post position. I've been at the Globe for far too long. If I stay much longer, no one's ever going to take me seriously!"

Seeing the look on his face, she set her utensils down. "I'll be fine! I'll write anonymously. My editor will let me. No one will know."

"Did you already ask him?"

"No, I'm going to ask him after I surprise him with the article."

That reduces the number of targets.

He shoved another bite into his mouth.

You have to, Aaron.

"Does this upset you? I wasn't going to tell you, but we're almost man and wife. Shouldn't we be sharing secrets?" She had that little sad pout on her face.

Be quick. If you don't want to hurt her, don't let her suffer.

"No, you're right. I guess I'm just being paranoid."

Aaron put the fork down on his plate. He stood up, came around the table, and pulled out her chair.

He wrapped his arms around her and gave her a hug from the back. He kissed her neck. "Congratulations. You really did it."

She hugged his arms and leaned back against him. "I couldn't have done it without you."

He loosened his hold on her. "Yeah. I'm sorry."

She frowned and turned to look at him, but there was a sudden pain in her stomach.

She looked down. The handle of a blade was stuck in her stomach. "Wha-"

He laid her gently on the floor.

"I didn't think it would be you. But... I guess I didn't think about a lot of things when it came to you."

You're making this more painful for her than you need to.

"I never imagined I would have to kill the woman that I love to protect my nation." He kissed her forehead, and brushed his lips over her wide eyes. "No one must find out about AEX. You cannot understand."

"Bu- How- what-" She choked a little, as tears leaked out from the corner of her eyes. She convulsed in his arms.

"I love you."

As the pool of blood spread under her, it looked like two red wings fanning out from her body until they connected to form a circle.

It had to be done.

Thorn

Interview Room   October 25, 2018
10th Floor, K-Pharma   9:15 p.m.

Thorn didn't know why she was here. At AEX, checking in on the girl she had kidnapped from the hospital.

Her mission was over. She should rest. She didn't need to check in with Eve. She had to grade and lesson plan for this next week.

We have plenty of time to prepare for class.

Kenzie was finally stable enough to interview.

The girl still looked half-dead. Pale skin, lingering sweat, dead eyes, limp body. They should have waited another week. But lately, for some reason, everyone at AEX was speeding, pushing deadlines.

"How is this any different than whoring myself out? That's less painful, apparently."

"Is it?"

"Death is painless. Except when you don't it well and someone saves you." The girl's voice was so soft that Thorn had to focus on reading her lips.

"You are not selling your body. You are helping us make the world a better place, while becoming stronger."

"Why do I want the world to be a better place?" Her voice was a whisper. "I want it to burn. It ignored my brother's mental illness, put him in prison to be "cured," and did nothing while he was beaten to death. Now, I can't even die in peace."

"That anger, you can-"

"Honestly, I don't care. I just want to no longer exist."

The doctors looked around, unsure of what to do.

Thorn opened the door just enough to speak.

"Give her some time. She's clearly in no state to be intimidated."

Dr. Faye nodded to Dr. Stewart and Dr. Marcus. "That's true. You might have too much on your mind. Why don't you take a few nights to sleep on it? And then tell us."

Thorn

Dining Area   October 28, 2018
11th Floor, K-Pharma   9:45 a.m.

"Do you ever wonder if you made the right choice?"

Thorn paused in her eating and set the toast down.

Since Thorn had interrupted the interview three nights ago, Kenzie had bonded to her. Thorn was no mentor and she repeatedly told the younger girl, but Kenzie was persistent.

It was exhausting speaking to someone with so many questions. Especially when she had to deal with that in school every day.

But Thorn couldn't just ignore her. The girl was defenseless, completely lacking in confidence and self-awareness. Even when she spoke, she couldn't meet Thorn's eyes.

Thorn couldn't walk away from that.

"No."

"Why not?" The girl hadn't touched anything on her plate.

"Because I couldn't afford to consider alternatives."

The girl considered her answer. "So you never regret the fact that you gave up your freedom for a life that goes against your morals?"

Thorn bit back laughter. "Freedom? You were about to be jailed for being sad. Mental health is still seen as a disease. Suicide is seen as a moral failing. You know the world out there. You see the stigma, you see the blame, you see the sweeping under the rug. Did we have freedom?"

Hesitantly, Kenzie shook her head.

"The world's morals are fucked up. True freedom and morality doesn't exist anymore."

"But you're actively working for the people who do this to you." Makeup had failed to hide the girl's puffy eyes. Her chewed fingernails held onto the table.

Thorn nodded. "If the world around us lacks morality, then why should I beat myself up over it?" She touched the gun at her hip. "We're doing what we have to."

The girl poked at her plate. "It's... So strange. I understand what you're saying, but... How do I choose? I hate this world but how could I inflict even more damage?"

"Do it or don't. There is no buyer's remorse." She paused, hearing Khara's voice come out of her mouth. "This is self-preservation."

Kenzie shook her head. Her fingers had a pinching hold on her stomach. Thorn turned her eyes away and tried to ignore it.

"But you should decide soon. Khara's not going to like it if you wait until the last moment and fail a mission."

"I-I just don't know if I can do it."

"Do what? Kill?"

Kenzie nodded.

Thorn gave her a long look. "You don't know what you're capable of. None of us are. It's best if you don't think too much about it."

Thorn
Memory

Office of Duke Marcus
9th Floor, K-Pharma   (Two years ago)

"Shouldn't I have more training?" The gun in Thorn's hand felt heavy, and she had no idea what to do if people shot or rushed at her.

Dr. Marcus didn't stop his physical probing. He shone a light in her left eye, then right, twisted her head left and right, and pulled her left arm, the one holding the gun, out and up, wrapping a cuff around her bicep.

This all seemed so mundane. She was supposed to kill people, wasn't she? This seemed like a regular doctor's visit.

Without answering her question, he proceeded to inflate the cuff, slapping her hands upward when it dropped below a certain height.

The pain of holding the gun up outweighed her willpower. Her hand dropped a few centimeters.

He slapped it up without even turning in her direction.

Her arm was screeching at her to let it rest. "Don't you have lighter guns?"

He ignored her.

In order to distract herself, she shifted the gun in her hand.

She pointed it at the window. Her arm moved horizontally until her barrel sight pointed at the back of his head.

Her finger was on the trigger.

It felt so sleek and nimble, and her fingertips tingled as she grazed the plastic. It seemed so light, so pretty, so... Comfortable.

Her finger jerked towards her and she heard a soft click. The doctor turned his head around and gave her a raised eyebrow.

"You should check your chamber and magazine before you point it at anyone."

"You're telling me I can point it at anyone, even you?"

He pressed the blue button on the strange octagonal machine. She hadn't noticed it earlier since his body was blocking it, but it looked like a part of a practice drum set with two buttons along each edge.

"You're in the business of killing people. Pointing it is your job. It's actually more dangerous for you to have it unloaded."

Thorn found it strange, that they gave her tools before teaching her how to use them.

"There is a method to this, I assure you," he continued, as if he heard her thoughts. "Sometimes, no matter how comprehensive VOS can be and how permanent that voice is in your head, sometimes your body will just reject externally-directed violence."

He motioned towards the gun in her hand. "As much as certain individuals hate, they may never be able to internalize the idea of killing someone else. And so they live in a state of constant conflict- unable to pull a trigger or slide the blade across a throat, but unable to ignore the voice that tells them to.

"And this is after they spent hour after painful hour of treatment. Along with hundreds of thousands of dollars invested." He put his hand on her weakening arm, now starting to tremble, and pushed down on it. "Wasted."

Relieved, she set the gun on the chair beside her.

"But your subconscious accepts the gun and what it represents. Now the real work can begin."

Thorn's gaze went back to the octagonal machine. "What's next?"

"Your VOS will be your guide. It will be able to process the weapons, training, and mission information much faster than your conscious mind. During the time you're processing the pictures, words and videos on that screen, your VOS will have absorbed the information embedded in the video."

"So... I'm going into these situations knowing nothing about self-defense or guns... And praying that this so-called voice will tell me in time?"

Thorn laughed, this time a little unsure of what she was doing here. "I mean, I am suicidal, but that seems a bit unnecessary."

The smile he gave her was all teeth. "Don't worry. Your VOS will not disappoint. They are all about self-preservation, after all."

Not reassuring at all.

Anthony

Warehouse in the Arts District   November 1, 2018
San Francisco, California   11:20 p.m.

Anthony ran, face bruised and bloodied. His body was sore, muscles overextended, adrenaline depleted, and yet he kept running.

He looked over his shoulder, feeling eyes on his back.

It should have been impossible for someone to track him, find him, catch him unawares. That was his job.

He was the predator, the chaser, the winner.

His VOS had betrayed him.

But the skull was right there with him. His new friend who whispered hope into his ear.

Warehouse door to the right. Find a weapon and a dark hiding spot. We need to rest and find out what we're up against.

He reached for a loose wooden plank before his eyes even fell on it. Anthony walked along the wall, not picking up on any threats coming from in front of him. He scanned the area once more before sitting down, his back to the corner, and breathed deeply.

The skull watched, right next to his shoulder.

AEX must have sent someone after him. He didn't predict it would be so quick.

The man had come out of nowhere.

Cornered him in his own home, so silent that even the skull took a full second before recognizing the danger. The man slammed Anthony into the door, hands coming up to grab his neck, but Anthony maneuvered to the side. Anthony ran a few feet before the man chopped at the pressure point between his neck and shoulder, and Anthony fell to his knees.

The man turned him over with a flick of his foot, and began punching. Anthony definitely heard a few cracks on his face and ribs, but the man didn't seem to be doing anything lethal. No knives, no guns, nothing sharp enough to pierce through the skin. The man merely wanted to incapacitate him.

Anthony could have been dead, but the man's weakness in letting him live gave him strength.

Anthony had taken the closest object to him- the desk chair- and slammed it onto the man. It bought him a few seconds, and he turned and ran.

He needed to regroup.

And now he was here, stuck in this warehouse, hoping to catch a few moments of peace before he had to fight for his life again.

The skull's mouth moved. Was blood dripping from its jaw? Where did the blood come from?

You know who he is…

When he tried to move his leg, he found that he couldn't. It was so dark that he couldn't see what had happened. Sliding his hand against his leg, he felt a small dagger jutting out from his upper thigh.

"You're a hard man to track down, Anthony."

Streye. Of course.

Anthony hadn't thought of him. To him, the older man was weak, unable to be a full agent.

"How long have you been hunting me?"

"For a while."

Anthony leaned back. "I did what was right. It's a shame what she did to all those girls."

"What you're doing is worse."

"I am doing AEX's work." Anthony tried to remove the blade from his thigh, but he only succeeded in pushing it more into his flesh.

He stopped trying to move it. "They're too bogged down by the details to even fulfill their vision. So focused on funding, and support, and politics, that they forgot that they were created to rid the world of evil."

"Fisherman's Wharf was helping the world?"

"That was for my VOS. It was a small price to pay."

"Your VOS."

"He needed proof that I wanted him back."

"Do you realize that you've lost it?"

"HA!" Anthony's hand accidentally slipped into the pile of blood pooling underneath his leg. "You really believe all that?"

He coughed. "Don't you think it's a little fishy that some evil is taken out, and others are permitted and even encouraged, to flourish? Your VOS should have deciphered and analyzed that. Don't you think that's a bit... Hypocritical?"

"You still murdered innocent people."

Anthony's eyes flashed in the dark. "I followed AEX's mission! How I did it went against those precious rules, but what I did was right! It's what they told us we'd be doing as agents, not picking and choosing evils!"

Anthony tapped his head against the wall.

Streye's voice was calm. "I suggest you don't move. If you cooperate you can still get out of this alive."

No you can't. They'll torture you, make you bleed, watch you squirm, until they get bored. And then they will kill you when you're of no use to them anymore.

The skull... did Streye not see it? It stood right in front of him.

"No I can't." Anthony felt the blood, his blood, puddle beneath his leg. His fingers dipped in its warmth.

Still no pain though.

You must wound him. In your state, you cannot be his match, but if you can wound him...

"Streye... Remember that time I asked you why you revived me after my suicide?"

"Yes."

"I think we all serve a purpose. Sooner or later we fall by our own hand, but the timing has to be just right, so we know we lived our life to its last good drop."

He removed the blade from his leg.

Before Streye could react, Anthony jammed it into his own neck.

Alden

Police Department
Los Angeles, California

November 2, 2018
9:10 a.m.

"What were you doing at Stephen Libbe's house?" The chief's face was almost the same color as the apple on her desk.

"Chief, I had to follow up on the lead. I was concerned about him." Alden sat with his back straight against the plastic chair.

He was exhausted.

Ever since he stumbled onto the crime scene, he'd been dead tired. Stumbling onto Stephen's still warm body, and the body of his mistress...

He couldn't get them out of his head.

He wanted to do so much and yet could do so little. The fact that he was moments too late, that he didn't believe Stephen, that what he stumbled on could very well a part of the conspiracy...

All those thoughts ate at him, at his very core, throwing his judgments and values into question.

"Your responsibility was to man the telephone. I gave you direct orders. Who told you to follow up on the lead?"

"No one, ma'am."

"So you decided to take it on yourself to do a little investigating. Left the phone ringing for hours. No one could reach any officer in the department. Even city hall received calls about your little faux pas."

"My instincts were right, ma'am."

"Your instincts should have told you to call the patrolling officers in the area. Your instincts should have told you to stay put, instead of being nosy and getting yourself caught up in the fucking case."

The chief twisted the ring on her finger. "I don't know what kind of tricks you used to play in your old departments, but I regret ever accepting your goddamn application."

"Ma'am-"

"Do you know why you're being questioned in this room?" Alden looked around at the sparse, dirty interrogation room.

"No."

"Because we can't vouch for your innocence."

Alden was speechless. "What? That's ridiculous."

The chief crossed her arms. "Of course. Oh, I found them like this. It's the perfect cover. No witnesses, no alarm, perfect alibi."

Alden couldn't believe what he was hearing. "I was the one who called it in! There is no evidence linking me to any of that."

"Right. Because as a police officer, you wouldn't know how to cover your tracks."

"Why are you trying to pin this on me instead of going out and looking for-"

He stopped mid-sentence, and stared at the police chief. He didn't like what he was thinking, but that would actually make sense.

"You're getting rid of me."

The chief raised her eyebrows.

Alden didn't say out loud that he suspected the chief of being part of the conspiracy that killed the media owner, that she was being used by someone greater, that Alden was a scapegoat because he asked too many questions.

He didn't say out loud that he suspected the chief would get rid of him as quickly as they got rid of Stephen, if he mentioned those suspicions.

Alden wasn't sure if staying quiet helps his chances of survival, but he wasn't going to take unnecessary risks.

"What do you plan to do?"

"I don't plan on doing anything. If you decide to take care of it yourself."

"I see."

Alden still suspected that the chief was planning a different end to their relationship. There was no way someone with that much to hide would just let him walk.

But at least to his face, she was giving him a way out.

AEX

Interview Room   November 4, 2018
10th Floor, K-Pharma   9:45 a.m.

"You will never speak to Khara directly. Your handler will instruct you on the target and the mission. If your handler cannot be contacted for some reason, you will report to Streye, who is in charge of personnel management."

Kenzie had the biggest eyes on her face as the stone-faced instructor threw rules and regulations at her. Habits, procedures, hierarchy, agents, compensation, and requirements. Nothing was written on paper except for the address of the house she was assigned.

She wasn't going to remember all of it, especially with the headache.

"AEX doesn't have the money to be tapping phone calls, bribing people, or giving you fancy James Bond gadgets. Once you're on the field, you're on your own, aside from your handler."

When she'd agreed to the doctors, she had hoped they would just put her under, do the experiment, it'd fail and she'd die. They said there was a high likelihood of that.

So why didn't it happen? Why did the treatment have to be successful?

The instructor slammed his hand on the whiteboard, violently jerking her out of her confused daydream. "You are now officially a member of AEX. Any action that you do or do not do reflects on us. While the public may not recognize the danger you pose, AEX is in a tenuous position with both the government and the public. Any incident you have outside of the bounds of any mission is grounds for criminal action against AEX." He gave her a pointed look. "You'll be *terminated* if that happens."

She shrunk back in her chair, her body still weak. It probably didn't help that the dopamine they pumped into her for the VOS treatment made her head feel like it was expanding and contracting.

Her eye sockets throbbed. Her vision was getting fuzzy.

Don't shame yourself, fatty.

Her eyes jerked open, and she looked around, frantically searching for the male voice that had just spoken into her ear. There was no one else around.

The instructor gave her a long look.

You should tell him that the VOS procedure was successful.

"What?" She didn't realize she spoke out loud until she heard her voice, delayed through the fog dampening her senses.

The instructor's face softened. It was the first positive emotion she's seen in him since they started training orientation five hours ago.

Don't force it. Just let me be in you. Open up your mind.

The man checked off something on the clipboard, and spoke in a gentler voice, "Let me find your handler. It's time for her to bond with you and your VOS. She'll be managing you on your missions."

As the instructor left the room, Kenzie finally slumped a little in her seat, just enough to get comfortable.

Lazy already? Come now. Stand up and walk around the room. You can't be useful if you get a heart attack while running.

Thorn

Interview Room   November 4, 2018
10th Floor, K-Pharma   10:42 a.m.

The beep in her ear brought her back to the present. Thorn frowned, watching Kenzie communicate with her newfound voice.

No Dr. Marcus to assist her, no Khara to question her, no Dr. Faye taking her vitals.

The VOS discovery process had become hurried, mechanical.

Thorn cracked her shoulder.

The recruits were by themselves, each trapped in their own minds and physical rooms, separated by an emotional wall that few could penetrate.

It was a lonely existence. While you knew there were others, you could never interact with them, bond with them, because you never know when they would disappear. Eternal loneliness.

Her eyes closed briefly, breathing in the light comforting scent that permeated each interview and observation room in AEX. The only thing that was comforting.

Time to prepare for your mission.

Thorn

Putem Residence   November 8, 2018
Long Beach, California   5:20 p.m.

Thorn loaded the full magazines into her now empty guns, checking them to make sure the chambers were loaded. She tucked the guns back into their holsters, patted her knives, and made her way around the bullet-ridden house, stepping over pools of blood.

As she walked around shattered tables, broken lamps and still bodies, her eyes fell on the framed images on the intact bookshelf.

Pictures of a group of white and Hispanic men, hugging in front of a golf course; two children- one about four and the other nine- laughing at the camera. They were dressed up, probably for a photo shoot.

You should leave this one for the cleanup crew.

The younger child looked... familiar, although Thorn couldn't place exactly where she knew her from.

Her eyes moved on to a different picture, of the target and a black woman standing in front of the ocean, faces pressed together. They looked exuberant.

Her eyes fell on the target. Don Putem. His eyes were closed, but his hand was wrapped around something in his jacket.

Keys? She pulled out his arm and noticed the small silver locket in his palm, wrapped around his finger.

He must have grabbed it before the shooting started.

We should leave.

"Not yet." She needed to organize the place for the clean-up crew.

Her hands had barely put on gloves when she heard the insertion of a key into the front door lock.

Leave. Now.

Thorn had never heard the voice tell her to run away, especially when it came to finishing the job. Even as her brain processed the warning, her body was already in motion, sliding against the pillar of the wall between the kitchen and the entranceway.

Her knife was in her hand before her back hit the wall.

She couldn't retreat, tail between her legs, before the job was done.

It is not worth it. Leave.

Thorn ignored her VOS, and flicked the blade open.

As the person stepped past her, she grabbed the waist, swung her legs to kick the knees – the woman went down too easily – and was about to slit her throat when her target wriggled out of her grip and turned.

Both of them stared at the other. Thorn's eyes widened.

For the first time, her blade hesitated.

"Ms. V?"

Alie.

The girl sported a large bruise on her right cheek. Probably from her mother.

You know what you must do.

Now it all made sense. VOS had recognized the face in that picture...
If she had listened to it and left when she could, she wouldn't be
forced to do this.

But if she had, Alie would have been someone else's problem,
someone else's body to dispose of.

Alie turned away. Her eyes fell on the dead target, his hand still
clutching the locket.

She reached for it at the same time Thorn took a step behind her,
grabbed her hair in one fist, and plunged the knife into her neck.

As if in slow motion, the girl fell to the ground, her hand still
reaching out for the man, as the pool of dark red blood expanded
under her torso, soaking her clothes.

Her eyes were still partially open, dimming as her blood spread
further and further away.

Thorn removed the knife. Her eyes scanned the rest of the room.

No movement. Still dead.

It was her job after all, to eliminate witnesses.

A strict AEX code.

She couldn't not do it. But...

"No witnesses."

She wasn't sure if she was speaking to the dead in the room or to
herself. The house only echoed the silence that followed.

Thorn

Putem Residence   November 8, 2018
Long Beach, California   5:40 p.m.

She couldn't stop shaking.

Her hands, her arms, her legs, her head, her torso. It felt like she was being rocked in every part of her body, without a solid still limb.

Even her vision seemed to seesaw.

Thorn cringed as she stepped on a bone she thought was part of the tile. It crunched and bits of blood and marrow clung to the bottom of her shoe.

She tried holding onto different parts of herself but that didn't work.

She tried to grasp the wall, heavy objects near her, the bookcase, the desk, the chair, but she couldn't seem to contract her hand muscles. Her palm promptly slid off whatever surface she intended to use to stabilize herself.

Thorn turned her back to the girl lying there, neck sliced open, blood pooling underneath her, dead eyes unseeing.

She set her almost uncontrollable limbs on a chair that wasn't upturned or broken, and leaned forward, pulling herself into the fetal position. As she tried to clip the knife back onto her hip belt, she had to give it three tries before her hand stabilized enough for her to insert it into its respective place.

She pressed the phone on her ear.

Van's voice answered on the second ring. "That took longer than I expected."

"More people here than expected...this place is also a lot more like a home than a drug den."

"Don't let appearances fool you. Homes are the best places. How many bodies?"

"S-seven."

Her eyes fell on the most recent body. She tore her eyes away

"I just phoned the crew. They'll be there within 20 minutes. Because it's in a busy area, we'll have to stage as opposed to remove. Take the rest of the day off. Tomorrow we'll do the post-mission training."

Thorn

Training Arena   November 9, 2018
11th Floor, K-Pharma   8:55 a.m.

She froze.

For the second time since she became part of AEX... She hesitated. Her hand wavered from the dummy's head, blade mere centimeters away from the upper neck. The dummy was made of straw, wrapped in rubber and covered with the paper image of a cartoon, resembling nothing but a cheap attempt to cover up the straw.

But she saw Alie's face, felt the blood drip down onto her hands, felt the dagger rip through flesh and cartilage until it escaped in a stream of warm blood, heard and felt the thud of her body as it dropped onto the floor.

Most of all, she saw Alie's eyes, accusing and then empty, on the face of the dummy.

A casualty, that's what she was. A necessary elimination.

Cut it.

Her body felt like lead, and she heard the thudding of feet and the shouting of words, but she couldn't process what was being said.

Her vision focused on the dummy's neck, inches from the base of the head, covered with a piece of elastic. Her arm shuddered as she tried to force the blade to go through, but something prevented her from actually moving her hand.

As if coming out of a vacuum, her vision zoomed out, her breathing steadied, and her hearing cleared up.

Cut the neck.

"Thorn, what are you doing?" Van was a few feet away from her, motioning for her to do something.

Cut it.

Thorn glanced at the dummy, now just hay covered in plastic, and sliced the head off.

The timer in the room stopped, and a buzzer indicated that the session was over. The door unlocked.

Thorn threw the dummy off to the side, where a small pile of headless and limbless dummies lay. She made her way through the maze, testing her blade on the meaty part of her index finger.

She needed to sharpen it.

Van appeared on her right as she exited the maze. "What happened out there?"

It wouldn't be wise to let him know about Alie. "I was overthinking again. You know how VOS gets when I try to control her."

Thorn

Vaughn High School   November 11, 2018
Los Angeles, California   10:00 a.m.

"Local residents Don Putem, Richard Diaz, and Charlie Barnes and three unidentified individuals were found dead after an illegal poker game gone afoul. A teenage girl was also found at the scene."

"Turn that off. You know cell phones aren't allowed in class."

"But miss, I think they're talking about Alie."

"-in their home. Neighbors reported hearing pounding, screaming, and gunshots an hour prior to the arrival of the police, but there were no reports of anyone fleeing the scene. We-"

She took the phone and turned it off. After dropping it into her desk drawer, she turned to address the class. "Until we hear from Alie's family, we are not going to start rumors about her."

The silence only lasted a few seconds.

"Her dad never came to parent-teacher conferences. They say he was selling drugs-"

"I heard she was using too-"

"No, not Alie. She was going to Harvard. I don't think she wanted to be the daughter of some low life criminal."

"Her mom left him so Alie wouldn't have to-"

"He beat her-"

"No, her mom was the mean one. Her dad treated her like a princess. She always had the biggest smile on her face when she talked about him-"

"If I was him I'd be so pissed she took my daughter away; I'd murder her-"

Thorn's headache throbbed behind her eyes. "The next time I hear gossip, I will make you write standards."

Someone else's phone began to play a video. "The young female victim has been identified as Don Putem's daughter, Alie Johnson, a senior at Vaughn High School."

Before she could confiscate the cell phone, she felt a wave of bile rising in her throat.

She barely reached the trash can in time.

"Miss, are you okay?"

A few students stood up, but she lifted a hand, motioning for them to stay in their seats. "It's fine. Jay, can you call the office and have them send someone up?"

As the boy called the office on the room phone, she remained at her desk, huddled over the trash can. The students stared at her sympathetically.

"It's okay, Miss V. This happens all the time. You'll get used to it."

"Yeah, you can't live in this area without losing someone."

She could only pretend that their words comforted her, but her nods were empty.

Thorn

Thorn's Apartment   November 11, 2018
Los Angeles, California   10:15 p.m.

Thorn tried to push herself up on her elbows, so her face wasn't directly in the toilet bowl. But it was too hard, took too much energy.

Put yourself together. Drink water. Eat some-

"Shut up." Her voice slurred, Thorn could barely even hear herself. She leaned against her left forearm, perched on the side of the bowl. It trembled, tired from supporting her torso for the past two hours, as she emptied the contents of her stomach, over and over.

She had stayed for the cleanup.

Thorn sat there, watching them remove all signs that anyone else had been in the house, place poker chips, cards, and money on the table, and rearrange the bodies.

She watched it all through a haze.

Everything was fine. So she had thought. Until the training. Until the news report in class.

Thorn made her way home from school – how she wasn't sure – but she made it. Just barely. The short walk home was like swimming in molasses: slow and suffocating. With just two thoughts running through her head.

VOS lost control of her thoughts.

She lost control of her body.

Thorn
Memory

Observation Room   When Thorn was 23
10th Floor, K-Pharma   (Two years ago)

Thorn's mind was still reeling from the colors and images. Even when she closed her eyes she could feel the trees swaying in the breeze. See the people stabbing each other with their knives…

One.

Two.

Three times, on rhythm, like robots.

It was all a blur of motion and shapes and pictures, with no real plot or connection.

She picked up her pen, her grip shaky. The dull ache in her head throbbed a little harder, and she felt the blood pulsing in her neck.

"Answer the questions." The command came from the overhead speakers. It did nothing to offset her headache.

She looked down at the paper in front of her. Her eyes caught the first question, after skimming over the page multiple times.

WHAT WAS THE 24TH LETTER IN THE LETTER?

What? She tried replaying the video in her mind but she definitely did not see any letter. She was about to turn her head around to ask, but the speakers clicked on.

"Set your pen closer to the paper. Let your hands relax."

The moment she held the pen tip to the paper, the shakiness in her hand stopped. She couldn't recall one answer to the questions, but her hand started to write answers in cursive.

A part of her wanted to jerk the pen out of her own hand, but the other part was curious. Intrigued.

She kept on writing, even as her hand began to cramp. The font grew sloppy, but her hand didn't stop.

Was she possessed?

They said that she would have another presence in her mind. Was this what they meant? Something taking control of her limbs?

She was more scared of the fact that she wasn't terrified – as if she was totally okay with something else controlling her body.

Her hand continued to write.

How was she processing her own thoughts when a different part of her brain was answering questions?

Only after she had completed the worksheet, put her pen down and leaned back in her chair did she realize her headache had worsened. She was gnashing her teeth together. The inside of her mouth tasted bitter, like blood, and her gums were sensitive to any jaw movement.

Each heart beat that passed through her head felt like she was being lifted off the ground while someone stuck a needle into her eye socket.

She released her breath.

AEX

Roder Residence
Santa Clarita, California

November 14, 2018
7:40 p.m.

The feedback from the earring phone squealed.

Wincing, Kenzie tried really hard to keep focused. It was hard enough keeping her nerves calm – only her third mission and somehow they already moved her to a kill assignment.

It was empowering that AEX's CEO had personally selected her for this mission, even though she was still new.

But it was also strange that she had access to a high level mission so early on.

Things felt... rushed.

The information on the target was sparse, and some pieces were altogether nonexistent. Why did Bill Roder deserve to be killed? AEX dealt with criminals and those who kill. Was this businessman in any way detrimental to society? He made a lot of profit, yes, but he also gave generously to charities, like the Food for Friends and Doctors without Borders programs. He volunteered on several local and national governing boards, taking very consistent, pro-environment and anti-violence positions.

She couldn't find anything during her research that made him a target, and so urgent that it needed to be done immediately. But her VOS had convinced her to obey orders.

So here she was, waiting for the right moment. He was in his study, door locked. No maids or manservants.

Shouldn't criminals be more cautious than this?

She wanted to observe more, gather more intel, but her earbuds screeched, indicating that the cleanup crew was ready.

Bill didn't hear the flick of the knife or feel hot blood spurting out of his neck. He was dead before he realized he wasn't alone.

As his hand dropped from the keyboard, something on the computer caught Kenzie's eye.

The words "AEX" and "psychological manipulation".

She leaned over his body to read what was on the screen. Her eyes shifted to the papers underneath his hands and head, stacks of papers with–

A piercing screech paralyzed her. She grabbed her head and dug her fingernails into the temples.

Her eyes flew back to the papers and the computer screen. While she recognized the words, she no longer understood them. She tried to focus on the words, but all she heard was more screeching.

Kenzie's thoughts jumbled together as her brain shut down. Nothing.

Her finger found the earring and pressed it. She heard Khara's voice before the light behind her eyes dimmed and she dropped to the ground, unconscious.

Her eyes slowly rolled into the back of her head as her body twitched.

AEX

Office of Evelyn Wells
9th Floor, K-Pharma

November 19, 2018
9:00 a.m.

"I haven't seen you in a while, Thorn."

Eve was surprised the agent had shown up. She knew something happened on the Putem mission – she was at the post-mission training – but she didn't know what.

Eve fully expected that the next time she saw Thorn, the agent would be haggard, a wreck, someone who was recovering from a malaise. That's what Eve always thought the VOS was – an illness.

She expected a painful, teeth pulling, putting-the-pieces-together session.

She definitely didn't expect this. Thorn standing in the same spot, one leg cocked against the wall, hand holding a bottle of tea, hair brushed back into a high ponytail. Her shirt said 'forget but do not forgive'.

Thorn dipped her head. "It's been a busy two weeks."

Eve opened the door wide, motioned for Thorn to step in, and stepped back to observe.

The agent's steps were regular. Her shoulders were straight and her face was calm.

They both sat down.

Before Eve had a chance to speak, Thorn leaned forward.

"I killed one of my students." She twisted the cap to the tea, her eyes following the movement of her fingers. Her hands were steady. "One of the students of that teacher mission."

Eve definitely didn't expect to leap into it so quick.

"She was one of the best." She set the bottle on the table between them, and ran her ponytail through her fingers. "Although that shouldn't matter, should it? She was just one person. But she was… different."

Eve crossed her legs. "What happened?"

"Mission was a success. She just happened to stumble on the scene at that time."

Silence.

"Did they have a relationship?"

"Target was her father."

Silence.

"Did you know about that relationship?"

"No. But if I had just left… if she hadn't come in. It's just… such bad timing." Thorn bit her finger. "I can't continue that mission. I can't go back to that school, to those kids, look them in the eyes, and pretend like I'm not a killer. I can't."

Eve nodded. "I will let Khara know."

"You're not going to persuade me to stay on a mission?"

"That's Khara's job. I'm here to make sure you're okay. " Eve met her eyes. "How do you feel right now?"

Thorn's eyes held Eve's for so long the older woman didn't think she would answer. "I don't know."

Eve would have prodded further, but Thorn seemed genuine in her uncertainty.

Eve waited. The room was silent for two whole minutes.

Thorn twisted the cap off of her tea. "I had three days of intense guilt. Gut-wrenching, nauseating."

She paused. "The second night, I dreamt that VOS was filtering out those negative emotions. She told me that I could not have prevented it, that everything was according to the books. That there was nothing wrong. In the grand scheme of things, everything worked out. The mission was a success, and no unrelated civilians were harmed."

She twisted the cap back on. "Technically she's right. Whether or not I feel bad doesn't matter. A major criminal and his closest men have been dispatched, along with a daughter who may or may not have tried avenging his death. The world is a safer place."

She set the bottle back on the table.

"I'm always waiting for the next hit of guilt. The kind so visceral you bend over and scream until the pain lessens. VOS keeps trying to get rid of that negative energy."

"And?"

"It's lessened. Some mornings if I'm not careful, I'm back to normal."

"You don't want that?"

Thorn rubbed her forehead. "I don't want to lose myself. I know VOS wants to protect me by repressing the memories. But I can't let her do that. I would be disrespecting Alie if I allowed her to be removed so easily."

"How is VOS responding to your defiance?"

"I'm not sure. She definitely disagrees. She wants to keep me from remembering it, to make me more effective in the field, to heal. But she hasn't... she hasn't forced me to forget. If I try, I still remember it. I remember Alie's face."

Thorn swallowed. "I remember it all."

"Why are you consciously forcing pain on yourself?"

Thorn finished the last of her drink. "I don't know. I feel like it's the right thing to do."

Eve set her hands on her knees. "Not listening to VOS could have its consequences, Thorn. So far nothing bad has happened, but it could. You have to let it guide you."

Thorn said nothing the rest of the session.

AEX

Observation Room   November 21, 2018
10th Floor, K-Pharma   6:10 a.m.

"Don't touch me don't touch me don't touch me. Fuck!"

Kenzie was curled into a fetal position in the corner of the room, her hands covering her face. Her feet were turned towards each other, toes curled, as her shoulders slammed against the walls.

Her bloodshot eyes were barely open. The hospital gown had been ripped so many times that most of her skin was bare. The only other garment she was wearing was a loosely wrapped loincloth.

Broken ceramic vases littered the floor. The bed was made, with the covers tucked under the mattress, pillows fluffed and set over the double-flipped cover.

Kenzie was shivering, crying without tears, as her cracked broken voice kept telling whatever it was to not approach her.

Her eyes focused on the pile of broken vases and torn up flowers. She straightened her legs and leaped from the ground, stomping on the flowers until the petals bled.

The hallway door opened.

Thorn turned to greet the nurse. "Rita." She looked back into the window of Kenzie's room.

"She had such potential."

Kenzie was still muttering to herself, occasionally screaming, and pulling at the remaining clothes on her body. Rita checked the contents of the desk and closed the drawers.

Thorn didn't turn around. "Do you see a lot of this?"

"Sadly, yes. But most recruits fail at the very beginning, as opposed to her." She watched Kenzie flail around inside the room. "Without a VOS removal process, they remain like this."

"VOS removal?"

"A procedure to flush VOS from the subconscious and conscious brain, bringing the recruit back to the time before VOS was implanted. Dangerous. Removing any part of the memory unrelated to VOS would be detrimental to their identity."

"Any luck?"

"So far, no." Rita sighed. "Zero successes. We couldn't even get as far as the actual removal procedure. All of our subjects failed the removal priming."

"What happened?"

"The VOS shut down."

"That's good, right?"

"No, quite the opposite. VOS had become the brain, controlled it completely."

"And?"

"VOS shut off their system completely. We didn't even have time to call in resuscitation teams."

"Why would you resuscitate them? Why not let them die?"

"Dead people are worthless to a research facility. We need to find out why and how we failed, and learn from our failures. So far, we have nothing."

Thorn looked at Kenzie, trying to see who she was before. "Why do some fail the VOS process at the beginning and others fail after it's complete?"

Kenzie climbed onto the bed, squatted on her heels, and rotated her head, left to right.

"Individual brains are fickle things. Sometimes the subconscious wants to accept the voice, other times it fights it. With her..." she pursed her mouth, "I don't think it's the procedure that broke."

"How so?"

"If she had failed her first or second mission, I would say that VOS didn't bond as fully as we thought, and continue with the VOS treatment. But she completed them successfully."

"What do you think it is?"

The nurse poured three ounces of clear liquid into a small vial, and inserted the vial into a silver machine the size of a microwave. Into another opening of the machine she dropped three red pills.

"The VOS is a voice, but it's also a code, right? It's basically all the values, rules, and procedures that AEX requires agents to abide by. The recruit then acts on both personal and the VOS's will."

"Right." Thorn's eyes followed the nurse's actions as she pressed multiple buttons on the machine in sequential order. The device whirred to life.

"What's to say that personal issues never conflict with the code?" She tapped the glass gently, but the girl inside didn't notice at all.

"So you think her code conflicted with VOS."

"Then the entire system shut down. That's my guess."

"What do you think broke the code?"

"Bill Roder was the primary drafter of the most recent transparency bill sponsored by the President. He somehow got wind of AEX. From where no one knew, but Khara had to remove him."

"So he technically didn't do anything criminal."

Rita nodded. "And Kenzie's VOS picked up on that when she killed him."

They looked at each other, unsure of what to say. The pinging of the machine brought them back to reality.

"What is that?"

Rita took the vial out of the machine, its contents now slightly pink. The pills had dissolved. "It's a concoction of alcohol and barbiturates, designed to work with what's left of the VOS to control the physical behavior of the recruits. Every five hours, we dose unstable agents and recruits. It keeps them conscious but not dangerous."

"You can't give it to them in a cup?" Thorn watched warily as Rita inserted the contents of the vial into a syringe.

"In her state? Do you think she's going to take it that way?"

Thorn looked back at the girl, now with little more than a quarter of the robe on her body. "No, I suppose not. But won't injecting alcohol directly into the bloodstream kill her?"

"VOS treatment induces a high tolerance for alcohol. Injecting them with the combination of the alcohol and pills is the most effective. Other injections take too long and wear off too fast."

Thorn

Third Street Promenade
Santa Monica, California

November 22, 2018
3:00 a.m.

Thorn mindlessly stopped at the bus station.

The codes that Rita was talking about… what exactly were they?

It took her a few moments to notice the yelling.

Thorn tried to ignore the man as much as she could. After all, this was not her mission.

She tried her hardest not to look in that direction or even turn her ears towards the commotion.

But when she heard the slap and the woman's involuntary whimper, she squeezed her eyes shut and realized she couldn't ignore it.

Thorn, don't get involved. This isn't your mission. VOS repeated that twice, but then became silent. A mild throb replaced her voice.

She turned to look at the man, who was standing over the woman cowed against the backboard of the bus stop. She had her hand clutched to her left cheek and turned away when she saw Thorn watching.

The man turned.

Crew cut, shaven face, and button-down shirt. From the woman's demeanor, his stance, and the entitled look he was giving Thorn now, it was pretty obvious that this was a habit.

"Can I help you?" His voice was gruff, but completely devoid of shame. His eyes crudely examined Thorn from head to toe.

The woman looked away again, her face a mixture of anger and sadness.

The man sneered.

Thorn considered her options.

This is not your mission...

As the man watched and the woman kept her gaze in the opposite direction, Thorn unholstered her Glock, pointed at the man's forehead, and fired two shots. His eyes barely registered her weapon before he fell.

The woman screamed.

Thorn went over to the man, his brains and blood splattered on the sidewalk, and examined his head. Both bullets were still in there.

She flicked her blade open. As she got closer, the woman slid on her knees to be right next to the man.

"Please, please! Please, what did you do? Oh God, he's dead!"

The left side of the woman's face was developing a bluish tinge from his fist. Her body blocked some of the man's body, but her tears were what Thorn wanted to get away from.

Thorn was not in the mood to talk. She was in public and her hands were about to get sticky.

She hated when both things happened.

She nudged the woman to the bench, but each time Thorn moved towards the dead man, the woman fell back on the ground, blocking Thorn's access to the body.

Thorn sighed impatiently. "Do you have a heart condition?"

The woman, confused, managed to stutter, "N-no."

"Good." Thorn stabilized her with a hand, and slammed her elbow on the nerve between her neck and collarbone.

The woman collapsed.

Thorn turned her attention to the man.

Her newly sharpened blade entered his skull.

It only took three back-and-forths before her knife touched the bullet. Then a few more for the second.

She tucked both of the bullets into a small plastic bag at her hip. Now she had to wash up.

Her head felt like it was being squeezed by a metal clamp. She saw red behind her eyelids.

Her VOS was suspiciously quiet.

Tucking her knife back into its sheath, she looked at her watch and then at the man whose dead face had the same entitled look he had when he was alive.

She was going to let the police handle this, for once.

Wiping her fingers on the man's shirt, she melted into the darkness.

Alden

Palazzo Pizzeria
Los Angeles, California

November 24, 2018
2:15 p.m.

Alden sat in the pizza shop. Disgraced, lost. Even the best pepperoni pizza couldn't keep his mind from spinning.

He had no job, no friends, no leads.

Despite hours of research, he still had no solid connection between the department, the missing persons, the crime rate...

If he was smart he'd leave town and find a place that wanted a good cop. But he couldn't. He knew something was going on, and he had to do something.

He set his head in his hand, as his right hand prodded the pizza in front of him.

His eyes drifted to the window, watching cars cruise by. The calm outside definitely did not make him feel any–

There she was.

He'd recognize that stride anywhere. And that dyed red hair.

The woman who had escaped into thin air.

She was strolling along the other side of the street, her face still as unreadable, her hands fisted at her sides.

He reached into his pocket, took out his wallet, and put a ten-dollar bill on the table. After loudly sliding out from the booth, he waved an apologetic hand to the woman he had bumped in the back.

He couldn't let her disappear this time.

The bell on the front door clanged as he left the restaurant. While it wasn't loud enough to draw attention, her head turned towards him.

She turned away and continued walking.

His cover, or at least, his observation, was blown, but he couldn't just ignore his gut feeling. He followed her.

Six blocks away, she entered a bakery. She came out, minutes later, holding two pastry bags. He was wondering who the second bag was for when he noticed her crossing the street towards him.

He kept his eyes on her as she walked up to him.

She thrust a bag at him.

His first reaction was to hit it out of her hand, but he didn't. As he patted the place that usually housed his gun, he remembered that the chief had taken that too. His personal piece was back at his house, a depressing little hutch he hadn't gone back to in days.

She raised an eyebrow at him. "For a police officer, you sure are forward."

She was talking to him?

She winked at him. Right after the wink, her eyes glazed over for a moment, before turning back to him. It was as if she wasn't there for that brief moment.

How strange.

"I'm not a police officer." Anymore.

She seemed to analyze his words. "You don't seem to be lying."

"I'm not."

She swung the paper bag at him, indicating that he should take it.

He reluctantly took the pastry bag. Inside was a chocolate croissant.

"Not very often that strangers come up to you."

"You tried doing that last time."

Something was different about her. Something that wasn't there the last time he saw her.

Why was she talking to him now when she avoided him so well before?

There was definitely something about her that piqued his interest. He wasn't sure if she had any connection with the murders and the police chief, but he was going to find out.

It wasn't as if he had anything else to lose.

He noticed the dark circles under her eyes, the defensiveness of her posture, and the tucked hip. What was most interesting was her face.

Her expressions alternated between happy and stone-like, back to happy and then stone. Her tone of voice stayed the same, but it was as if he was watching a two-person show play out in front of his eyes.

Her phone rang. She turned away as she put the phone to her ear. As she walked away, her voice faded with each step.

She made no effort to say goodbye.

AEX

Research Laboratory
11th Floor, K-Pharma

November 24, 2018
9:15 a.m.

"You cannot go around murdering civilians!" Randolph slammed his fist on the desk six inches from Thorn's face. She didn't flinch.

This was the man who wanted to rule the world, and he was acting like a spoiled child.

No, she wasn't afraid he would touch her. He wouldn't dare.

Thorn looked into his eyes. "He was a woman beater."

Don't anger him further.

"You were unauthorized! You do only what we tell you!" Spittle flew out of his mouth, and Thorn kept a close eye on his flying arms and hands. "Do you have any idea how the media is going to spin this? 'Why is there homicide on the street right outside?' 'Who is this murderer? Bring him to justice!'"

'I did bring him to justice." She curled her upper lip. "Plus, the police covered it up just fine."

Thorn, stop talking back to him. Your words cannot overpower his anger.

Just as Randolph leaned in again, Khara caught his shoulder.

"Thorn, you understand that what you did went against AEX policy, the one you signed to uphold."

Thorn nodded warily.

Khara gave Randolph a look. He backed away. "You understand what can happen if AEX is exposed."

Nod.

"And I understand why you did it. The wife did confess to being beaten on a regular basis. But we have bigger problems."

Khara walked closer. "You murdering," she said with intonation, "the man, even if he was a wife beater, does nothing but bring unwanted attention."

Khara set a hand on Thorn's shoulder, the strength of her grip making the agent wince. "This is your only warning. You are my property. If you ever bring this much attention again," she leaned down to whisper into her ear, "I will kill you myself."

Khara motioned towards the T-machine. "You and your VOS need to be retreated, since you both have clearly forgotten the rules."

A small part of Thorn told her to run out of the room, to not allow them to put the cap on, but she remained firmly seated.

You must answer for the violation of the code.

Khara motioned for Van to bring the electrode cap. "Next time you blatantly disobey instructions, remember what this feels like."

Thorn promised herself not to scream.

She could not keep that promise.

Thorn

Research Laboratory   November 24, 2018
11th Floor, K-Pharma   10:15 a.m.

What felt like eons later, they removed the cap off of her limp head.

"--------"

Thorn tried to focus her attention on whoever was in front of her, whatever they were saying, but all her senses were mixed. Her hearing seemed to taste, her eyes seemed to feel. The only thing she knew for sure was that she was sitting down.

"-------------------- too much."

Th---n, t---- to k--ck yourse- out of it.

Nothing was making sense. She still felt the electrical waves on the top of her brain, but the presence, the feeling of warmth, had dwindled.

"Thorn! Focus yourself."

Her senses came back to her in one sweep, entering her body with one sudden intake of breath.

We are fine.

Thorn couldn't help the feeling of distaste that accompanied her relief.

"Thorn. Listen to me."

The agent swung her attention to the woman standing in front of her.

"We're going to change up this next mission for you. It takes a little more... planning.

"You will still eliminate all targets, all underlings of Blade and Clamp, but you're going to get their money. And their drugs."

Thorn started to ask why, but the sudden loud buzzing in her head stopped her short.

Khara leaned back. "That's your VOS telling you not to ask questions. After all, you only carry out *our* orders."

Khara, Randolph, and Van stared at her in the chair, fighting herself. A few minutes passed before she shakily rose from her seat.

Khara

Research Laboratory   November 24, 2018
11th Floor, K-Pharma   10:35 a.m.

Van heaved a long sigh after the door shut behind her. "For a second there, I thought she was splitting in half."

Randolph continued to stare at the door. "Her VOS is still powerful enough to control her."

Khara remained silent. They got lucky this time. Especially since the timing for her misbehavior was so perfect.

Anthony couldn't carry out this mission, nor any other missions, and Thorn usually shied away from missions with interrogation. Now, because of the retreatment, Thorn had to obey her VOS for the next 24 hours.

Without argument.

But Khara was beginning to worry.

Thorn's VOS was usually the most reliable. And the fact that she could so easily eschew AEX code without the same effects as Kenzie was worrisome.

Dangerous.

Outside AEX

Carter Residence
Los Angeles, California

November 27, 2018
11:20 a.m.

Isaiah hid in the closet, behind the shoe stand filled with his mommy's shoes, behind the heaviest coats and jackets, exactly where his daddy told him to stay. His back was pressed firmly, almost painfully, against the wall.

His back hurt, his butt hurt, and he was afraid, but he needed to listen to his daddy. When the door exploded, his daddy threw him in with the clothes, making him promise to not make a sound or leave the closet, no matter what.

His daddy wouldn't let anyone hurt him. His daddy was powerful, and strong, and everyone was afraid of him.

"I'm telling you nothin', bitch!"

Isaiah pulled back slightly. His uncle Roddy never sounded like that, not in the six years of his life that Isaiah had known him. Uncle Roddy was always kind.

Isaiah huddled even farther from the closet door, pressing his hands to his ears, wishing to wake up now, in his bedroom, with his mommy and daddy sleeping in the bed next to him.

A gunshot.

Uncle Roddy's screamed. Isaiah had his hands over his ears. Why, why won't the sounds go away? Isaiah told himself that everything was going to be okay, that he heard gunshots all the time, that this was just a normal day, that when he opened his eyes, the guns and the gunshots would be far away, and no one would be hurt.

He thought he heard a woman's voice. It was soft, calm… like his grandma and mommy. It calmed the fear in his chest, and he leaned away from the wall, hoping to hear more of this voice. It was cultured, like his teachers, but sharp, like the Mr. Blade who dropped by every month.

"…want to have to shoot your other kneecap, Rodrick." Shuffling. "It's not every day that I get to play with a whole group, and let me tell you," shuffling, "I consider it a privilege to leave something personal… with you, if I can call it that."

Isaiah thought he heard other people groaning, but he couldn't tell if it was from Uncle Roddy, Taylor, or his daddy.

Now that there was a woman in the room, Isaiah felt calmer. She must be someone nice, someone to help his dad, help him, to get out of here. There's no way that this woman wouldn't help his daddy, right?

He inched closer to the closet door, hoping to get a glimpse of her, maybe let her know that he was here.

"…are you doin' here? This is no place for people like you. Who sent you?"

Footsteps went towards the voice. "You don't need to know all that, Devon. I just want to know where your money and drugs are."

"Then just keep me! Let them go!"

Isaiah gathered courage from his daddy's voice, and he inched closer to the door. His left side now pressed against the shoe stand.

The sound of metal striking flesh echoed in the room. A groan followed, along with sniffling.

"Now, now. You're in no position to negotiate. Why don't you stop acting dumb and help me help you?"

Devon released a snort of laughter. "You're government. There's nothing you can do to us that can't be prosecuted."

This time it was the woman who laughed. Isaiah thought it sounded like bells chiming.

"You're a lot dumber than I thought."

Gunshot.

Muffled curses, and Devon's surprised gasp.

"First of all, who are they going to prosecute, if you're all dead and there are no witnesses?"

Another gunshot.

"Second of all, I do what I want." She sighed. "Now look what you made me do. I didn't want to kill Taylor just yet."

Footsteps going away from the closet. "You know what I hate more than wasting time?"

Silence.

"W-wai-wait. Please."

"Then answer my question."

"No, no I don't."

She sighed.

"I hate proving my point to someone just because they want to call my bluff. Call it a serious pet peeve."

Another gunshot.

More muffled screaming, this time more terrified and panicked than before.

"I literally hate when people doubt what I say. Poor Rodrick. Is he ever going to walk again? Tell me where-"

Isaiah scooted closer to the door. His arm caught on a jacket sleeve, and he slid out with too much force.

The shoe rack tipped, balancing on two rubber ends.

Isaiah prayed to God that it wouldn't fall, that it wouldn't splay the closet door wide open, that he wouldn't break his promise to his daddy.

Thorn

Thorn's Apartment
Los Angeles, California

November 28, 2018
4:32 a.m.

One moment Thorn was reaching for the child, and the next thing she knew, she was at home.

She lay on the couch, eyes wide open, hand mindlessly stroking the couch fabric as she tried to remember what happened.

Alie happened again. But this time, VOS actually erased the memory.

She killed another child.

The ceiling was dark, riddled with shadows, a convenient distraction for the issue at hand. Her mind was trying to piece together the present and the past, desperate to fill in the blank where her memory should be.

The closet door had flown open. Tumbling out alongside tennis and platform shoes, wearing a gray t-shirt and jeans, was a boy of about six. Thorn had breathed a sigh of relief that he was not a combatant. But she still had to eliminate all witnesses…

You have to kill him. Use him to pry more information out of them, but you cannot leave him be.

She ignored the pleas of the men.

She ignored the thuds of the chair legs against the hard surface of the floor, shuffling of clothing, the creaks, and a crash of a chair on the floor, followed by a grunt.

They couldn't break out of their restraints, no matter what they did.

Thorn reached for the boy and took him by the shoulders. She paraded him in front of the two men still alive, now with very different looks on their faces.

The one who fell in his chair attempted to make his way towards the boy. His eyes darted about, followed the movement of her left hand as she stroked the boy's head. The right hand still held the gun, but it was pointed at the ground.

The other man kept his gaze on the boy.

Thorn put her hand on the boy's shoulder. "Go help your dad."

The boy stumbled and walked towards his father, who watched his son approach. The boy held one arm of the chair and tried to lift it but it was too heavy for him.

Devon's eyes met his son's, and his face turned back towards Thorn. "It's inside the cushions of the couch in my mechanic's warehouse. All of it."

"And the money?"

"In the textbook cabinet of his teacher's classroom, hidden behind stacks of manuals and booklets, tucked into a box that says 'old'."

His eyes ran over the boy's face again. "Just please, don't hurt him."

Thorn lifted the gun and fired two shots into each man's head.

Her last memory was seeing her hand reach for the boy, who started to scream.

AEX

Observation Room
10th Floor, K-Pharma   (Two years ago)

The three figures standing behind the wall watched Thorn through the one-way mirror, and analyzed her work through the four cameras pointed at the table. The images appeared on one 90-inch television.

Two assistants sat behind computers, recording and transcribing what was happening in the glass box.

"She was quicker than anyone else we've tested."

"Did you see her face though? She had no idea what was happening."

"And yet she allowed it. Encouraged it, even."

They watched her pen as it circled the images in the matrix and matching test.

"We haven't done the real life testing just yet. Finding patterns and subconscious recall is good but we need to see if she can handle time and physical constraints."

Khara

Office of Kharavera Terraza   November 29, 2018
9th Floor, K-Pharma   9:15 a.m.

Randolph stared at Eve over the brim of his water glass.

"You say her VOS is stable. But I'm not so sure. The retreatment might temporarily keep her in line, but it's risky. I don't want another Anthony situation."

Randolph stroked his chin. "What if we partner her? Clearly we need her skills but we also want someone to keep an eye on her."

Eve shook her head. "I don't think VOS works well with partners."

"We don't have any evidence of that."

"The way VOS is designed, two agents might destroy each other."

"We don't know until we try." Randolph leaned back, hands behind his head. "We have to use Thorn, but she has to be supervised."

Khara looked pensive. "Streye?"

Randolph nodded. "He's consistent, controlled, and could take her down if we need him to. "

Thorn

Outside Café Bonne   December 4, 2018
Los Angeles, California   12:20 p.m.

Thorn felt the hair on the back of her neck tingle.

Her senses sharpened with each breath she took. She was never sure if the sensation of time slowing down was a side effect of the meds, or her VOS was trying to keep her alive. But it happened every time.

Her eyes took in more color contrasts and individual movement. Her nose flared, catching different scents from different direction, how far away they were, and what it was. Her skin became a tactile machine, hair follicles calculating wind direction and strength. Most notably, her muscles contracted and relaxed, and her entire body becoming primed for quick action.

There was no sudden movement, but her pupils dilated and contracted with each shift of her body.

She turned her body towards the right.

She saw him.

Black hair, prominent brow, broad shoulders. Red collared polo, black jeans, lace up military boots. Dark sunglasses but just light enough to reveal his narrowed hawk eyes.

He was looking away but she knew better.

She walked towards his table.

He didn't react aside from a twitch of the hand closest to his belt – a weapon, perhaps – and a twitch of his jaw.

Without asking, she pulled out the chair and sat down, leaning forward. Her entire body was flexed, ready for an attack.

"Are you following me?"

The man turned to look at her, but didn't pull off his sunglasses.

"I've been sitting here for a while." He flashed a smile, but she didn't reciprocate.

She crossed her arms in front of her chest. "I've seen you twice already. Who are you?"

He didn't budge.

She would provoke him, but she had no proof. And VOS has been extremely clear that they were not going to break rules again.

It had physically restrained her, and took over her completely.

She still didn't know what she had done to the child.

But VOS… she knew what VOS would do. And if she wasn't in control at that moment, then there was only one thing that could have happened.

Thorn felt lightheaded now, and her forehead was burning. The headache was coming back.

Giving the man one last look, she stood up, pushed the chair back in, and walked away.

Streye
Introduction

Cedars-Sinai Medical Center
Los Angeles, California   (Five years ago)

He was numb. Numb all over. So numb that even Ana's bawling was muted, shoved into a far corner of his mind.

It was so cold, why was the room so cold? Just moments ago it was boiling hot.

He took her hand, tried to hold it tight between his, but he couldn't bring himself to caress her. He wished he could comfort her, hug her, love her, as her body was wracked with sobs.

But he couldn't. Even holding his fiancée's hand was making him nauseous, filled him with a hate so ferocious he felt like it was eating him alive.

He did this. He wasn't good enough. Now he couldn't protect her.

He hated himself with a passion he hadn't felt since the war.

"I'm… I'm so… sorry…" She managed to choke out those words, in between hiccups. He turned to her, wanting to say all the right things, all the words to make her realize this wasn't her fault, that none of this was, but the words were caught in his throat, blocked by the all-encompassing numbness.

He choked down the disgust.

Was it worth it? Did it matter? Did anything matter?

His words didn't mean anything anyway.

He could keep holding her hand, hoping, wishing, that it was enough. But he knew it wasn't.

Not this time.

He gave it all up for this? He gave up himself just for heartbreak?

He felt another wave of nausea, disgusted with himself. How could he think that? This woman loved him, dedicated her life to him.

"I know you... left for me, for us. If you want to go back-"

"It's okay, Ana. This is not... your fault." Even as he said the words, he knew they sounded mechanical, forced.

He meant every word. Didn't he? "We can... try... again..."

For a third time? No, he couldn't.

You are truly selfish.

Yes, he was. That's who he was. He couldn't keep pretending that he was the loving, supportive man she thought he was.

How does it feel, to finally be free from your self-deception?

Ana's eyes finally closed as she drifted into a morphine-induced sleep. He released her hand, tucking it under the blanket.

He managed to pry the infant one piece out from her other hand. Without looking at it, he threw it into the trash can.

Moving to sit in a chair by the door, he retreated to his own dark place.

Streye

Outside Café Bonne
Los Angeles, California

December 4, 2018
12:30 p.m.

Keeping his eyes on her retreating back, Streye reached for his phone.

"How did it go?"

"She noticed. Seems like her VOS is still in good shape."

"Good. You'll be working with her on missions from now on."

Streye felt a twinge of irritation.

"Partner missions?" Having someone watch his back was always shit.

Yes, because you're probably the one to kill them.

"Why?"

"Her VOS is acting… a little unstable. We can't afford to bench her, and we figured her VOS would have fewer problems with yours."

Failure. "I don't want another Anthony on my hands, Khara." That was still too fresh in his mind.

"She's been mostly stable. We just want you to keep an eye out."

"Great."

Khara

Office of Kharavera Terraza   December 4, 2018
9th Floor, K-Pharma   5:25 p.m.

"I'm pairing you with a partner."

Thorn opened her mouth to disagree.

Just agree.

She stayed silent.

Thorn didn't want to risk another retreatment. Not when she was still trying to remember.

No matter how much she wracked her brain for an answer, it was still an empty black hole.

Khara's face was resolute.

"It seems like you already made up your mind."

Khara nodded.

"Who's the agent?"

"You've met him already."

Thorn
Memory

Research Laboratory   When Thorn was 23
11th Floor, K-Pharma   (Two years ago)

The first day they met was underneath a blinding white light, electrode cap attached to her head, her body wracked with pain.

Two weeks since AEX found her by the fountain, lying in a pool of her own blood, and brought her back to AEX headquarters. Two weeks of enduring blood transfusions, strictly planned meals, and social isolation for two weeks.

She enjoyed each moment of pain. It was such a strange feeling, to be so stimulated by hurt.

It was almost… comfortable.

What she didn't take into consideration was the extensive injections. They strapped her down, as tightly as the bands held. They placed a cloth and metal cap on her head (half of her hair had been shaved) and inserted needle after needle into her body. IV drips for pushing fluids in, catheters for getting fluids out.

She had drifted off to sleep before the procedure was finished.

When she woke up, she didn't know how much time had passed but she knew three things: her head was immobile, there were two tubes inserted into her head and each limb, and the screen in front of her was intensely bright.

The screen was large, taller than a person and wider than a car. She was so close to it that it enveloped her. Absorbed her.

They made her watch repeated clips of death, sex, abuse, religion, parenting, job interviews, and news reports. There was no semblance of any pattern. As she watched, the tubes sent electricity into her head, her brain. It tickled her just a little painfully from the inside, but she had to keep staring at the screen.

Her subconscious mind occasionally directed her attention to something that had happened. She couldn't turn away.

The jolts became increasingly painful, and the fluid going into her veins burned. It felt like they were shoving hot coal into her arm.

Her vision fizzled a few times as her eyes reflexively closed during and after the waves of electricity. She tasted blood as her teeth clenched, but she couldn't move her head or her arms. Her hands were clenched into fists, and she couldn't even feel her legs.

Her eyes kept focusing back on the screen, trying to distract itself from the pain.

She felt like sawing off her limbs.

The videos repeated, this time on mute. She saw black as electricity ran through her, buzzing, causing her body to feel weightless.

The videos became unmuted.

It was only after they debriefed her afterwards that she found out sound was playing throughout the entire treatment but her mind had shut out the noise. The doctors never found out why.

She lost the ability to ball her hands into fists. Her head was now a throbbing bomb, and the inside of her skull felt elastic, pushing out against the bone.

Her eyes were on fire, as dry as sandpaper, and were swollen, protruding from her face. Her lips tingled and her ears felt like they were being pulled apart and rotated. Her legs kicked as much as the straps would allow, and her toes curled.

From a distance, she heard a sweet calming noise. The pain in her body began to fade away.

"...get the AED, she's flatlining..."

"...one..."

"Don't take that out! It's-"

"Goddamn it, turn that shit off!" The room darkened as the screen faded to black.

A smile curled weakly on Thorn's lips. It felt like the hands were touching her from outside a bubble. Sounds faded away, the burning in her arms subsided and the headache became a pleasant memory.

The rubbing of her brain against the inside of her skull had stopped, and the piercing pain dwindled until it was just a dull ache.

She felt the straps being tugged from her body, her gown torn open, and two disks placed on her chest.

Her body flexed as they restarted her heart, but the constant high-pitched beep continued with only a blip in its screaming.

Her head felt like it was underwater, but she wasn't drowning. It was a womb of comfort and she didn't want to leave. Her body twitched.

I'm here.

In that moment, everything stopped. There was no more movement, no more sounds, no more pain. All that existed was the feeling of freedom, of comfort.

The voice belonged to no one familiar, and yet she felt she had known it her whole life.

AEX

Research Laboratory   December 5, 2018
11th Floor, K-Pharma   9:00 a.m.

Dr. Stewart milled about the room, retrieving parts of electrode caps and wires from different drawers. Rita and Taylor stood in the corner, monitoring the two agents' vital signs.

Thorn and Streye were lying on two medical chairs shoulder to shoulder, hands and feet restrained by cuffs.

"Thorn, you don't need to clench your fist so hard on the chair. It's done nothing to you."

Dr. Stewart didn't even need to turn around.

Thorn unclenched her hand and glanced at her partner. He had his eyes closed, almost like he was sleeping.

"Don't let him fool you." Rita walked over to readjust the cap. "When he does that, his VOS is extremely active.

"Rita." Streye opened his eyes to glare at the woman.

"You're going to be fighting alongside each other. She'll find out sooner or later."

"Sure. But what if I have to hunt her down too?"

The room became silent.

Dr. Stewart, ignoring the exchange, attached the last free-standing wires to the machine behind them. "Okay. We're ready."

As the nurses turned to recheck the monitors and the readings, he stood directly in front of both of them.

"As you know, VOS bonds through trauma. That's why T-treatment tends to be so painful. Now, instead of bonding you to your VOS, I will be bonding your subconscious to each other."

Streye's feet crossed at the ankles. "Do you mean the VOS?"

"No. Each of you has a subconscious, which the VOS draws from. VOS is a separate entity, one that includes parts of your subconscious but not all of it."

Thorn waved at him. "Okay, so what's going to happen?"

The doctor loosened the cuffs for the hands closest to each other. He set Thorn's hand in Streye's open palm, and readjusted the restraints.

"Uh…" Streye kept his hand flat.

"If you both experience the T-treatment without touching, it's going to just be a regular retreatment, animating your individual VOS. But if a part of your body is in contact with hers, the treatment will actually bring the two of you a mutual trauma. Hence, better bonding."

Dr. Stewart stepped back and motioned for the nurses to start the electricity.

They both grunted in pain, squeezing their eyes shut, as the machine buzzed to life.

He was pleased to see that Thorn's fingers extended across Streye's palm, as Streye's fingers wrapped around hers.

AEX

Training Arena
11th Floor, K-Pharma

December 7, 2018
8:10 a.m.

Thorn's fist almost connected with his eye socket. She pulled back just enough so that she didn't take out an eye but it landed solidly on his cheek. He winced, but didn't make any attempt to attack.

He took two steps back and put his hands in front of him halfheartedly. His eyes didn't even follow her movements.

She stepped in towards him so that they were nose to nose. "What is wrong with you?"

He bounced on the balls of his feet and met her eyes for the first time. "What do you mean?"

"Why don't you stop acting fussy and actually fight?" She stabbed a finger into his chest. "You don't want to be here. Do you think I do?"

He narrowed his eyes on her.

She stepped back from him. "If you want to be a man about it, go take it up with Khara instead of half-assing this shit."

She was going to do some target practice.

By herself.

Thorn

Waterhours Bar
Tujunga Canyon, California

December 9, 2018
7:15 p.m.

AEX could have waited a little longer before sending them on their first mission. They hadn't properly trained once.

She hadn't even seen him around after that first "session," if she could even call it that, and was starting to wonder if he'd even show up to the actual mission.

She glanced at him in the other room, cornered into a small hutch, surrounded by the members of the cult.

She wasn't sure her VOS liked Streye.

Focus on the mission at hand.

She turned back to her own problem.

Fifteen of them. Blocking every exit out of the room. They were young and old, male and female, but all were half-naked with blood smeared on their bare skin. All of them wore the same emotionless look on their faces as they advanced slowly towards the bar.

Thorn glanced at their hands. They held no weapons, but all of their fingernails were kept long and cut into triangles, forming pointy tips at the end.

According to the ML, that was how they murdered their victims.

Without averting her eyes from the crowd, she patted herself down. She only had two magazines, and her blade was almost useless against so many.

Her hand started reaching for the liquor counter.

Use the glass bottles - don't even go for your weapons. It's too close range for the gun.

Her fingers gripped the long neck of a vodka bottle, and she set two in each hand, one neck between thumb and forefinger, and another between the middle and fourth. She gripped them with her fingers curled towards her palm. Without turning away from the mob, she did the same on her other hand.

The mob moved slowly, walking with the same feet at the same time. It was as if they had trained to be in sync.

She lifted and dropped the bottles alternately to test the grip, and threw her arm high before smashing the glass on the counter, turning the bottles into weapons.

Liquor spewed and dripped off of the counter, exploding over the wooden top. It slid along the neck of the bottle and over her fingers.

The stickiness of her fingers became an additional layer of friction against the smooth glass.

She heard metal clanging in the kitchen. Streye.

The clanging stopped.

She heard the slide of his gun release.

As he fired the first bullet, the mob rushed at her.

Thorn

Outside Waterhours Bar   December 9, 2018
Tujunga Canyon, California   7:45 p.m.

Covered with blood and sweat, Streye planted himself next to her on the curb to wait for the cleanup crew.

"Next time, you should use your gun."

Thorn shot him a look from the corner of her eye. "Why, exactly?"

"While using the beer bottles was very creative, it also was slower. It took too much time."

"Hmm." Thorn felt a tightening of her chest, and she heard her heartbeat pound in her ears. She wasn't sure what the feeling was, but it felt familiar.

In the bad way.

No.

"This time you didn't call out or cover me. Next time we need to communicate better."

She edged away from him. "We didn't get in each other's way, completed the job."

"That's the minimum." He patted her knee. "We need to be able to go in knowing what we're doing, not making up plans as we're being surrounded."

"You didn't have an idea beforehand."

"We'll have to figure this out."

VOS was quiet.

His electronic notepad beeped. He pulled it from his pant.

"Our next mission."

"So soon?"

"Yeah, they want us to do this by the end of the week. In and out, undetected."

They both read the ML.

"What do you think?"

Thorn faced him. "An hour window is short, but there are only five targets."

"We'll split the house. Front and back, or side to side. No guns." He set his hands on the curb next to him. "We will be fine."

Thorn raised her eyebrows. Was he trying to reassure herself? Or himself?

Right. He had a voice too.

Thorn remembered a moment during their bar fight.

"You seem to have quite a bit of experience, seeing you move. Were you a civilian?"

"No."

He didn't offer anything after that and she didn't ask.

Streye

Outside Waterhours Bar   December 9, 2018
Tujunga Canyon, California   8:10 p.m.

He didn't know what to make of her. Thorn, this partner that he was now somehow bonded to.

She was talented and bright, but also extremely awkward and direct. He didn't fear for his life while working with her, but a part of him feared her.

Despite her tough exterior, she couldn't take criticism. When he had mentioned that she should have used her guns, her body language completely shut him out.

He didn't understand why she took offense. It was standard protocol to never spend more time on a target than you need to. It made you vulnerable to other threats.

It was a comment, not a criticism. But he wasn't going to defend himself.

They sat here in silence for so long he could almost forget that he had a partner. She wasn't much for small talk.

He appreciated that.

It's because she doesn't want to talk to you.

They heard wheels crunching on the asphalt.

"Cleanup crew's here."

They stood up, brushing dirt off of their pants. He turned towards her at the same time she dug her fingernails into his bicep. Throwing her entire body weight down, she wrestled him onto the ground.

As he hit his back on the side of the curb, he turned angrily towards her. "What the-"

The wall next to them exploded in a barrage of bullets. Debris exploded from the side of the restaurant as the car got closer.

He was thankful that the restaurant had a low brick wall in front, giving them some protection.

Didn't even sense it, did you? You're just a failure.

"I guess it's not the cleanup crew." He could barely hear himself above the screaming of the bullets around them.

Whoever was firing was not stopping.

"Guess not." Thorn winced as a piece of flying plaster slashed her cheek. She reached down to her hip and took out her Glock.

She patted the pack she carried on her back. "I have about 120 rounds."

"They have a machine gun."

"Sooner or later they'll run out of bullets. And then they'll have to send people to come find our dead bodies."

There was a blush on her cheeks, a liveliness that wasn't there two minutes ago. "How many rounds do you have left?"

He patted his pockets, checked his Sig. "Ten. Maybe twenty."

She gave him a long look. "Rethinking your advice to me?"

She's smarter than you too.

She motioned at him with the Glock. Her other hand trailed down her other side and produced a second Glock.

The machine gun fire was slowing down.

There was a moment of complete silence, as both parties held their breath.

A shoe crunched near them.

In one smooth movement, Thorn stood up, knocked the man down, and put a bullet between his eyes. Before Streye could even react, she had flipped onto the street.

Take his gun and go help her.

He took the dead man's gun, and pushed himself off of the wall. There were four bodies around the truck, and gunfire was now farther away.

He made his way around the car.

The driver was trying to get back into his seat and had started the engine. Streye grabbed the man with one hand as the gun in the other took out the rear tire.

He threw the man on the ground just in time to see a woman aiming her gun at him, and threw himself on the ground.

The shot pinged off the side of the truck.

A moment too quick…

When he lifted his head, Thorn had the woman pinned against the wall, and was kneeing her repeatedly in the side.

That girl really preferred hand-to-hand over guns.

The man in front of him attempted to take someone out of his jacket.

Streye shot him.

He spared the man a quick look just to make sure he was dead, before circling the premises, checking for additional fighters.

He didn't hear her until she was next to him. "Done playing spy?"

Startled, he swung his gun towards her. In three moves, she batted the gun out of his grip and disabled it. She scattered the pieces on the ground.

His VOS laughed at him.

Without waiting for his answer, she turned away. "They're working for the government. Their clothing was untagged but they're definitely Feds."

"Why would the government be after us?"

"I don't think they were."

"The cult?"

"It seems like. I'm going to go ask Khara about this. If the government is involved, then we should be as far away from it as possible."

She tucked her guns back into their respective holsters. "Next time you should save your guns and bullets for the big leagues."

She was definitely going to get on his nerves.

Thorn

Outside Kharavera's Office   December 10, 2018
9th Floor, K-Pharma   9:50 a.m.

Thorn was about to knock to announce her presence, but her hand stopped inches from the wood.

"...she's telling us to get rid of this one man, but -"

"She's made more enemies?"

Thorn stood with her back against the wall, but she could hear Randolph fidgeting in his chair.

"Just one. Apparently one of her men was repeatedly defiant and she had to get rid of him. The man was there moments after Stephen's death."

"Why didn't she take care of him?"

"She doesn't want to get her hands dirty. Dirtier."

"Sure." Khara's voice was firm. "But you know this sounds more like petty revenge, not furthering our cause at all."

"What if the man goes after us?"

There was a silence. "We can't keep doing political favors for her.

The police chief needs to be able to clean up after herself."

"Oh, come on. AEX benefits as much from police cooperation as we do. Just have Thorn and Streye go – they should have no problem with cleaning duty."

"Their partnership is not so we can wipe everyone's ass."

She sighed. "With Stephen gone, we can't risk media attention. Now we need to stay in the shadows, hunt down only those who won't raise suspicion. We can't be bold with our missions anymore."

Randolph was suspiciously silent.

"Oh just say it."

"What about Roder? That was pretty bold."

"He was too close to revealing AEX. Much too close."

Randolph breathed out through his nose. "I think we should get rid of the nosy officer. What if this comes back on us? What if that guy finds out about AEX? He's nosy."

"Oh please." Khara scoffed. "Even if he was suspicious, he wouldn't know where to start."

Thorn
Memory

Navarro Residence
Sacramento, California (Two years ago)

Every part of her body was sweating. Even her eyelids were leaking. It took everything in her to keep her breathing quiet enough to hear the ticking of the timer on her watch.

A bead of sweat ran down her forehead and stung her eye.

She could only blink the pain away. Any unnecessary movement could betray her.

Her hands were wrapped around her gun, but she didn't want to let go in case her reflexes weren't fast enough.

Thorn licked her upper lip nervously.

But…this was exciting. This was danger and realness and alive. She hadn't been this nervous since... Well, she couldn't even think of a time when she felt like this. She just hadn't cared enough. Feeling again – it was as if she had regrown a long-lost limb.

Her first mission. She had to do well.

Thorn

Cemetery Canyon   December 10, 2018
Castaic, California   2:30 p.m.

Thorn sat on the rock under the sprawling tree, her eyes closed. Walls of giant stone pillars stood at her back and sides. Her mouth inhaled and exhaled to a steady rhythm.

Here she felt safe. She could breathe and think and do the things she couldn't around people. Grasping the rock under her with open palms, Thorn tried to fade away.

Alie's face flashed behind her closed eyelids.

Immediately it was gone, replaced by VOS's presence and voice.

You could only do what you could.

That little boy's face.

Think positive. I need your help archiving these memories so you don't think about them.

Will the reactions ever dull?

Not until you stop fighting me.

Image of Stephen Libbe.

Image of Blade.

The memories were appearing one by one, but with each image she felt less of the emotional reaction.

Image of Clamp.

Try to let them go. The people, the feelings. We must process these thoughts before they evolve into something else.

Bodies of targets sprawled in different stages of death. Thorn had stopped consciously recognizing who she was recalling.

And then Streye's face.

VOS was quick to remove it. But his presence lingered in her mind. Never before had a non-target appeared in her vision.

She turned back to the stone walls.

The first time she wandered onto this place, it was an act of rebellion. Her mother had ignored her when she tried to speak about the incident.

Thorn decided to run away. She didn't care where, as long as she could get away from the place she called home.

She ran to six parks and wildlife preserves, only to leave after not liking any of them. They were too crowded, too small, or too dirty. One had an old man watching her every move. She was tired and hungry and dehydrated. The food she packed lasted only two days.

As she was making the journey home, she took a detour.

And found this place, hidden behind a cemetery, a desert canyon with no name, no hikers, no tourists.

Just silence.

From that day forth, this was her spot. Her sanctuary.

Thorn

Alleyway   December 14, 2018
Lancaster, California   10:45 p.m.

She knew this partnership was a mistake. On their second mission, and already she knew she was going to kill him.

Streye side-stepped her feint, and kept his hand wrapped around her upper arm while the other quickly immobilized the arm going for her gun. Her knee was about to make friends with his testicles, but he sidestepped again.

The bastard.

She was on the balls of her feet.

"Why did you do that?"

She wanted to beat his face in.

He observed her face for a second. "I completed the mission."

Thorn, what are you doing? Calm down.

"You killed a fucking dog. It didn't do anything to you." She turned to leave the alley. Her foot had just rounded the corner when she felt his hand grip her arm like a vise.

Streye pulled her away from the main street. "What are you doing?"

His fingers dug into her arm.

Thorn jabbed at his neck and made contact, forcing him to let go of her arm. She twisted out of his grasp. "Next time you touch me like that, be prepared to lose a hand."

"The dog was drawing attention to us. You know that's protocol." His face was close to hers. Even when he whispered like he was doing now, it sounded like yelling. "It was quick and painless."

"It barked once." She bared her teeth at him. "You could very well have walked away from it."

Thorn.

"I removed all signs and clues that could give us away. AEX policy demands that of its agents. You know this."

She tapped her foot twice, trying to reign in her frustration. She pinched her lips together.

"I can't even understand why you're like this." He ran a hand through his hair. "It's AEX protocol to eliminate any source of discovery. If Khara knew that you hesitated because of protecting some animal's life..."

"The mission was a success. All five targets were eliminated. We were on our way back."

"It wouldn't have been a success if someone came to check on the dog." He threw up his hands. "Where is your VOS? She should be telling you that what I did was standard procedure."

Only when he brought up VOS did she realize it had barely spoken to her during the mission.

Thorn didn't remember the particular principles that Streye was talking about. Was he right? Was she ignoring protocol?

Without saying another word, they both headed back towards AEX.

Thorn

Miyori Sushi and Grill   December 20, 2018
Santa Barbara, California   3:00 p.m.

Thorn had a plate of sushi and sashimi in front of her, and Streye had rice and teriyaki chicken in front of him. A half-empty plate of tempura and two sake bottles sat between them.

As Thorn leaned back, she caught Streye's eyes focused on something behind her. She picked up her chopsticks and leaned in, making the appearance of eating so she could get close enough to whisper.

"What do you see?" She picked at the grains of rice that had come loose from the rolls.

He glanced at her before redirecting his attention to his plate. "No, I don't think it's anything." He took a sip of his sake. "We have someone watching us."

"Threat?"

He made a small shaking motion of his head, and took a bite of his chicken. "No, he doesn't have that look." He poured some soy sauce on his plate. "More of the deer-in-the-headlights kind."

"Maybe you should stop looking at him."

Despite his nonchalance, Thorn felt a pit grow in her stomach. She put her utensils down.

Her VOS didn't say anything. But her gut feeling spoke volumes.

Streye met her eyes. "It's not that. Would you like to take a look?"

Thorn nodded.

They switched seats but she made sure not to look in that direction until they switched their plates. Her eyes looked around the outside patio, waiters, cars, and buildings, before landing on the boy.

It felt as if she had been struck by lightning. Her vision momentarily blacked out, and she had never been so glad to be able to control her facial expressions as she was now.

Her fingers clenched white on the underside of the table.

She didn't remember him.

Her VOS commanded her not to remember him, had even blacked out a portion of her memory.

That face...

VOS had stopped her from actively remembering what happened on that mission. But now with him right in front of her, VOS could no longer deny that she had let him live.

The boy.

VOS had blanked her memory to protect itself. By letting the boy live, VOS had gone against the most fundamental of AEX codes. By blocking her memory, it could deny its own violation.

He looked exactly the same.

She met the eyes of the little boy who should have burned to ash in the house along with his father, mother, and uncles. For some reason, Thorn had one moment of rebellion even during that 24-hour retreatment period and left him alive. She didn't know if she asked

VOS to erase the memory, or if VOS decided to do it without her consent.

Did he tell the police? What has he said?

And now here she was, looking straight at a witness she failed to kill. If what Rita said was true, about breaking code, then it was just a matter of time before she lost her mind.

Somehow the VOS hadn't broken yet, hadn't revealed her secret to AEX, hadn't done anything except hide the memory from her.

Streye watched her carefully. "Do you know him?"

Thorn thought very carefully before she spoke. She desperately wanted to tell him, to share the burden of this mistake, to cajole out of him some sort of sick forgiveness.

But it was too risky. She couldn't tell him. The secret that she had failed a mission. Kept a witness alive. Defied AEX's code and VOS.

If AEX found out, her meltdown would be the least of her problems.

"No." She swallowed. "But his face looks familiar."

Streye seemed to accept that explanation. "It's nothing to be afraid of. People thinking you're someone else happens all the time."

Thorn's eyes flew to his face, trying to decipher how much he knew. But she relaxed. If he knew, there was no way he would be content with inaction.

He was management, after all. He'd kill her.

The boy was still looking at her, but he didn't make any attempt to communicate. She lowered her eyes to the plate.

"Yeah, you must be right."

She took a large gulp of sake, hoping that the burning trail it left in her throat would help her ignore the boy's gaze.

Streye

Interior Park   December 23, 2018

Huntington Beach   2:35 p.m.

Thorn constantly defied him and his orders. How she could be so defiant and yet so efficient he had yet to understand, but it was getting dangerous. By not listening to him, she was putting the entire mission in jeopardy.

"Tight black top and boots. You just had to wear that."

You like that, don't you?

Thorn rolled her shoulders forward. "It's better access to everything. You know how dangerous she's supposed to be."

"Our mission is to blend in to get close to her."

Her eyes flashed at him. "That's what you think we should do."

"No one wears that to the beach."

How would you know? You've never gone. Or taken anyone else.

Thorn shot him an irritated look. He tried to ignore her. He just didn't have the capacity to deal with her right now.

Not today.

His jaw clenched.

"She's staring. Can you not look like you're in pain?" Thorn set a hand on his thigh. "You're the one who looks out of place. Couple's day out, remember? Look happy."

He looked at the reflection of their target on her sunglasses. The target really was staring.

Can't even do this right.

He looked away, far off into the sky.

Today was supposed to be a day of drinking, of unconsciousness and thoughtlessness. It's been the tradition for the past four years.

It's your fault.

Morning liquor. Lunch liquor. Dinner liquor.

How do you call yourself a man?

He had to force himself to be upright and conscious, because AEX didn't want Thorn to suffer a breakdown. Well, fuck if he wanted to be here. Khara knew today was his day. Khara knew. And yet–

"Streye."

He sat there, across from a woman he knew nothing about, both throwing their lives away for nothing. They were two strangers who were from the same hell and living the same nightmare, and yet nothing alike.

You can't possibly fuck this up too, Streye. You always do.

Darcy, their target, called over one of her henchmen, and whispered in his ear while staring in their direction.

"Fuck."

"I told you."

What are you going to do, Streye? If Darcy makes a move here, a lot of innocents will die. Do you want that again, Streye? Do you want to live knowing you caused innocent deaths?

Like Will? Like Damien? Memories of his squad mates appeared.

Like your unborn children?

His voice wouldn't go away. It was at its harshest, knowing exactly where to strike. That was why he needed his liquor.

His gaze fell on her hand, still lightly draped on his thigh, giving the impression that she actually wanted to touch him.

How could she? He was even repulsed by himself.

You are disgusting. A piece of shit.

How would it be to touch her?

"Streye. I thought you said you had the plan figured out."

Would she be soft and yielding? Or hard and angled? Would her lips taste like the blood she's spilt? Or would they taste like the sweets she so loved?

You know it goes against AEX code. You're going to fuck up her VOS, just like you–

He leaned over, took her chin in his hand, and pressed his mouth to hers, opened slightly in a surprised 'o'. The hand on his knee tensed and balled up. He set a hand on top of it.

His voice had nothing more to say.

It was silent. Blissful, peaceful silence.

His other hand wrapped around the back of her neck, fingernails gently scraping her skin. He pulled away slightly to look at her, still as composed as ever, except for the pink blush on her cheeks. His thumb brushed against her lower lip.

As she made an effort to move away, his hand came up her thigh to cup her waist.

Still, silence. He hadn't known this silence could exist.

Is this what it's like to be free?

He'd been running from himself, his internal voice, for years.

He thought about letting her go, but her body was tempting and distracting, just as effective as getting plastered. He pulled her in towards him with a hand in her hair, and set his lips on hers again. This time they opened easily, allowing him access to her soft mouth.

She tasted like pastries.

She pulled away to take a breath.

Setting a less than stable hand in between them, she made a quick note of where the target's bodyguards were, and turned back to him.

She eyed him warily.

She brushed a hand across her mouth. "What… what was that?"

"For the mission." Even to him, that excuse seemed flimsy. "She noticed us. Had to do something."

Asshole. Selfish asshole. The voice was back.

Maybe he just needed to touch her for the voice to leave him alone.

They both caught movement from the left side of the bench. He pushed her behind him as he grabbed the gun from his belt and pointed it at the shuffling leaves.

Nothing appeared.

Thorn made a gesture to get up but he pressed his body aggressively against hers, motioning for her to stay seated. She narrowed her eyes at him, but didn't make an effort to rise.

Trying to feel like a big man, Streye? Some things just don't change.

He went the opposite direction as the noise, supporting his gun hand with his left.

Some wood chips out of place. Leaves pushed to the side. Footprints.

He heard two silenced gunshots behind him. Rushing back to the bench, he made it just in time to see a man fall face-down in front of Thorn, a suppressed Glock in her hand.

She's making you look even worse, you incompetent dumbass.

Her implacable mask was back in place. "I'll go check on her other two bodyguards. Seems like your ploy didn't exactly work."

He needed to see her soft and vulnerable again.

So you can feel good about yourself? You're a fool.

She was in the process of standing up when he reached over and pulled her against him. The fact that her loaded gun slid right against his leg made it even better.

Hotter.

She didn't fight when his arm grabbed across her stomach.

Holding her tight against his torso, he used the muzzle of his gun to lift her chin and pressed her head back towards him.

Thorn started to speak, but his lips crushed down on hers.

Ah, there it was. Sweet, blissful peace.

He barely felt the gun go off by his ear.

Thorn

Exterior Park   December 23, 2018
Huntington Beach   3:18 p.m.

She glanced at him out of the corner of her eye.

He was silent, lost in his own world. His eyes stared straight ahead.

After she shot the man who was coming up behind them, his eyes searched her face for a long time. The longer he stared, the colder he became, until he finally stepped away.

They hunted and eliminated Darcy in silence. The only time he spoke since then was to call the cleanup crew.

She wanted to touch her fingers to her lips, to feel that heat again.

It was such a strange feeling. She wasn't sure what it was.

"You could have warned me about the man standing there." He rubbed his ear. "I think you pierced my eardrum."

"I was trying to. Then you kissed me. So I got rid of the threat."

He became silent again.

Thorn felt that discomfort again, the same one she felt as they sat outside the bar in Tujunga. She still couldn't pinpoint what exactly

275

she was feeling.

All she knew was that the wonder and warmth she felt only moments earlier, was gone.

Her head began to throb. Again.

She resisted holding her hands up to her head. And succeeded, only barely.

--n- become --e of ----.

VOS repeated it two more times. But Thorn still couldn't make out exactly what it was trying to say.

Thorn
Memory

Training Arena
11th Floor, K-Pharma   (Two years ago)

Her frown deepened into a scowl as she realized this was not going
well. Her confidence from her first mission plummeted with each
shot, jab, or hook Van directed at her.

Where was VOS?

She needed to regroup, but he was giving her no time. He was both
everywhere and nowhere. Her body parried automatically but her
mind was completely blank.

What was her method of attack? How should she approach? Should
she trap him?

"Let your VOS come out. Stop forcing your mind to reach for it."

He sent a right hook and she dodged, but only barely. The knuckles
grazed her jaw enough to send her into another panic.

He wasn't wearing protective gear; she wasn't wearing any armor-
what if she actually hurt him? More likely the case, he would actually
hurt her. They weren't taught to pull back or hold out on punches or
attack. They would actually be hit. A punch to the face could take her
out. And then how else would she be able to do more missions?

How could she face them all? That would be so embarrassing.

She didn't see his hand and reacted a second too slow. He flipped her on her back, landing with a heavy thud, the wind knocked out of her lungs.

She closed her eyes.

He stood over her, not even breaking a sweat. "Why are your eyes closed? You could be killed doing that."

He leaned down and slapped her face, two times across each cheek, hard enough to sting. A rush of tears formed in her vision, and she shot up in a seated position.

She had just killed a man, and now she was crying. She was supposed to be ready. How could they have seen it in her? She was no one, and had no training. They were just cracking jokes at her expense.

How stupid. She pushed herself upright and turned away.

"Stop. Where do you think you're going?" Thorn wanted to run out and never come back.

But his voice stopped her. "We're going to stay right here until you allow your VOS to do this."

She wanted to yell. To scream. Let her hide.

Where was VOS?

Alden

Entrance
K-Pharma Complex
Casmalia, CA

December 30, 2018
8:45 a.m.

Alden stood at the base of the K-Pharma building.

It was a huge complex, miles and miles across, bordered by residential areas, layers of fencing, and security. A lot of security, both human and machine.

K-Pharma was well-known, considered one of the fastest growing, philanthropic companies of the century. In the medical technology and pharmaceutical industries, K-Pharma owned 60% of the market, more than any other medical company. In its rise to fame the past ten years, it has driven hundreds of medical companies out of business.

A powerhouse.

This was where the girl had gone after their last encounter. She had been quick and careful, taking long stretches of road and detours, even changing cars, but her escape this time was significantly different from the last.

Even while she was still alert, Alden had no trouble tailing her. It was so easy he feared he was walking into a trap.

But he hadn't.

She had parked her car two miles away, walked around to the back of the research building and went through the double doors.

That was two weeks ago.

He knew there was no way he could just barge in on a corporation the size of a small city, so he bid his time and made a plan.

He needed to understand if what Stephen said was true, and if so, why wasn't there any information on it?

Who was controlling the operation?

Taking a deep breath, he stepped into the rotating doors.

Two armed men in suits approached him. "Sir, can we help you?"

The receptionist standing at the front desk rushed over, and handed Alden a temporary badge. "This gentleman is with me!"

Turning to him, she smiled. "Mr. Hardt. Welcome to K-Pharma."

Thorn

Chinatown
Los Angeles, California

December 31, 2018
4:48 a.m.

The axe came down towards her.

She didn't have time to evade the swing, so she leapt toward the broad-shouldered Asian woman, whose face was covered by a bandana.

"What godawful mission did Khara send us on this time?" She pushed the woman with all her might, feeling like a squirrel fighting a brick wall. She kicked, punched, swung, but none of the contact seemed to affect the rock-like warrior.

She ducked as the axe flew over her head and thudded back into the woman's palm.

"Who the hell are these people?" Streye was caught up in his own fight against three fighters. He had parried and landed blows, but they seemed tireless.

"I," she ducked and threw herself toward the woman's legs, "told you something felt off. They're getting," she rolled into an attack position, clenching and unclenching her hands, trying to ignore the dull aches and tight muscles. Trying to stay in one piece had never been harder. "So complicated."

As she got to her hands and knees, she saw her gun laying ten feet away, kicked from her hands before she got a chance to fire it.

She only had one of her three blades left. The rest were broken by the woman's superhuman aim.

Where was VOS? It crackled earlier on in the night, but had since disappeared.

The ML was also blurry in her mind. She still remembered key points of the mission, but could not recall the exact logistics. That's never happened before.

Even worse, her reactions were slow.

Streye slammed one of the men on the metal shelf, breaking the glass bottoms. Something cracked.

Thorn wasn't sure if it was a human bone or the metal contraption, but things were happening too fast for her to do a double take.

"They must have some reason."

Thorn's body was thrown in between Streye and his opponents. She kept on rolling, shoulder over shoulder, until she tilted her feet to the ground and propelled herself into a crouched position.

She stopped mere inches from the wall. Her tumble, tuck, and crouch took a total of two seconds and one smooth motion, but she stumbled as she got up.

Her knees wobbled.

A quick palm to the wall stabilized her.

Thorn shot Streye a quick glance. "Your faith in AEX is commendable."

A line of blood trickled from her right hairline to her cheek, and she swiped her forearm over the right side of her face. She held herself up with one arm on the wall, as her eyes tried to refocus on the woman, who was heading towards her.

The two remaining men glanced at her, then at the giant woman, and stepped aside to let their teammate walk by.

Thorn licked blood from the corner of her mouth.

The woman wasn't even breathing hard. Carrying that axe should at least be wearing her down.

Streye opened his mouth. "Hey-"

Thorn rushed at the woman with her last remaining dagger. She zigzagged around, making a few cuts on the woman's clothes while the bigger woman swung her axe.

Thorn had already dived for her gun when she realized she was heading right to where the woman was swinging. With a muffled curse, Thorn slammed her elbow on the ground to pivot her in the opposite direction.

But she was too late.

The axe came down with a deafening thud on the concrete.

Thorn heard herself scream as she felt the thick metal slice through her thigh.

Streye

Emergency Room   December 31, 2018
Cedars-Sinai Medical Center   12:45 p.m.

Six hours since the surgery started. Six-and-a-half hours since he burst into the emergency room with her in his arms, blood staining his shirt and pants.

Her blood had stopped streaming and started leaking, her body going into shock from the amount of blood she lost. She had gotten colder and colder, her breathing getting softer against his chest.

Useless. Another death, on your-

AEX was too far. Cars, people, animals, streetlights, everything was so slow. But he couldn't just run every red light, run over every elderly person.

Most importantly, he couldn't call an ambulance.

Halfway through his journey, he realized that she would die if he didn't get her medical attention soon. She had lost too much blood too fast.

There was no way she could make the hour-long trip back to the medical sector of AEX.

So he took her to the closest hospital.

He'd never thought he'd be back in this particular one. Not after all the memories associated with it.

But it was this or she was dead.

Thank God the doctors didn't ask any questions. Not yet anyway. He wouldn't know what to say. How did the injury happen? Where? Who?

If he didn't get arrested first.

He had washed his hands and changed into clean clothes, but he hadn't left the waiting room for anything else. There was no telling what could happen, who'd come in, and who he'd have to kill to protect AEX's secret.

The sliding doors flew open.

"Khara."

They looked at each other, him sitting down, her standing a few feet away.

"Why didn't you bring her to AEX?"

He turned away, knowing that she'd sense his distaste if she saw his eyes. "If I could, don't you think I would have?"

"I don't know, Streye. It's like you've been a different person lately."

"The codes are still active, if that's what you mean."

I don't know about that. You've found a loophole, after all.

"Sure." Khara crossed her arms. "You're still management, aren't you? I hope you haven't let your loyalties stray."

Bitch.

For once, he agreed with his voice.

"What happened with the mission?"

"They've been eliminated."

He sat up. "Why were there trained assassins protecting these small time criminals? What happened to big name criminals? The ones that actually matter?"

"I'm not sure who these fighters are, but as long as you complete your mission, we're fine."

"Right."

"You don't need to know the answers to everything."

"So now you don't trust me."

Probably with very good reason.

She didn't respond. Instead, she sat down a chair away from him and crossed her legs.

"She couldn't complete the mission." She took out her electronic notepad. "Maybe her VOS really is weakening."

"She did complete the mission."

Khara narrowed her eyes on him.

Streye released a breath. "The fight was slow. Even against Thorn, the woman was not weakening. At this point, we had been at a stalemate for a good hour. The axe hit her thigh."

Khara nodded. "That's what you told me on the report."

"I made my way out from those two wiry motherfuckers, when I saw her get up. She had this look on her face."

He tried to come up with a word, but gave up. "She grabbed the dagger off of the ground and leapt on the woman." He looked at his hands. "I have never seen a look of such inhuman focus as she was stabbed the woman. In the neck. The face. The entire time, her leg was gushing. On the woman, on the ground."

Khara's expression didn't change.

"After the woman finally fell, Thorn leapt off her back. Her face was so pale, she was still bleeding. She didn't even register my presence."

The phone at the nurse's desk rang and they both looked up.

"One moment she was lying on the ground screaming, the next she was up, a monster. She chased down the guy closest to her, broke his neck. The next guy, she rammed his face into the wall repeatedly until he had no features. Then the third guy, who I already disabled. She stepped on his throat until... well, you get it."

Khara's hands had clasped in front of her. He didn't need to finish his sentence.

Streye ran his hand through his hair. "I have never seen anything like that." He made a small explanatory gesture with his right hand. "Anthony was different. His was calculated, with intent... Hers... it was primal. Desperate."

His eyes went to the sign over the door. "After making sure they were all dead, she just fell to the ground. Didn't look at me. Just fell."

"No wonder the cleanup crew hasn't gotten back to me."

He nodded. "There's a lot to clean up."

Her face softened for the first time since she'd stepped inside the hospital. "You know that bringing her here creates witnesses."

"I'll take care of the loose ends. Just... don't tell her I brought her in."

Khara gave him a measured look.

"That's probably for the best."

Thorn
Memory

Corra Residence
Palmdale, California

When Thorn was 21
(Four years ago)

There was a soft knock on her door.

Thorn turned to see her mother standing in the doorway, hair pulled up into large curls, dressed in her classic business suit. Her heels clicked on the wooden floor as she walked in and sat by her daughter on the bed.

She caressed Thorn's face gently. "My beautiful daughter. I'm worried about you. You don't sleep, you don't eat, and you don't even enjoy your weekends. What is going on?"

Does she really not know? Or is she pretending not to, so she doesn't have to live with the guilt?

"I'm fine, mom." It was the only thing she could say to her that wouldn't start an argument. She had tried, and she was tired of trying.

They had isolated each other in their own spheres, separated by a distance no amount of talking or touching could fix.

They both remained silent, Thorn's features stoic as she tried hard not to cry.

Grace touched her leg through the comforter. "You have to get over this. I have tougher things to get over, but I did it for you. Can't you be happy? For me?"

"Mhmm." Thorn's voice was small, and was blocked in her throat.

She wished she was somewhere far away, away from these pretend niceties, away from a home she felt like a stranger in, away from everything she knew.

She wanted to disappear.

Thorn

Thorn's Apartment
Los Angeles, California

January 7, 2019
1:20 a.m.

She couldn't seem to remember the details.

The specific time, date, mission logistics... Everything was so hazy, especially the memory of her missions. Thorn rubbed her temples, unsure of how to proceed.

Making sure not to move her leg, she pulled the leather-bound journal from its resting place under her coffee table.

When VOS had first started fading, Thorn hardly noticed. VOS spoke to her less, but was still there for her when she needed it.

Then VOS had removed the quick understanding of the mission. Prior to its disappearance, it had taken Thorn at most twenty minutes to process all of it. Now Thorn read the ML for hours, and she still forgot important details.

The silence then became the loss of muscle memory, which almost got her killed multiple times.

Like that time with the axe woman. How she got out of that she didn't know, but her near-failure was because her VOS was retreating. Only by pure luck and exhaustion did she come out victorious.

Thorn was slow. And tired.

She was becoming worn down with each battle, when before she used to gather strength from them.

Now her memory was starting to go. Thorn was losing track of all the people that she interacted with at AEX: the doctors, the nurses, the other agents… had she met all of them before?

But what scared her most was that her prior memories, from before her suicide, before AEX, were coming back.

She needed to forget the past.

She needed to.

She couldn't go back there.

But there have already been mornings when she's woken up, thrown back in time, thrown back into that nightmare.

The nightmare of who she was before AEX saved her.

She felt panic rising in her throat, and had to dig her nails into her uninjured thigh. She felt the nails form crescent trenches into her leg, but even that didn't provide the relief as she wanted.

She took a few deep breaths, and turned her focus back on the journal.

Her eyes blurred.

Had she taken VOS for granted?

Streye

Streye's Apartment   January 14, 2019
Westwood, California   11:00 p.m.

He stood in the shower, water streaming onto his face, steam wrapping itself around his body. The peppermint scent of the body wash soothed the cuts on his skin as it calmed his mind.

Calm, for now.

He leaned towards the showerhead, letting his eyes close so the water sluicing down his hair didn't run into his eyes.

The heat shocked his skin. A good pain.

The shower curtain flung to one side, metal rings pinging against the shower bars. His face lowered, body priming itself for defense against an intruder.

Her scent hit him faster than his eyes could process.

Thorn's eyes pierced him, undeterred by the haze of steam swirling around them both.

While keeping her eyes on his, she unbuttoned the loose gray-green shirt, fingers caressing each of the buttons before sliding them through the hole. The top one was already open, revealing the smooth triangle of skin at her neck. Her hands glided over the middle, starting at the second highest button.

Her index finger circled the button, moved like molasses down to the next, revealing more and more of her bare skin.
A black bra, black ink...

Streye held her gaze as long as possible, but the steam forced him to blink.

When he re-opened his eyes, his gaze fell on the exposed chest, the rise and fall of her breasts behind the confines of the bra, the scars on her skin, the gauze on her thigh…

Her fingers unhooked the last button.

Keeping her hands still, she slid the shirt slowly off her torso. It pooled into a pile at her feet.

She stood there, in her bra and panties.

His mind was pleasantly blank.

He took a step backwards, toward the inside of the shower.

Without removing the rest of her clothes, Thorn stepped over the edge of the bath, pushing him toward the tiles. His back hit the cool white ceramics, and her chest pushed into his.

The showerhead drizzled over them, hiding their bodies and their secrets from the world.

Alden

Security Room   January 25, 2019
10th Floor, K-Pharma   12:10 p.m.

Two hundred and thirty employees.

There were people in every section on every floor, making his
investigating more difficult than he expected. Security was also tight,
making rounds and double checking ID. He couldn't even stay after
hours because they checked everyone out at the same time.

There was no escaping the guards.

He also couldn't just keep looking at security footage he'd hocked
while sneaking in during their lunch break. Nothing was on there.

In the four months he's been a K-Pharma employee, he's only found
several coworkers having sex in the "private" bathroom and a few
recordings of embezzlement.

He'd made friends with the workers around him, and been privy to
their conversations. But the only thing that was suspicious was the
high quality of benefits they received.

He went to his desk.

Why was their security so tight? Nothing the floor worked with was
in any way secretive. It was mostly analysis of the footage of the

chemical labs, to make sure no one tampered with anything.

Alden pushed his chair back, making sure that he didn't draw attention to himself. He shuffled some papers, set them on the desk, and got up from his chair.

"Watch my stuff, will you?"

The skinny woman working at the desk across from him nodded, and gave him a thumbs up.

Making sure no one was following him, he made his way to the HR hallway.

There was one man inside. Duke Marcus.

Alden only met him once. Marcus was leaving the R&D department and had grinned at him. His eyes were bloodshot, his face sweaty.

Dr. Marcus was sitting with his left side to the front door, fingers frantically clicking on his keyboard. A folder of loose papers and pictures slid around to the left of the computer.

Alden tried to look closer at the pictures, but they were farther away. He leaned into the door with the small glass window.

His badge clicked against the door.

Dr. Marcus' head immediately turned. Alden silently cursed, and hurried around the corner towards the interior of the building.

Made it just in time.

Right as his shoulder disappeared from the main hallway, the door opened and the doctor's head stuck out to look to the left and right.

"I swear... these files are making me crazy," Duke muttered.

His head and body went back inside the room. The door shut behind him.

Thorn

Outside L.A. Live
Los Angeles, California

February 1, 2019
12:20 a.m.

"I'm going after the one that ran." Streye's strained words could hardly be heard through his labored breathing.

She really needed to talk to Khara. This time, it wasn't the presence, or absence, of her VOS.

Something was wrong. She knew, but…

Her VOS still hasn't spoken to her.

"O-ka-y."

Thorn grunted with effort. Her hand was wrapped around the neck of the hitman. In this case, the hit-woman. She slammed the petite assassin against the wall with enough force to stun her.

Thorn's bloody lip stung, and she laved the blood with her tongue.

Her ears still rang from the slap.

Thorn knew she had to go on the offensive. The woman was good. And with Thorn in a non-VOS, semi-handicapped state, the woman was definitely better.

While the woman was stunned against the wall, Thorn checked her for weapons. Patting her body suit quickly she found and discarded brass knuckles, two syringes, three blades, and a Taser. No firearms.

Strange.

The woman regained her bearings, and twisted her legs to kick at Thorn's midsection. Thorn swatted them away, slammed a hand to her face, and twisted the woman's arms behind her. Using the woman's own weight as leverage, she dropped her to the ground.

Thorn tucked and rolled to get her gun and skidded to the other side of a heavy trash can. She holstered it.

She tried to recall what the ML sheet said about this particularly target.

Unknown sex, with an emphasis on her connection to the Triads.

Yet nothing about the woman screamed Triads. She wasn't anywhere near their bases, didn't seem to care about their storefronts. Her technique… she wasn't meaning to kill.

What's more…

When Thorn had landed her kicks and punches, she felt the hard flexibility of AdKev. It was a new and advanced form of Kevlar that was fire-, heat-, and water-repellant, and was bullet-proof against steel core and hollow point bullets. They bounced right off.

It was not only expensive, but tailored and very limited in its production.

The Triads shouldn't have access to it. AEX didn't even have this technology.

No…

The answer hit her like a cold blast of air.

The woman didn't seem like a Triad.

This mission was hurried and completely out of the blue.

Randolph was adamant on completing this soon.

The woman's gear was only accessible to R&D groups with close ties to the U.S. military.

The woman wasn't a target because the government wanted her dead. This woman *was* the government.

Why were Thorn and Streye sent after government? Did Khara and Randolph know?

Of course they did. How could they not?

She signed on to rid society of criminals. Not commit treason.

The woman rushed at her. Thorn feinted a headlong rush, but stepped to the side and lifted her arm so the woman ran into it. The woman tried to stop and turn, but she was too quick. She fell, but was still conscious.

As soon as the woman's back hit the ground, Thorn was on top of her, keeping a hand on her throat, legs around her torso.

Why was the mission to get rid of someone from the military? Was it because they thought she had turned Triad?

No... It didn't feel like that.

"So it's... True..." The woman was turning purple, but she kept her eyes on Thorn.

Thorn released the pressure on her throat, even though AEX code and training told her not to.

"You.... Exist..."

The woman coughed and took a breath but didn't say any more. Her eyes were closed but Thorn didn't let that fool her. She tightened the grip on her throat. "What is true?'

The woman tapped the heel of her boot on the floor and a blade slid out from the toe. Thorn dodged just in time to avoid the blade, but she had to let go of the woman.

Rolling away, the assassin retrieved and threw three blades at Thorn. Thorn barely had enough time to dodge, her thigh still weak.

When she turned around, the woman had disappeared into the underground tunnel.

As she turned to follow, Thorn fell to one knee.

A blade had found its mark, and sliced into the right side of her ribs. "Ah, fuck."

She touched the blood seeping out from her side, and gritted her teeth before applying pressure on the wound.

VOS...

It remained silent.

Was this connected to the bar incident?

Streye arrived through the same tunnel. He had dirt and blood on his body and a self-made wrap on his arm, but he was alert.

"She escaped?"

Thorn nodded. Her head throbbed.

"Can you move?"

"Yeah..."

"You're not going after her?"

"She's gone. With my thigh the way it is, I doubt we'll catch up."

His look was a second too long, but he nodded.

Randolph

Washington Dulles Airport   February 1, 2019
Washington, D.C.   5:30 a.m.

"Some things don't change!" The President stepped out from the car, his angry face illuminated by the overhead lights.

Randolph's surprised look was completely unplanned. "Mr. President."

"I knew something was off. Your secret little absences and unanswered phone calls. Now when the election is only months away I find you sneaking off to L.A. doing God knows what."

"Sir-"

"I trusted you! And you... How... Exactly like your father are you?"

Randolph's face drained of color. "How dare you."

The Secret Service stepped out from the shadows, hands on their weapons. The President really did come prepared. Eli and the two other men eyed them warily, not sure what their rules of combat were for the Secret Service.

"I knew you were hiding something. But I wanted to give you a chance. Where are your assassins, Randolph? It's only a matter of time before I find them."

Randolph took a breath, released it. "What exactly do you think I'm involved in?" His mind raced.

The President scoffed. "You can stop pretending. One of mine recently got involved with one of yours."

Motioning toward Randolph, the President wordlessly indicated for his men to take him.

Randolph held up a hand. The Secret Service stopped, not sure what to do. "You clearly have no idea what I've been working on, and you won't believe a word I say."

Langston didn't say a word.

"Let me show you."

"So you can lead me into a trap?"

"I may have shortcomings, but attempting to harm the President of the United States is not one of them."

The President glowered at him.

Randolph's mind raced with possible explanations. There was no avoiding showing him something… but if he could spin it in just the right way… he might be able to escape from this.

"Langston, let me show you why I could not reveal it to you before."

"If it has something to do with the mass murderer, you better hope you're wrong."

"It does not. It's directly connected to the Suicide hotline bill I had passed."

"Don't tell me-"

"No, it's nothing like what you're thinking. It's something that K-Pharma wanted to tackle. They didn't want other companies to steal the idea so I had to keep it a secret."

Everyone was silent. The Vice President looked at the President, President looked at the Vice President, and the guards looked at both men, torn between their orders and the tension. The mercenaries waited, looking bored.

More silence.

"Fine. But you ride with me. No bodyguards."

Eli was about to speak but Randolph nodded.

"Understood. Eli, you follow us."

"No. No bodyguards at all."

There was a mutinous look on Eli's face, but when Randolph nodded again, he shrugged.

As Randolph stepped into the President's car, he knew he only had one chance to explain this lie. Thoroughly.

He hoped it was enough. Khara was going to be mad, but he couldn't go to jail.

Not now.

Not when he was so close to fulfilling his father's dream. His own dream. The dream that multitudes of men had before him.

By the time they get there, it will be late anyway. No workers or nurses to refute his explanations. No Khara, no agents.

He looked out the car window as they made their way to the airport.

Thorn

Hallway   February 2, 2019
9th Floor, K-Pharma   9:00 p.m.

Eve had to know something. Anything.

Thorn may not trust Khara to tell her the truth- the woman was a true enigma. But Eve... Eve she could ask.

Thorn didn't trust her completely, but she knew the woman was a good person. Eve wasn't going to ignore the bigger picture. She also wanted answers, no matter if they were good or bad.

Was AEX taking out agents of the government? And if so, why was it so unsettling? It was like a pit of rocks had settled in her stomach.

Her VOS had deserted her and taken with it, her peace of mind. Slowly. Chipped at her skills and memory, and now even her internal calm was in jeopardy.

She was still capable of carrying out missions, but for how long?

What was her VOS doing? Had it cracked? Was it because she had gone against the AEX code? Was it the boy? The wife beater? Streye? Why had her VOS not broken down? Why wasn't it doing anything except stay silent, when she was going completely against basic code?

Now that she was thinking about it, she had done more than a few things against code.

Even with the government assassin…

She had asked questions and failed to complete the mission. Normally she would have immediately gone after the target, wounded or not. But she didn't.

Thorn needed answers to questions she shouldn't be asking. Trusting that person not to betray her. And while she shared her body with Streye, she just couldn't trust him.

God, her head hurt.

It was past business hours, and the building looked dark from the outside. But the R&D sector that housed AEX thrived at night. They even hired special teams to make sure that no one went in or out without permission. 8-hour rotation of secretaries, 4-hour rotation of guards, and rooms of analysts reviewing the recordings and tapes.

The receptionist smiled.

Thorn nodded and pulled on the door the same second the buzzer sounded. She made her way through cubicles, conference rooms, and connecting interior bridges, until she came to a new interior building. The steel door was labeled R&D, its metallic sheen a stark contrast to the light beige, almost white colors of the surrounding walls.

She flashed her hand in front of the scanner, and the mini-computer picked up on the ID chip inserted into her hand. The deadbolts on the door unlatched. Thorn waited for it to be half open before she stepped past the threshold.

She kept her strides long and her breath even, as her thoughts pounded against the inside of her skull.

Wanting answers, wanting relief, wanting numbness.

She saw the light under Eve's doorway, and quickened her pace.

Thorn

Office of Evelyn Wells
9th Floor, K-Pharma

February 2, 2019
10:10 p.m.

The older woman knew even less than her.

Since Eve's most recent disagreement with Randolph and Khara, their interactions were few and far between. She was even excluded from their regular meetings.

"Where is VOS? What did she tell you?"

Thorn debated what to tell her. She may trust Eve enough to ask questions, but not enough to expose herself.

"She told me that it was a government assassin, but the woman was quick, and escaped before VOS could detect anything else."

Eve nodded. "So tell me about the ML."

Thorn felt another wave of panic rise in her throat.

The ML.

The ML she tried to memorize for hours, and yet the details were still a fuzzy haze in the back of her mind. That would never happen if VOS was still present. If she stumbled, Eve would know that her VOS was malfunctioning.

"It was a regular mission. Our goal was to isolate the right hand of the Triads. Once we got there, Streye was targeted by another woman. They took their fight elsewhere. We still hadn't located the target so we split up. When I found her, she seemed surprised that I called her a Triad."

"You spoke to her before the mission?"

Thorn forgot. Agents were not supposed to converse with targets.

Fuck.

She pretended like Eve didn't ask. "The kind of combat gear she was using... That wasn't a standard vest. It was government-issue, military grade.

I had her pinned down, and she said something, something about the fact that "you really exist". Before I could question her, she got away."

"Question her? Aren't you supposed to kill first?"

Thorn hesitated. Another weak point.

AEX code prioritized the mission success before curiosity. Death before clarity. If there was a possibility that a target would get away, the first issue to deal with was that. Questions were unnecessary.

The mission always came first.

"I wanted to ask her questions."

"So you failed the mission."

Thorn leaned back and sighed. "Eve, I want to know if AEX is somehow targeting United States government." She grabbed onto the arm of the sofa. "That's treason."

"Technically everything that we're doing is treason." Eve stared at the wall behind Thorn. "But you're right."

Eve rubbed her scalp with her fingers.

"Thorn, I have no answers for you. I'm sorry."

Thorn watched the older woman's face, looking for any trace of deception, but she didn't see any.

Then again, without VOS, she wasn't even sure if she'd recognize a combatant from a civilian. Standing up, she let out a breath.

A sharp pain pierced her head. It was so sudden that she couldn't hide the wince.

"Thorn?"

"No, it's nothing." She turned towards the door. "Thanks for coming in, Eve."

Thorn shut the door behind her.

The sharp pain had diminished, leaving a buzz in her left ear.

She almost made it into the main hallway of K-Pharma when the door in front of her slammed open and a slew of Secret Service operatives filed out.

She saw the President and Vice President at the same time the Secret Service saw her.

Great.

"Hands up or we'll shoot!"

She had nowhere to go.

Randolph's head shot around. His eyes narrowed.

The President glanced from one to the other. "Randolph, who is this young woman?"

Randolph managed a smile. "Sir, this is Patient B."

The President's eyes widened, and he motioned for his agents to lower their weapons. Stepping forward, he clasped her hands in his, and gentle shook them. "Precious girl."

Thorn's left eye started to twitch. She managed a smile, a curling of her lip.

If the President was here, why wasn't he ordering for the whole place to be shut down?

One glance at Randolph told her everything she suspected.

More lies.

Khara was going to kill him.

"Sir, could you wait here as I take her back to her room?"

Thorn wanted to tell the President everything just to see Randolph get what he deserved, but she didn't want to be arrested with him either.

The President nodded. "Yes... go. Do you need one of my men to help?"

Thorn had to give credit to Randolph. His "no thank you" was both well-timed and earnest.

As soon as they were out of the group's earshot, Randolph, whose hands were tight bands around her arm, pulled her in front of him and lowered his voice. "You better not mention this to anyone."

Thorn didn't say anything.

She could almost hear her VOS laughing in the back of her head. But that might just be a side effect of the piercing headache plaguing her for the past few months.

It was time to go to the Medical ward.

Thorn
Diary Entry

February 3, 2019

I don't know why I feel this way. It might be infatuation and it might be something more, but I can't help being completely and utterly fascinated and annoyed by you.

I dreamt of losing you. Multiple times. And the sadness and despair that it inspired in me scares me. I don't want to be dependent on you for my happiness. I don't want to be dependent on anyone, least of all a man I've known for so little a time.

I want to be with you all the time. It makes absolutely no sense and it terrifies me beyond all belief, because I am no longer me. I want to be "us." I don't like it.

I want to say everything to you but I don't want to say anything. Because I don't want to make this fleeting vulnerability permanent. Because that would require me to admit that I need you. Every moment I'm not with you I want to be with you and every moment I'm with you I want it to last forever.

I can't concentrate when I'm not with you, because my mind wanders to you. I really do like us. I adore us. We are good together.

I just want you to need me as much as I need you.

Khara

Office of Kharavera Terraza   February 3, 2019
9th Floor, K-Pharma   5:50 p.m.

"Give me some good news, Johann."

Dr. Stewart sighed. "Khara, I'm sorry."

"What do you mean? You must have found something. I've given you more than a few subjects to work with."

"VOS removal is tricky. Trickier than VOS treatment."

"What about Trent? Kenzie?"

"Trent's was already malfunctioning, Kenzie's was too broken, and the others weren't fully formed yet."

"What happened?"

Johann shook his head.

"What happened?" Khara gripped the table with a white fist. "What do you mean? It's been months! Haven't we progressed at all?"

"As soon as the procedure started, Trent was dead. He flat lined before we could complete the procedure." He blinked a few times. "Kenzie... wasn't so quick."

Khara waited.

"The procedure went well until the second stage. She began seizing. We tied down her arms and legs, but her entire body bounced on the metal seat like it was electrified."

"Didn't you inject her with the muscle relaxant?"

"We did. And we injected her with more. But she kept seizing and started frothing at the mouth." He swallowed. "We had to put her down."

Khara ground her lips together. Her eyes no longer focused on him, but on her computer monitor.

"What do you need to perfect it?"

"Subjects with working VOS." He patted her shoulder. "I know. There's only seven. We've spent so much money making the VOS that it seems ridiculous to try to spend even more money destroying it. But that's what we need."

Khara didn't respond.

She glanced at the monitor showing Eve's office, watching the recorded interaction between the psychologist and Thorn.

Thorn

Thorn's Apartment
Los Angeles, California

February 7, 2019
8:30 p.m.

For the tenth time, Thorn realized that the partnership and their relationship, whatever it was, was a bad idea.

When he spoke, it was always condescending. When she spoke, he looked away, attention turned elsewhere, distracted.

Something else was always on his mind, someone else, a different time.

They had nothing in common except for the bloodshed and the sex.

She knew exactly what was happening. She saw it all before. The same things her mother cried and raged over. The depression, the loneliness, the uncertainty.

Her mother trusted no one, but she also was never satisfied with herself. Grace never felt safe or complete, because she couldn't truly "be" with people or her own thoughts.

The only person she could share freely with was her daughter. To Thorn, Grace spoke of things she could not tell anyone else.

Because Thorn's mother had acquaintances, not true friends. Because she had lovers, not husbands.

Grace spoke of things no daughter wanted to hear, or should have heard, at such an age. She unburdened herself by sharing her secrets with her daughter, not knowing or understanding the damage that could do to a young girl's mind.

Thorn couldn't refuse. Her mother only had her. She had to be Grace's everything. Her closest friend and confidante. A caretaker even before she learned to be a daughter.

 And that is how she felt now. Burdened with some unspeakable weight, unsure of her own thoughts and feelings.

Trapped in a place she could not leave.

Thorn

Medical Sector
11th Floor, K-Pharma

February 8, 2019
9:15 a.m.

The pills slid easily on her tongue but caught in her throat. Her esophagus contracted, trapping the three capsules between her jaw and throat. Coughing, she spit them out.

She gave her palm a look of relief and disgust.

Bemused, the doctor reached into an overhead cabinet and took out a clear tumbler and a bottle of wine, half full. As she popped open the cork and filled the glass half-way, she gave her a gentle smile.

"This should help." She lifted the glass toward Thorn, who looked from the wine to her face, with an incredulous arch to her eyebrows.

Thorn made a motion toward the glass. "Alcohol and medicine...?"

Something passed through Thorn's memory, almost like she was forgetting something. Something important... something to do with alcohol and medicine. But she just couldn't remember.

The doctor's face lit up with sudden realization. She laughed. "No, no, no, killing you is not anyone's intention! My apologies for the misunderstanding. I forgot that this was your first time coming in here for medication."

She took two steps closer to Thorn, who leaned back, trying to gauge this woman's intentions.

"Most recruits are in here the second or third day. It's hard to believe that you suffered two years of that. Taking it with alcohol is more effective, gets into your bloodstream faster."

Thorn kept a wary eye on her.

The doctor set the glass on the counter and unlocked the right-hand drawer with her key. She flipped through a stack of different colored papers, and pulled out several sheets folded into three sections, brochure-style. She set them on the counter next to the wine, as she put the stack back.

"Here. I know you don't believe me, so you can judge for yourself." She handed the papers to Thorn, who took them from her slowly. The doctor looked at the glass of wine. "I suppose it'll be a waste this time."

Thorn's head seemed to be ebbing and flowing with pain, her periphery flashing white. It felt like fire dancing on each of her nerve endings.

Her hand reached out and took the papers from the doctor's hand.

"Why alcohol?" She glanced down, intending to skim through it, but as her neck arched, her head pounded even harder.

She looked back up.

"VOS has an aptitude for alcohol. AEX agents have an extremely high tolerance for it, and it seems to improve their skills and the VOS's communication with the host."

Again, that same feeling like she was forgetting something. She slowly shook her head to get rid of whatever it was.

"So because VOS has a positive association with alcohol, it makes taking the pills easier?"

"We believe so." The doctor poured the wine out, and rinsed the glass. She set it inside the sink. "I don't think your reaction is to the painkiller, but to the two other pills."

"How do you mean?" Thorn massaged the paper in between her thumb and index finger.

"Your VOS is part of you all the time, even when it's not speaking to you. Whatever you know, they know. They know the pills limit their control over your mind. They don't want that. Assuming that they want what's best for you, they don't want their reactions impaired if you do need them. So the VOS tries to prevent it from entering the bloodstream."

The doctor reached into her white coat and took out three blue bottles. "Here are the pills. Read the pamphlets, and let me know if you have questions. Dr. Marcus can also help you too."

Thorn reached over and took the bottles. She would have nodded but her head was already about to explode.

Thorn
Memory

Corra Residence
Palmdale, California

When Thorn was 20
(Five years ago)

"I don't understand why you're still crying."

"I just don't feel good."

Grace had patted the top of her head. "You know kids will be kids. Don't let them get to you."

"They got me fired!"

"You'll find another job soon, Thorn. You just need to be strong. Now, wipe yourself off. Mac's coming over. We need to look pretty."

"I want to stay here."

"No, we have to eat as a family. You know how much he means to me."

"Yeah, but-"

"Really, Thorn. It's not that serious."

A sharp pain pierced Thorn's chest. "I-"

"Don't you love me? Do this for me, sweetheart."

Thorn had learned that she did not matter, and her tears were worth almost nothing. She was there as a limb, as an extension, of the person who had birthed her.

Like children who stop crying after caregivers stop being responsive, she stopped trying to speak.

Grace stood up. "Come on, get up. Stop being selfish."

Thorn was trapped between her comfort and her mom's love, between her will and her mom's happiness.

So she always chose her mom, because that was the right thing to do.

She brushed away her tears and put on the dress Grace had set on the chair.

AEX

Office of Kharavera Terraza
9th Floor, K-Pharma

February 8, 2019
9:35 a.m.

"You risked everything by being a selfish asshole." Khara shut the door with a resounding BOOM. "You treat AEX as if it's your own, abusing your goddamn privileges, overstepping boundaries like they don't apply to you."

"He was going to arrest me. I had to give him something real. The only way to throw him off AEX's trail was to show him the work we're doing with rehabilitating suicide victims. At least, that's what he thinks we're doing."

"Did you even give one thought to the fact that he wouldn't find anything? He had suspicions, not evidence. And now he knows exactly what you're involved in and where to find it."

"You supported Phase 2. He knew you were in on this already. Please."

"In on Phase 2, not a completely different project. Do you even realize what you did? You bet my entire life on a gamble. That he wouldn't look deeper. That he wouldn't suspect anything further." She took a drink of the water, her hands claws around the glass.

Randolph ignored that. "He was on the verge of commending us."

"If my father didn't owe yours a favor, I would kill you right here."

"That's rude. I have done so much for AEX. What would your agents say?"

"They'd agree. They know better than to panic and give out secrets. They'd process through every possible scenario, every outcome, and stick to the one of long-term gain, not shortsighted idiocy."

Khara slammed her hands on the arm rests of his chair.

"AEX is mine. K-Pharma is mine. You may think you're some political talisman that made this happen, but you're not and you didn't. I created AEX."

She paused. "I know you like to tell your little underlings that you did. I don't care about that. But this time you risked my whole life, my company, because you panicked. That is unforgiveable."

"Are you done being emotional? Everything turned out fine."

Randolph refused to admit that she did have a point. The President only had suspicions, nothing bordering on evidence. Even if he had searched his car, his bodyguards, his phone, his office, questioned everyone, he wouldn't have found any proof of AEX.

He wasn't going to tell her this. She was too much on her high horse already.

As if switching masks, her face smoothed into a smile, a baring of teeth. "Get out."

"What?" He wasn't sure he heard correctly.

They stared at each other for a long minute in silence.

"Get out of my office before I rip out your fucking throat." The smile never left her face.

He got up to leave. Neither of them said anything more.

Khara watched his entourage get on the elevator and called in Penny.

"Take his name off of any sensitive, processing, or R&D file. This company no longer recognizes him. And I want you to take away his access privileges. I don't want that man getting anywhere near K-Pharma or AEX."

Penny wrote down all her instructions and started to walk away.

"Wait. Make sure we have all his files. If he tries anything, he's going down with us. I doubt he's that stupid, but we've misjudged him before."

Khara tapped her pen on the paper.

"Also, tell Dr. Stewart to start considering VOS removal for Thorn."

Penny looked up. "Thorn?"

Khara nodded. "He needs viable test subjects. And she's getting to be more of a liability than an asset."

Thorn knew too much. And her VOS was becoming unstable enough for her to break AEX code.

Randolph

Duarte Residence
Baltimore, Maryland

February 9, 2019
1:10 p.m.

"Thorn needs to be taken out as soon as possible." Randolph took a long swig of his whiskey and a puff of his cigarette. His bodyguards stood against the walls of the study, hands clasped behind their backs.

"Not Khara?"

"She I can still handle."

They nodded.

"Thorn is the one thing that might take me down. Khara values her precious K-Pharma too much to fight right now. But the President is definitely going to try to bring Thorn in for questioning. You all know how she feels about me."

"She would rat out AEX?"

"We can't take that chance. Whether she does or not, we need to take her out."

"What should we do?"

Randolph took another sip. "You guys sit out the first round. If it doesn't go well, you can get your hands dirty."

"You don't need us to do it?"

"I have some companies that would love to get their hands on some psychotech ideas. And have men to spare." He puffed. "I can't believe Khara thinks she can beat me at this game." He shook his head.

"Which companies?"

"Medtech."

"The one with connections with the CIA?"

He nodded. "They owe me a big favor."

"What are they going to do?"

"They can do whatever they want with her. As long as she disappears. And if they fail, you will finish the job."

"What should we be doing?"

"Track her. Keep close notes on who she comes into contact with on a regular basis. Do not let AEX or her know of your presence." He lifted a finger. "If MedTech fails, send in a group you trust. Don't do it yourselves. She already knows your faces."

"What if the President makes a move?"

Randolph ground his teeth slowly. "Let him take her. But not alive."

The men nodded solemnly.

Khara

Office of Kharavera Terraza   February 10, 2019
9th Floor, K-Pharma   3:00 p.m.

"The removal machine is being primed."

Khara nodded at Penny and ran her hands along the side of the desk. "Getting Thorn is the hard part."

Her secretary-assistant shut the door behind her. "Why not wait a little longer for Thorn's VOS? It's not broken for sure."

"We don't have the luxury of what if. Without Stephen, without Randolph, and now with closer scrutiny of the President, we can't afford for Thorn to draw any attention. It'll be too late to fix."

"So she's a liability. Why not kill her?"

Khara shook her head. "No. We can't waste her brain. We need to capture her to test the VOS removal procedure. She might be the subject we're looking for."

"What about the other subjects?"

Khara was silent. She shook her head again.

"What will happen if the removal is not successful?"

"*Then* we can dispose of her."

Khara

Office of Kharavera Terraza
9th Floor, K-Pharma

February 12, 2019
6:40 a.m.

Khara hadn't slept in two days. She was so busy reviewing ledgers that she didn't see the caller ID when the call came in.

Her hand absentmindedly pressed the phone to her ear. "Yes?"

"I hope you are not as rude when answering all your phone calls, Kharavera." Hearing that low, humorless voice along with her full name snapped her to attention. Her fingers froze on the keyboard.

"I received your message."

It was embarrassing and humbling that she could be reduced to a child by the mere sound of his voice.

She set aside the papers she was working on. "I didn't expect a call back so soon. Apologies."

He made a sniffing noise, and then blew his nose to the side. "I've seen the latest reports on K-Pharma. You're doing well."

'Thank you." Khara smiled, the first in a while. Her father's compliments had always been rare.

"I am concerned about your Vice President." He hocked.

"He's no longer in the picture."

"Hmm. We all must learn our own lessons." He took a quick pause. "You are a smart woman. I made you that way. You have the same logic, determination, and recklessness that I have, and are very much like your siblings. But," he hocked again, "you must be careful. He is the Vice President, but he is also quite dangerous."

Khara wondered how he knew everything at just the right moment. But she wouldn't ask, and he'd never tell. Secrecy was only one of the many traits that kept the man alive.

Alann was a wanted criminal in nearly fifty countries. Despite his constant appearance in the news, no one has ever gotten close to catching him. No one even knew he had children.

Part of her wanted to ask about her siblings.

Four of them in total. Two girls and two boys. He separated them as soon as they became of age.

Once given funding at 16, they were forced to change their names and renounce all ties with their previous life. They didn't know where the others were, what business the others were in, or if they were even alive. Forbidden from contacting one another, they became strangers to those closest to them.

Khara didn't know what his goal was for them, and he never talked about it.

He came back on the line.

"Religion is a powerful force. Politics and economics cannot ever hope to destroy that. You must understand its motivation, its manipulation, its brilliance, and harness it... But do not confuse that with business."

"Yes, dad." She heard it slip before she was even done speaking.

"Don't use endearments, Kharavera. You know full well what that can do one's ambition."

"Yes, Alann."

"Before I leave… What exactly did you say you needed?"

"A tracker."

"That's a slippery slope."

"I understand its implications. I wouldn't use it if I had any other choice."

A pause. "That serious?"

"Yes."

"I have someone in mind. I'll code you his information." His voice faded away briefly. "But he does have a hefty price."

"Of course. Money is a small price to pay for quality." He used to repeat that to them all the time.

"Good girl. Always look after your investments."

"You taught me well."

As Khara pressed the END CALL button on the phone, she released a breath.

Thorn

Thorn's Apartment
Los Angeles, California

February 15, 2019
9:50 p.m.

The pills stared at her from the bottle on the counter.

She frowned at them.

It's been three months since she had heard from VOS, and the pounding of her brain against her skull was getting worse by the day. VOS had done so much, kept the worst of the pain from her, and she hadn't even realized.

She rubbed her head. Did Streye take these pills? Are they as effective as–

White flashed across her vision as pain shot across her forehead.

Every time she thought of Streye...

Thorn felt the blood running hot through the veins in her neck, her fingers, her toes. She saw the flashes even as she closed her eyes, and her body rolled forward into a fetal position. Her mouth tasted like copper, and her face scrunched in agony.

She couldn't think about Streye without reeling in pain, but she also didn't know how to not think about him. Just picturing his face eased the loneliness in her chest.

Her hand arched over her head to grab the bottle, tucking it into her palm with so much force her fingers turned white.

No, she couldn't do this anymore. She needed those pills.

Her thumb popped open the top of the pill bottle.

Its semi-transparency reflected the wild look in her eyes, the shaking of her whole body.

She turned away.

What have I become?

Without looking, she dumped four pills in her palm. The other hand grabbed the handle of vodka sitting beside her. Closing her eyes, she planted her palm on her face and threw the pills into her mouth, washing it down with the burning liquor.

With the help of the vodka, the chemicals slid into her stomach.

She set her head against the top of the couch, waiting for relief to slide through her body.

Thorn

Fashion District   February 17, 2019
Los Angeles, California   1:00 a.m.

She was high.

So high.

The headache was a haze, along with the memory of the past two days. She wandered the city aimlessly, with just a passing notion of where she was, when it was.

No missions, no Khara, no Streye, no Eve. Just her and the endless cloud that she floated on.

But…

Even with that high, she smelled the ambush.

The men, the cars, the guns, the unnatural silence.

Streye's face appeared in her mind. And with it, the screeching pain that accompanied it. Thorn's hand reached into her belt pouch and produced a small pill bottle. She poured the contents of it directly into her mouth, forcing them down her still rebellious throat.

She tucked the bottle back into her pouch.

No, it was up to her. She had no one else.

She climbed through the window into the nearest building, and held her back against the wall.
Was this the Feds?

Thorn crouched in the far corner of the warehouse, keeping her eyes on the closest exit, two aisles away.

No, it couldn't be. The time of night, the area, the technique... whoever planned this knew her and her style. By keeping the ambush in a large area, they put her close-range combat style at a disadvantage.

Her brain wanted to focus, but her memory kept showing her Alie, Isaiah, and... her mother? She shook her head.

The headache was back.

She had her guns tucked into the holsters, but she kept her Python in her right hand. The only way out of this wasn't to shoot blindly.

She had to be smart about this.

Except her VOS was gone. And with it, her technical advantage. Now her only goal was to survive. Get out of this.

Easier said than done, especially since her body was still high on those pills.

She glanced at the main entrance, lit only by the exit sign.

Thorn barred the door with heavy boxes, old machines, and a broken desk, before tying a nearby chain on the handles. She tucked it around the metal as tightly as she could, but didn't have a lock to secure it.

Voices got closer, followed by yelling and the clink of guns against gun belts and ammo bags. Her heart began to race, and she ran towards the storage shelves near the back of the dark room.

Where are you? I need you. I have no idea how to get out of this.

No response.

VOS was not coming to her aid.

Her throat closed and her entire body felt hot. Her vision started to blur, and she realized she was fainting. Her heart pounded louder and faster in her ears.

Her fingers reached into her belt pocket.

She wasn't addicted to the pills, she told herself. This was only temporary.

The doors shook as she swallowed the second set of pills, keeping both the entry and exit doors in sight. She still felt her heart racing against her neck, but it was slowing down.

All she wanted to do was curse at VOS and then crawl into the ground.

Streye...

No. She wouldn't think about that.

She took a deep breath and forced distractions out of her mind. At this point, it'd probably get her killed.

The thought of potentially dying filled her with a strange sense of delight. One that she had not felt in a long time.

Feet pounded against the hallway outside.

Streye's face flashed before her for a brief millisecond. She saw the negative image behind her eyelids even after she closed her eyes.

At least that pain was dulled.

She made her way to the top shelf, and plastered her front against the cold metal.

The door shook violently, heaving back and forth.

Almost open.

She tucked the knife back into the belt, took out her guns, checked the magazines, and reholstered them.

It hit her just how lonely she was without the voice guiding her, especially in moments like these.

What could she say to herself?

His face appeared again. Her chest felt heavy.

But she'll make it. She had to.

The door crashed against the wall and five armed men streamed in. The leader shouted at the others to search the room. As they split, the leader stood in front of the closest door, blocking one of her two ways out.

No escape.

Thorn
Memory

Corra Residence

Palmdale, California

When Thorn was 18

(Seven years ago)

Curled up in a corner on her bed, Thorn looked out the window and hated.

She hated school. She hated the kids who gossiped about her and called her names. She hated her mother for not understanding, for not trying to understand.

She hated the world for not believing her.

But mostly, she hated herself. Hated that even three years later, she was as affected by the rumors and the looks as that first day.

Hated that she doubted herself.

After all, if everyone said it happened because of her, then it must have.

How could everyone else be wrong?

Thorn

Fashion District   February 17, 2019
Los Angeles, California   3:30 a.m.

Thorn could no longer run. Her lungs hurt, her thigh ached, and blood ran down her arms.

She could hear the voices get louder, behind her, in front of her, but she couldn't focus on the words being said.

All she knew was that they were close, and they were coming for her.

She'd failed before.

Two missions. But it wasn't because she couldn't complete the mission. It was because she chose not to, even when it meant defying her VOS.

Now, in a moment like this, she realized that she would fail because she couldn't do it. Physically, mentally, emotionally.

She didn't have a choice in the matter.

Everything about her was falling apart. No VOS, no strength, no memory... But she couldn't just give up. She had to take out as many of them as she could before they got their hands on her.

The voices were louder, more demanding, their nasally sounding commands sending chills down her spine.

VOS was gone. And this situation was worse. Instead of being locked in an institution to have tests run on her, she was going to die at the hands of the enemy.

She shook her head.

No, there was no way that being a lab rat was in any way better than dying on the battlefield. At least here, she could have some sort of honor.

Some blood on her hands. Some pride to maintain.

She kept running, keeping her hands along the wall, feet one after the other. She was half-blind from the headache but she had to keep going.

She felt her knees buckle.

Outside AEX

Undisclosed Location
Somewhere in California   February 18, 2019

"Lift her head."

The man lifted the harness attached to Thorn's head. She was tied with her arms behind her back, kneeling in front of a deep trough. Her ponytail was tucked into the space in the back of the harness, and a clip was attached to her nose, forcing her to breath with her mouth.

As soon as her face left the water, she gasped painfully. Her eyes were still shut, eyelashes framed with clear droplets. Water sluiced through her hair, down her face, making their way down her neck and her shirt.

The man was completely silent.

Why? Shouldn't they be interrogating her?

Thorn coughed, hacking up water. VOS had appeared for every life or death moment during missions before. Except for that axe woman, but she had extricated herself from that.

But now…

This was it.

"You're strong. No wonder Summer couldn't take you down."

Without waiting for her response, the figure motioned for the man to dunk her again. Her head hit the surface of the trough with a large splash. As her face sunk in, she didn't struggle, and no bubbles rose from her facial orifices. The rest of her body was still.

The man in command stood farther away, hands clasped behind him.

The girl seemed to have excellent training, but didn't live up to the hype. Randolph had complete faith that the girl would decimate them. Hence why Arthur had to send four different teams to retrieve her.

She put up a good fight, but not four teams' worth.

"Send Delta and Epsilon Teams back. We'll handle it from here."

A few bubbles rose to the surface of the trough.

He motioned for the man to lift her head. A few more times. Just to weaken her enough so that transport wouldn't be a problem.

First though, he was going to show her to Hannah. He promised Randolph he wouldn't, but the Vice President should have known better than to trust him. It baffled him how the man thought a favor for him was a greater deal than for the President.

Randolph really thought he was special.

Hannah was going to love the girl. Not only will it help them with the problem of Randolph, but the things they can learn from her... it was going to change the future of U.S. military.

One that Arthur will definitely benefit from.

"When she comes back up, attach the leash."

"Yes, sir."

After two more dunks, the man unclipped the harness as he pulled her head up. She sputtered.

A third man appeared from the shadows, his hand grasping a round metal contraption.

"Will this be enough, sir?"

"Yes. It should be more than enough. If she goes beyond a ten feet radius, it will trigger the electric current. Her nervous system will crumble, and she will be forced to return."

They clicked the device around her neck, taking her ponytail out of the way.

Art patted the remote in his pocket.

"Prepare the plane."

"Yes, sir."

Streye

Streye's Apartment
Westwood, California

February 19, 2019
6:45 p.m.

It actually seemed like things were going well.

He didn't think it ever would. Not after his discharge, not after the two miscarriages…

Since he became aware of his schizophrenia and tried to commit suicide, he never relaxed, fearing that the voice would overtake him.

But lately, he finally felt like he could. Could let go, could release the tight hold on his conscious. Could live.

Even though Thorn would not have been his first choice.

You think you would be her choice? Think again–

He had seen enough of this world to dislike people and shun relationships. He had killed enough people to know how evil souls were, and how fragile physical bodies were. He had been in pain and caused pain, enough to know that everyone has a breaking point.

Everything ends, even something that seemed permanent.

His relationship with his ex-fiancée had proven that. Five years later, and he still kept the lessons he learned close to his heart.

He tried his best to fend off the pain. First with Ana and her wholesome goodness, and then with AEX and its rules.

But the hurt was always there, briefly hidden by the illusion of his control.

He never once realized that he himself, not others, was the source of the pain.

And then Thorn.

They didn't get along. Their interactions were volatile, bloody, and frustrating, but she put his demons to rest. The voices even settled within his mind when she was here.

Even she has more control over you than you–

They were complete strangers, even to this day, and yet shared an indescribable bond. They were deeply scarred by trauma, though neither talked about it.

He tried not to be taken by her unintended charm. But… it wasn't easy. He fell into an easy pattern, and so did she. Even their VOS seemed to get along, falling prey to none of the dangers that Eve had initially feared.

Streye hadn't wanted to interact with anyone, least of all someone so naïve with a subconscious that even Khara was scared of.

Thorn was an oxymoron, a juxtaposition of what an agent should be and yet what an agent could not be. He felt alive and anxious when she was near, reveling in the unknown and the unexpected.

He had lost whatever capability he had to love, but he knew that somehow they were important to each other. It didn't matter how.

She helped him manage the pieces of himself he couldn't show others.

The ringing of his phone tore him out of his thoughts.

Outside AEX

Milla Residence   February 19, 2019
Oahu, Hawaii   3:15 p.m.

The doorbell rang.

Ana put the apples away on the fruit rack, and wiped her hands on the towel hanging in front of the sink. As she passed by the stand near the hallway, her finger brushed over the delicate orchid petals.

Setting her braid on her left shoulder, she put her hands on the front door and looked into the peephole.

A tall man in jeans and a collared shirt, whom she had never seen before, stood on her porch. A large box sat at his feet, an electronic clipboard on top.

She opened the door but kept the latch attached. "Yes?" A wary speckled green eye peered out at him.

"Ms. Milla?" His voice was gravelly and held a hint of a foreign accent.

"Yes?"

"I have a delivery."

Ana looked at the box at his feet. It was a plain shipping box with no label. "I didn't order anything."

He took the clipboard from on top of the box. "It says Ana Milla, at 4508 East Drawer Drive."

"That's not mine."

Did Streye send her something? No, that couldn't be. They haven't talked in over four years.

She gave the man an apologetic smile before closing the door.

He sounded normal, looked normal, but something was off. Ana may not be the wisest, but her gut was never wrong. So she trusted her first reaction, which was to shut the door.

She kept her eye to the peephole, but didn't say anything. He just stood there, tapping his foot. A couple of moments passed, and the man left the porch but didn't take the box. Ana remained glued to the peephole. After making sure he wasn't coming back, Ana let out a relieved sigh.

Until she heard the doorknob to her back door wriggling.

Grabbing a poker from the fireplace, she ran to the back of the house. As soon as she turned into the kitchen, she saw the man trying to pry open the door, slamming his whole body against the wood as he levered a crow bar in the frame.

Ana ran to the door, and locked the remaining two locks.

Her heart pounded in her ears. Her sweaty hands were melted onto the poker.

The man finally let go of the doorknob. He looked into her eyes, and she flinched.

He turned away from the door and ran left, towards the bedroom. When she reached the bedroom, he had already pried the screen open, and his left leg was inside.

She went towards the window and tried to push him out, hitting his leg and arm with the poker. All it did was make him wedge himself into the room faster.

As he was about to be fully inside, she turned to run back to the front door, but he grabbed her ankle and pulled.

She crashed onto her stomach.

She kicked her leg as hard as she could, but his grip on her ankle didn't budge. Using her body as leverage, he managed to get his entire body into the house. He flipped her on her back, holding two of her hands over her head with one of his, and kept his legs over hers.

"Ana, you just had to make this difficult. I thought you could be reasonable."

"Who are you?" She tried to keep her voice strong.

"Package to deliver, darling." He brushed a finger on her cheek, along her jawbone. "He has good taste."

She shook her head. "Please, take whatever you want." Her voice was trembling. Ana was sure he could feel her whole body shaking.

"And Streye?"

Streye? What did he have to do with this?

She shook her head. "He-he hasn't lived here for years. Please don't kill me."

The man winked at her. "That's not what I was paid to do, darling. But I like the way you think."

"Just tell me what you want."

"You."

Outside AEX

Milla Residence
Oahu, Hawaii

February 19, 2019
3:20 p.m.

Ana froze, pinned to the ground by fear.

What did he mean?

"Give me your phone."

His finger grazed her neck. Its coldness sent shivers down her spine, causing goosebumps to rise on her skin.

"B-b-but it's not with me." She motioned towards the bedside table. "The landline is right-"

"I cut your line earlier. Your cell, honey."

She lifted her arm to point towards the bag in the kitchen.

In a blink of an eye, he was upright. He gave her a jerk of his head towards the kitchen. "Get up."

She pressed her palms to the floor beside her and sat up, fingertips grazing over the carpet fibers. She moved slowly, keeping her eyes on the ground, trying to come up with some plan to escape.

Normal people don't get involved in this.

Figures it'd be terrible taste in men causing all of this. She always liked them strong, silent, mysterious. Bad decisions never truly end.

She eased herself on her hips and turned her body to the right so her legs could press against the floor. As she was planning to kick out his legs, her gut gave her pause.

If he really wanted to kill you, he would have done it already. He wouldn't ask you to go get your phone.

She didn't need to anger him.

She stood up on shaky legs, and her arm shot out to stabilize herself.

His gun appeared in his hand. It was so quick that she didn't even see him pull it out.

She lifted both of her hands in a surrendering gesture. "I'm just getting up."

He cocked his head to the side. "Just making sure. Come on, get up."

She stood up, hands at her sides. He followed behind her far enough to see where she was going, close enough to catch her if she tried to run.

Her hands had barely brushed her phone when he grabbed it roughly out of her hand with his left, keeping the gun pointed at her. He dialed in a number, pressed the call button, and handed it back to her.

She took the phone from his hand, and pressed it to her cheek.

Streye

Streye's Apartment   February 19, 2019
Westwood, California   6:50 p.m.

Streye slammed the phone on the coffee table, forgetting that it had a glass top. Breaks in the glass speared out like lightning, and the bottom dropped out.

Streye still held his arm there, forearm balanced against the frame, hand mangling the phone.

"Fuuuuuck!"

His scream echoed in the nearly empty apartment.

The room seemed to be closing in around him, the furniture sucking the air out of the room. His voice rang in his ears, but all he could hear was the man's voice, rough, threatening, and Ana's… she sounded terrified.

What had the bastard done to her?

He thought he had avoided the particular kind of hell his mother had put his father through. She was some military spook who married his dad so their kids could have some stability. They were nothing alike, and she was almost never home. That marriage only lasted because they never saw each other, and the fact that Streye and his brother held them together by blood.

But their sham marriage wore on the sons, especially Alex, his younger brother. His genius brother, who could hack into anything, be whatever, whoever he wanted, began to act out, get into fights, all to get attention from their cold, distant parents.

Eventually, Alex took up crime to get attention. Burglary, grand theft auto, breaking and entering...

His specialty was arson, setting fire to stores, cars, homes, warehouses, whatever he could get light. After his fourth conviction, their father disowned him.

Alex left home without even a look back.

Streye didn't know if his brother was dead or alive. It felt like centuries since he's seen him.
s
His mother ran away, and Streye... He was left to pick up the pieces, by himself. After his father succumbed to alcoholism, no one else was left.

Being in Spec Ops saved him. And brought him to Ana.

She deserved better. While he couldn't give her the life she deserved, he could protect her from the darkness.

That's what he thought.

And like fate, irony was also a bitch. The very thing he had so feared was happening anyway, even after he did the right thing. And he wasn't even around to defend her.

Ana didn't deserve this. She had been with him for so long, stayed true, trusted him, honest and brave to the end. She didn't deserve this, not from him.

And Thorn...

He threw his phone at the wall.

AEX

Dining Area   February 20, 2019
11th Floor, K-Pharma   1:31 p.m.

"Eve!" Dr. Marcus had a manic look in his eyes. "Did you know about this?"

In his right hand he held a piece of paper and a DVD. His green eyes flashed at her under long, wavy bangs.

"What is it?"

"They're going to remove Thorn's VOS!"

She glanced at the two items, and saw the title of the transcript. "You're not supposed to have access to this." Her eyes roamed the page despite her words.

She felt her stomach sinking. *They finally…*

"Did you know about this?" His eyes dug into her face, accusing. "How could you do this? Thorn is our creation! And you know what happens to each one of those subjects."

Eve looked away.

"Did you agree to this?"

"I-I was there when they talked about it. But they hadn't agreed to anything. I didn't realize they would..."

"Why? Why would they do this?"

"Her VOS is evolving, Marcus. It's becoming something else."

"That's it?! That's why they're going to kill our best agent? Our best creation?"

His red face was so close to hers, she could see his pores. "Eve. I've seen the reports. There are no successes. Zero."

Eve wrung her hands. "Thorn's... VOS has changed. Because of that, I think Khara is scared that she's going to be Anthony. Or another Trent."

"You're missing the point, Eve. Her VOS has evolved. How is that even possible? How are we not trying to look more into that? She might be our only way out of this research slump!"

Eve bit her lower lip. "Realistically speaking, I agree..."

She sighed, and her eyes dug into his. "But Khara's set on testing her VOS removal procedure. In case it can fix some of the failures. She no longer cares about Thorn's VOS."

"We have to stop this."

"I don't know. I don't even know if we're able to stop it."

They kept silent, their eyes saying what their words couldn't.

Neither of them noticing the figure behind the far wall.

Alden was pressed as close to the doorway as possible without exposing himself.

So there was something going on. Finally. All these months of snooping was paying off.

Alden

Security Room   February 20, 2019
10th Floor, K-Pharma   3:45 p.m.

Alden sat at his desk, wondering if he should keep quiet or report it.

They seemed to be talking about human experimentation. Something that had nothing to do with pharmaceutical research.

At the rate his investigation was going, he wasn't going to get close to anything resembling the actual conspiracy. Not if he doesn't get to Khara. She was the key to all of this. He had to prove himself invaluable to her before she could trust him with anything. Anything he has access to right now wasn't worth his time.

His mind flashed back to the break room. The knowledge that Khara's people are hiding from her would be very valuable to Khara. And reporting it would ingratiate himself into her trustworthy circle.

Would she reward him? Or be more suspicious?

He needed to get this company's secrets.

It was the only way he'll get the truth. He wasn't sure what was going to happen to the two employees, but he couldn't focus on them now.

He needed to think about the greater good.

His gut had never been wrong.

And if he happened to see that girl again...

It would be all the better. He had a feeling she could answer some of his questions.

Streye

Streye's Apartment
Westwood, California

February 21, 2019
9:00 a.m.

The phone rang twice.

Streye waited, his palms pressing the cracked cell phone to his ear. His heart pounded, and his head hurt from thinking of all the possibilities, but his decision was made.

It was the best one, even if it wasn't comforting at all.

He had destroyed his room, but at least it had brought him some tiny measure of peace. Enough that he could stay still to call the bastard.

You really are a traitor. I don't know what she saw in you. What they all see in you. You're such a good for nothing, piece of sh–

The man answered as the third ring started, its cry cut off by his breathing. Streye waited, rubbing the back of his scalp, which had suddenly started to itch.

"You took your time." The man's voice was monotonous, robotic.

"You didn't leave me with an easy decision." He rubbed his face.

Foolish. How did you think–

"Did I not?" The man chuckled once. "While I give you credit for your skills, you do underestimate your peers, Mr. Hardt."

Streye tensed at the mention of his last name, his real last name, the one that he hadn't used since he was fifteen. Not at West Point, not in the military, not with Ana, not with anyone.

Get your mind back on the subject at hand, you fucking idiot. You truly are-

"Fine. I agree to your trade."

"Which one?"

Fucking bastard...

You did this to yourself. If you hadn't gotten involved–

"Let me talk to Ana."

"You are in no position to be giving demands."

"I know. Please. I just want to hear if she's okay."

How could she possibly be okay? She's involved in this because of you. You promised to keep her safe.

It was a lie, like everything else.

"She's fine. I have absolutely no interest in hurting her." The man said something away from the phone, muffling the speaker. "But if I didn't have her, would you even be talking to me right now?"

Streye rubbed the back of his head. The pain had subsided, but a nasty pit had formed in his stomach. "No."

"Glad we're both being honest."

The man went silent.

Streye leaned back against the flipped couch, opening and closing his mouth several times before sound actually came out.

"I'll do it."

Saying those words again felt like someone trying to rip out his lungs through his mouth and his stomach through his ribs. It hurt more than any physical damage he'd experienced.

"I'll bring Thorn to you."

Sharp needles poked into his skull and his hands.

"Please let Ana go."

Traitor. Useless.

At least Thorn will have a chance against the blackmailer.

"She'll go free as soon as you bring Thorn to us. Now," Streye heard him moving as the background noise increased in volume. He could make out soft jazz music and faint voices on a television. "Here's your reward."

The phone was silent for a few seconds before Ana's trembling voice came on the phone. "Streye?"

A bittersweet sense of relief washed over him. "Ana. Are you okay? Did he hurt you?"

"No, he's kept his distance." She breathed. "Streye, I don't know what's happening, but thank you."

"It's alright, Ana. This is my fault. Everything's my fault." Streye's voice held a calm he did not feel. "Things will be alright. Just bear with him. He doesn't seem to want to hurt you."

"I know."

Both of them went silent.

The man's voice came back on. "You have a week. Bring Thorn to us, alive."

Thorn
Memory

Applegarry High School
Palmdale, CA

When Thorn was 17
(Eight years ago)

It was a cloudy day in April, one of those mornings Thorn actually enjoyed getting up for school. She loved the grayness and the clouds, and the smell of water.

She took the stairs, grabbing her premade lunch on her way out the door. She made sure to lock the door and try it a few times.

Before living in the suburbs, she never enjoyed walking to school. Too many people, too many loud noises, and always so much construction.

But since her mom had found this new job, Thorn enjoyed being outside, breathing in the fresh air. She hadn't made too many friends but she also didn't have enemies. She never confronted anyone or tried to be the center of attention.

A perfect high school career, one that was almost over in a few months.

Thorn was lost in her daydream when she entered Applegarry High School's gates. She didn't notice the stares or the abrupt silences as she walked through the hallways.

It was only when she had sat down at her table that she realized someone had written "THORN IS A LYING WHORE" on her desk, covering its surface with hateful block letters. She stared at it for a few seconds and looked up. All heads were turned towards her.

Elana, the class president, a popular girl with skin like burnished bronze and curls that reached her shoulders, sat down next to her.

"How could you do that to Zaria's dad? He was such a good man."

"What?"

"Here we thought you were a good quiet girl, a nerd. Turns out you're a homewrecker."

A hand on her shoulder, fingers brushing her hair...

Another girl slammed a picture on her desk. A black-haired middle aged man with large ears. Thorn felt her stomach recoil, and her face flushed.

"I can't believe you thought no one would find out."

Thorn had to use all of her energy to prevent the bile from coming out of her mouth.

"My best friend is his daughter. She told me everything. You're sick."

"You said he touched you. Him, a good father and husband, touched this girl!" She lifted strands of Thorn's hair and felt it between her thumb and index finger. "You probably did it for attention."

Thorn felt the room was closing in around her, trapping her in this tiny box filled with so much hate.

"You probably asked for it too. But afterwards, you just couldn't face the fact that you're a trampy little slut."

Elana laughed, a cruel, harsh sound in Thorn's ears.

The laughter... It became louder and louder, echoing in her ears until it was all she could hear.

Thorn

Open Field
Outside Austin, Texas

February 22, 2019
4:30 p.m.

She did a lot of thinking on that flight.

They weren't in the air for long, but it's been weeks since she could focus. She still didn't know why her VOS had completely deserted her, but she had to take steps to get herself back.

She refused to be helpless.

She was going to end things with Streye. Her chest hurt just thinking about it, but it had to happen.

Her VOS left, due to her relationship with Streye, and she wanted it back. VOS was the one she needed.

Streye… he was just a replacement.

Thorn relied on him too much, and that gave him too much power. Despite how much Streye made her feel, she felt more alone, unable to trust, unable to laugh.

It was only after they captured her that she realized she couldn't afford to stay with him.

Her VOS, her pride, her life… he was dangerous to all of them.

It was time to take her mind into her own hands.

Thorn waited until the plane was landing, when they unconsciously began discounting her as a threat.

With the renewed energy that her decision had brought her, she disarmed both teams, and had a very intimate conversation with Arthur.

A mistake on their part. A lucky break for her.

She gave the plane behind her one last glance before she took the key ring and clicked off the metal around her neck.

Thorn really hoped Arthur found a flame to cauterize his hand.

Thorn

Cemetery Canyon
Castaic, California

February 25, 2019
10:10 a.m.

Thorn ran her tongue around her teeth, grimacing at the bitter aftertaste of the pills.

She should feel relieved, relaxed, as she walked to her sanctuary. But it wasn't her secret anymore.

She brought Streye here, and now he knew its secrets.

Another thing she lost.

A sense of déjà vu spread throughout her body. As her mind tried to make sense of the feeling, her hands clenched around the belt around her hips.

She felt strange.

Anxious was not quite it, angry not quite it, nor happy. It was as if she was standing a hundred feet over the ocean, and had just peeked over to see what lay at the bottom.

Her VOS was silent. She didn't expect anything more.

She was tired. Her body had spent the last of that energy getting rid of MedTech, and now all she wanted to do was rest.

For days, for weeks.

Maybe forever.

As her foot stepped over a pile of rocks, she finally realized what the feeling was.

The moment she finally sank the blade into her wrist. After standing there for hours. The moment everything made sense, that she needed to remove herself from a world she no longer recognized.

She didn't know this world. A world where a man had replaced a part of her.

She was a stranger inside her own mind.

It still scared her to say goodbye, combined with the fear that VOS still wouldn't come back.

Then she'd really be alone.

But what was she truly scared of? That loneliness was the world she came from, one she lived through. Not this strange one where a man was becoming more and more important to her.

She just hoped she didn't need someone else's help to go through with telling him it was over.

She needed to do it on her own.

Her stride automatically slowed as she approached the tree, even as her mind continued to race with memories and fears.

Her mouth dried.

She took a deep breath before stepping out from behind the large rock.

Streye sat there, under the tree, on the same stone that he usually does. Predictable.

He stood and greeted her with a half-smile as she approached. His gaze was as magnetic as ever... but... something was off. Maybe it was his facial expression, maybe it was his stance.

Did he sense what she was about to say?

"Streye, I-"

He pressed a finger to her lips. He took her into his arms, those muscular warm arms she'd fought alongside, been held by. She softened in his embrace but didn't return the embrace.

She just didn't know why it was taking her so long to open her mouth.

Something pricked her back.

She nudged his arms a little, but he didn't budge. She pushed a little harder at him. The pain from the prick was fading, replaced with a tingling numbness.

He finally pulled back, and in his eyes she saw a desperation she'd never seen before. Curious... she'd never really seen anything but anger in those depths.

But that didn't matter anymore.

Not now.

She fell to her knees, her fingertips tingling.

Well... at least he was making this easy on her. She didn't know if she could have gone through with it otherwise.

Still weak. Still so fucking weak.

Some part of her knew this day was coming. Deserved it. As she mashed the mud in between her fingers, she smiled a little.

But he misunderstood her.

Misunderstood her falling for complete numbness, hesitance for weakness.

She had experimented with all the poisons and drugs she could get her hands on before AEX found her. She failed to react to them then, which was why she had to resort to the knife.

She had to handicap him. She wasn't losing consciousness yet, but she knew the drug would hinder her reflexes.

He was talking, she realized. "I'm sorry… she doesn't deserve to die. I never wanted this to happen…"

She didn't process what he was saying. Couldn't. She had to focus on the task at hand.

She dug out her daggers and staked his foot straight into the ground with the one in her left hand.

His shocked gasp was broken by a clenched groan. He tried to back away from her kneeling form, but was held to the ground in front of her. Leaning down, he tried to pull it out, but it immobilized his entire foot.

Blood soaked into the ground.

She watched him through hazy eyes. "I…wasn't… expecting…"

He fell on his back as his face turned a sickening red and pink pallor.

"But… you… made this easier…"

"Trust me! I didn't want to… I didn't!" He groaned in his throat as he tried to pry the blade out.

Words… words…

Thorn crawled towards him, her hands unsteady. He must have given her a pretty high dose. She could barely feel her fingertips.

She took out another dagger and staked it into his right thigh. If she could get up, this would be a lot easier, but her legs refused to cooperate.

She had to immobilize him as much as she could.

"Yeah... thanks... I don't have doubts..."

Her forehead glistened with the effort to stay conscious. His forehead was layered with cold sweat.

She finally kneeled in range of his throat.

Before she dug out another dagger, he pulled out the one from his thigh and swung the blade up, slicing across her upper chest, from left shoulder to right. She swung her leg and dug her heel into his wrist, which cracked as it hit the ground.

He dropped the dagger.

She picked it up to try for his neck again, but she felt the ground spin underneath her.

She tasted copper.

As one hand stabilized her balance, the other stabbed the blade into his shoulder, the body part closest to her.

She had to get back to her car.

Thorn

Cemetery Canyon
Castaic, California

February 25, 2019
10:45 a.m.

Calm washed over her as she walked away, but that soon disappeared. Thorn leaned over and threw up, holding onto a tree.

Her arms couldn't hold her up as she wretched, and she fell, her head hitting the crispy bark. That pain woke her, just a little, from the numbness everywhere else on her body.

Thorn wiped her mouth and stood up shakily. She had to hold onto whatever trees were nearby, but she was upright.

Whatever drug he'd injected into her fought to keep her down.

The slash on her chest burned.

He was no longer with her. Literally and figuratively.

Hold out a little long, Thorn. You have to get home.

See, she could be her own VOS.

Are you there? She called out to the voice in her head.

No answer.

The journey to her car was the longest ten minutes she'd ever experienced. She was almost crawling.

As she turned the corner for her car, she saw three armed men in suits at different points around the secluded parking lot. They triangulated around her car, each facing away from it.

She pressed her body against the closest solid vertical surface. Even that sudden motion made her knees crumble. Closing her eyes, she planted her feet into the ground.

They couldn't possibly have just stumbled onto her location. Coincidences just didn't happen.

At least, not lately.

Did Streye lead them here? He was the only one who knew where she was going to be. Maybe they were here to collect her body.

No. It couldn't be.

Streye wasn't the kind to want or have backup. So that only meant one thing.

Multiple people wanted her gone, alive or dead.

It made no sense.

She closed her eyes. She was thankful she didn't use her gun earlier. Not only would it have revealed where she was, but she also would have wasted bullets.

She didn't need bullets for one man.

Even if it was Streye.

The nausea was back.

She could head out, on foot, leaving her car behind. Pro: she would not have to confront them. Con: that would take hours, and it was already past midnight. She definitely would not make it, even if the drug starts to wear off.

She could take them out one by one. Pro: no gunfire. Con: difficult, especially since they were positioned so close to each other and had those coms in their ears. She could do one, maybe two, but there was no way she could take down three in her current state.

They would capture her.

Third route. Shoot them down, take them out as quickly as possible. Con: the noise would attract a lot of attention; she wasn't sure if she had enough bullets. Pro: everything else.

Ah, fuck it.

She didn't have the time or the strength to do this properly. Taking the Glocks out of their holsters, she checked the magazines and patted her ammo belt to make sure she had fresh magazines.

Her vision was still blurry and she still felt like a rag filled with vomit, but she managed to stay upright.

"Don't give up on me now. Come on, keep it together."

Thorn

Thorn's Apartment
Los Angeles, California

February 25, 2019
2:50 p.m.

She felt like a stranger in her own home.

Everything about the décor and the furniture was still the same, but nothing felt familiar.

She set her hand on top of the closest object.

The table where Streye and she had taken apart and cleaned their guns, from midnight until the morning sun peaked over the horizon.

Her chest ached, and her face burned with the flying wood chip debris during the gun fight.

The bar area where they made love...

No, she shook her head. Not love.

If anything, VOS was the only love she knew. The only one that knew her, inside and out.

Stabbing pains ran through her shoulders and sides.

Yep, still alive.

Her hand slipped on the doorknob, slick with her sweat and blood. Her fingers trembled as she locked the door, once, twice, three times.

Where her body wasn't numb, it hurt so much that all she wanted to do was scream.

Thorn unlaced her boots. She clenched her fingers with each twist and turn of the laces.

She finally slid them off her feet.

As she let her clothes drop on her way to the bathroom, she ignored the blood and dirt she left in her wake.

The shower was so hot she felt her skin burn. Wincing, she cleaned out each wound and cut, her fingers prying apart the skin. She was going to have to suture the larger ones.

She fell to her knees and retched. The entry point of the needle tingled as water slid over it.

The numbness was slowly wearing off. She could move her fingers.

But as the numbness cleared, so did the fog in her brain. She could think again.

Streye betrayed her.

She hadn't wanted to realize, think, believe that the man... she...

What she did, she was protecting herself... but him...

She should not have been wounded. But his betrayal –so easy– made her slow.

She was both retching and crying at the same time, but she had nothing left in her body.

Thorn stayed in that position for a while. Until the steam was as thick as fog. Until her knees and feet began to cramp. Until she couldn't feel the temperature of the water.

She turned off the shower, wrapped herself in a towel, and popped a set of pills into her mouth. Her hand slipped on the side of the drawer, unintentionally slapping the pill bottle to the ground.

Thorn made her way to the couch, setting her feet on top of the cushions. She wanted to be distracted.

But she was tired of the lies on television. Music would help, but she was too restless. She had books, but she was exhausted.

Her eyes fell on the journal underneath the coffee table. The only place where she was completely open and honest. Even her mind had lied to her for so long that the only truth she had was on paper.

She couldn't relive the past few months. Not yet.

She sat up, noticing that the headache was back. She had nowhere to go, no one to see, and people trying to kill her.

Why? Why?

The question continued to bounce around inside her head.

She took the first aid kit on the underside of the coffee table, and began to patch up her wounds using gauze, ointment, and tape.

Thorn put on her clothes slowly, making sure she the gauze stayed.

She didn't need to know where she was going, but she couldn't stay cooped up here, with only her thoughts in this unfamiliar apartment.

Thorn
Memory

Corra Residence When Thorn was 15
Palmdale, California (Ten years ago)

Grace found them on the couch.

Thorn, disheveled, pinned between Jason and the armrest, blood splattered on her dress. Jason with a pen stabbed through his hand, fingers wrapped around Thorn's shoulders.

Thorn didn't said anything. She thought that it was obvious what had happened.

But she was wrong.

So wrong.

Her mother laid hands on her.

Over a man.

Who had tried to touch her underage daughter.

In that moment, the bond between mother and daughter was forgotten.

In that moment, everything broke.

Grace apologized, later, much later than she could have, finally faced with the fact that the man of her dreams was a sexual predator.

But she wasn't sorry for what she did. Not really.

Grace's mouth said sorry. But her eyes and her body said nothing.

Her apology didn't matter anyway.

Sorry was just a five-letter word, and no words were going to fix the crack that appeared in Thorn's soul.

Thorn

Corra Residence   February 25, 2019
Palmdale, California   7:30 p.m.

She drove aimlessly, without a thought in her head, and found herself in front of the place she used to call home.

Why was she here?

Her life before AEX was a fleeting memory, one that she never cared to explore.

Thorn felt dirty as she hid in the hedges of the front yard, peering into the living room and kitchen. And she looked, almost with masochistic curiosity, as the woman she used to call mother set the table for her new family.

The man's face was familiar. Thorn tried to think back to when they met. Or if they even had. Her memories from before AEX were so jumbled and out of order, that she wasn't sure if they were even real.

Was that the partner at the law firm who was a single dad? Or did she imagine someone like him as a fitting spouse for her mother?

Seeing the relaxed way her mother moved and hearing the soft laughter, Thorn knew she should feel happy.

Yet she only felt a strange disconnectedness, a bitterness that left a cold taste in her mouth. It was right in front of her, her own flesh and blood mother, and she couldn't feel anything.

It doesn't matter anymore.

She was no longer part of that world. It was as if she existed on a different plane, while the rest of the world went on with their lives.

Thorn, an invisible spectator.

It was better for all of them that she stayed that way.

She set a comforting hand on her gun before melting into the darkness.

Alden

Office of Kharavera Terraza
9th Floor, K-Pharma

February 26, 2019
7:30 a.m.

"You're sure about this?"

Khara leaned in from her side of the desk, calculating violet eyes locked onto Alden. Her room was darker than normal, the lights dim. She even sent Penny away so they could have complete privacy.

Alden felt sweat run down his back. He wasn't going to be intimidated. He had too much to lose.

Even the pictures on the wall stared at him.

His eyes bore into hers. "Yes, ma'am."

"Call me Khara." She set her chin in the palm of one hand, elbow on the table. "And when did you hear them talk about this?"

"Six days ago, ma- Khara. They were in the break room discussing something they had replicated. Something about Thorn and an evolving thing. And saying that you were going to destroy their creation."

"I see." Khara's eyes went to the posters behind his head. "What was your name again?"

"Alex Hardt. Security analyst."

"I see." She tapped the pen. "Did you get a look at the materials?"

"No. They were discussing this in a corner."

Alden thought about the assistant who was also there, but ratting her out to Khara had no purpose. She could be very useful to his investigation. If nothing else he can blackmail her for information.

"That was all?"

"Yes."

"Okay." She turned to her phone. "I will take care of it."

She graced him with a smile. Her intensity lessened. Only slightly.

"While this was directly outside of your purview, you did a good job. Do not say anything to anyone. As soon as this is all handled, we'll talk more."

He nodded as he stood up.

Khara watched his back as he left the room.

Thorn

Rooftop   February 26, 2019
21st Floor, K-Pharma   8:00 a.m.

The sun rose over the horizon, its red rays slicing through the darkness of the dawn.

Thorn held the Glock 17 in her hand, making sure to keep her finger off the trigger. It was hefty, but she no longer registered the weight of it. To her, it was an extension of her arm.

The handle was a little worn, the barrel dotted with pockmarks and dents. The magazines fit a little looser, but they were spotless.

Thorn shifted the barrel towards her, its black eye pointed at her face. Her finger was touching the side of the trigger, lightly sliding back and forth. No doubt a slip right now would kill her, but that thought bothered her less and less as the minutes rolled by.

Thorn slid the other Glock from its holster and held them barrel to barrel, the tops of the guns touching each other.

She pulled them slowly apart and held them on either side of her face, the left gun touching its right side to her cheek, the right gun touching its left side to her cheek.

She closed her eyes, enjoying the coldness, and remembered the first time she held them in her hands.

Thorn
Memory

Training Arena   When Thorn was 23
11th Floor, K-Pharma   (Two years ago)

Always hold the gun firmly. Your grip must be high and tight on the handle. You don't want it to jam.

Is that you?

I am.

I didn't know you could come out whenever. How do you know all of this?

You, and by association, I, have read all of these in training. I am merely directing you to the important parts.

I don't come out whenever; I'm always here.

It's still a little weird.

Thorn didn't even know how she maintained her calm. She just was.

Don't worry. I will help you reorganize, prioritize, and plan. Until the day comes that you decide I am less help than hindrance, I will be here.

Thorn

Rooftop   February 26, 2019
21st Floor, K-Pharma   8:00 a.m.

Thorn rubbed the tops of the barrels against her cheeks, soft at first and then harder, until her skin felt warm.

That was how Eve found her half an hour later.

Thorn sitting against the edge of the roof, her back towards the building and her face towards the rising sun. The guns were still pressed against her cheeks, but her hands were no longer moving.

Her eyes were closed.

"Thorn?" Eve stopped in her tracks. She made her way to the edge of the building.

Without opening her eyes, Thorn leaned her body to the side opposite Eve, giving her room to sit down.

"I'm done. I can't do this anymore."

Eve lifted a hand to comfort her, but then put it down.

"Thorn…"

"VOS is gone, and I no longer trust the decisions I make."

Eve didn't know what to say, so she decided to go with honesty.

"I know."

Thorn fixed her gaze on the older woman. "You did?"

"Of course. Things have been…off with you."

Eve sank down and sat next to her. "You changed. The manner you talked, the way you planned…you became more human as your eyes grew more desperate."

Eve paused.

"I attributed that to your relationship with Streye."

Thorn no longer had any reason to hide it.

"He was a big part of it. But it started long before…" She dropped her hands to look at the guns. "VOS definitely warned me against it."

Eve nodded. "She couldn't stop you."

"But I was wrong." Thorn turned to Eve. "Does Khara know?"

"Yes."

They were both silent.

"He drugged me."

"What?"

Thorn retreated from the question.

"MedTech, and then Streye, and then Randolph's men tried to take me. On separate occasions."

"VOS couldn't have sensed that."

"Even if she did…" Thorn shook her head. "My point is, I'm done. I've failed my VOS, and it feels like I've gone against everything I've fought for."

Her teeth felt strange in her mouth.

"But I didn't even have anything to fight for."

She tightened her grip on the guns. The tip of one touched the scar on her left arm.

Eve released a breath. "Your VOS... I don't think she just left. It's our guess that... she evolved."

Thorn made a sound. "Right."

Eve continued. "That was why Khara and Randolph were so scared of you, of what you could be." She bit her lip. "That's why Khara plans on removing your VOS."

Thorn didn't react, not sure if she heard correctly. "What?"

Eve nodded. "She's going to try to remove it completely. She thinks you're too unpredictable, uncontrollable."

"She wants to remove the VOS?" Thorn's voice was barely above a whisper. Her eyes took on a glazed look.

"She believes that if they come up with a successful removal procedure, we cure all of the unforeseen fails and AEX can spare more funding on experimenting and creating more agents."

Removal...?

As if reading her mind, Eve shook her head. "There have been no successes."

Thorn barked out a short laugh, startling Eve.

"Why haven't they just asked?"

Eve stared at her.

Thorn leaned back, a small smile on her face.

"You can't be serious. You will die."

Thorn's smile didn't leave her face. "What better chance than now? I have nothing, no one, and I'm tired."

She put the left Glock back into its holster. "Eve, maybe this is the answer. Maybe I need to start from scratch again."

Eve didn't speak.

Thorn leaned back against the side. "You're not going to try to change my mind?"

"Is there anything I could say to change it?"

"No." Thorn leaned back.

They sat there, silent, listening to the calls of birds and the breathing of the earth.

"He couldn't even do it right. He had to use a fucking needle to subdue me."

Thorn's chest hurt.

Eve kept her eyes straight ahead. "Perhaps he had a reason."

"Reason or not. He did."

Eve watched the rays of the sun until the light began to burn her eyes. "You can't let them kill you so easily."

"There's no guarantee of that. Who knows, Khara might be right."

"Thorn, this is suicide–"

And at that moment, Eve realized. "You're on a suicide mission."

Thorn didn't respond.

"Thorn, please reconsider."

Thorn set a hand on Eve's arm, the first time she's ever reached out and touched her. "You said my VOS was different, unique, evolving."

"Yes."

"I will let her decide what happens."

"You still have free will!"

"I've made enough decisions."

Thorn caressed the barrels of her guns. "If she doesn't want this to happen, she'll let me know."

Khara

Office of Kharavera Terraza February 27, 2019
9th Floor, K-Pharma 1:40 p.m.

"What did you say?" Khara never paced, but she was too restless.

"Streye never showed up. He didn't seem like the kind of guy to promise and not deliver, so I tracked his phone using your technology–"

"What?"

"And found him. In a canyon near the Lyons Cemetery."

He stopped talking.

"And?" Khara demanded impatiently.

"He was unconscious."

"So he's alive." Khara rubbed the corner of her eyes. Why did this have to be so hard? She was making the right choice, wasn't she?

"Not quite."

"What do you mean?"

"He's comatose."

Khara's body fell in her chair.

"Anyway, he's in your medical ward." The man started talking away from the phone, but then turned back around. "Thought you'd like to know: three bodies were also found a little way away, near a parking area."

"Who were they?"

"Military gear, ear pieces, nice guns. Mercenary trying to look government."

Randolph.

"What did you do with the bodies?"

He scoffed. "Nothing. I'm not your cleanup crew. My job was Streye."

Khara slid her fingers through her hair. "No, no, thank you. I will add the delivery to your fee."

"Yeah. The bodies were still there when I left. Although I'm sure they're long gone."

"Yeah."

"What do you want me to do with the girl?"

For a moment, Khara thought he was talking about Thorn. But reality sank in.

"Let Ana live. Make sure she doesn't speak about this."

"Got it."

Khara turned off the call and stared at the phone. She set it on the desk, and slid her body along the wood until her chest was touching the desk. She covered the back of her head with her hands and stayed there, silent.

She didn't make a sound aside from the slight creaking of the chair.

Five minutes later, she righted herself, and ran her fingers through her hair, smoothed her cheeks, and took a deep breath.

She picked up the phone and dialed a number.

It rang three times.

"Khara. I wasn't expecting you to call."

"I need to talk to Anthony."

Silence on the other end.

"Please."

"Khara, this is Elegrant, not a pet prison. We can't have inmates coming in and out like water."

"I know, James. Just let me talk to him."

He muttered a few curses under his breath, and called for one of his guards.

The silence while they waited was long and tense.

The squeak of wheels interrupted the silence. There was slight static as the retriever exchanged hands.

"Khara."

Anthony's voice was light, softer than she had expected.

"Anthony."

Khara had to prevent her voice from betraying her desperation. "How is Elegrant?"

"Great. It's like a personal hell. Death would've been better. Why did you keep me alive?"

"For a time when you could prove yourself again."

Silence.

"I assume it's now?"

Her own silence answered his question.

His laughter made her pull the phone away from her ear.

"You've caged and crippled me, Khara. I can't use my left hand."

"Your disability won't stop you. You know that as well as I do."

"You must be truly desperate to come to me."

"I am."

The silence held.

"You really have no one else."

Silence.

"So Thorn, Streye, and Aaron must be incapacitated..."

Silence.

"Or the target."

Silence.

"I would say you can go fuck yourself, but this is too good. I can't kill anyone in here."

"I need you to take her alive."

"Her?"

Khara paused. "Thorn."

"I see. You sure you're okay with setting me free? After everything you did to put me in here?"

"I can handle you. If not, then the chips in your neck and feet will."

"You know I'll be coming after you. After I peel apart pretty little Thorn."

"Of course." She touched her purse. "But I need her alive."

Silence.

"When can I get the fuck out of here?"

"Immediately."

"Then I agree to your terms."

As she hung up the phone, Khara felt a loathing inside her, a disappointment in everything she's ever said and done. After all the sacrifices she's made to stay true to her word and her science, this is what it's come to.

Relying on psychopaths, destroying her own creation, betraying her team...

But this was more than science, more than relationships. She needed to protect K-Pharma, her legacy. And if her science threatens the future of her namesake, then that's a sacrifice she must make.

K-Pharma will survive.

Even if she doesn't.

Thorn
Memory

Interview Room
10th Floor, K-Pharma   (Two years ago)

Dr. Stewart left the room. The next thing she knew, Khara was standing in front of her.

Thorn didn't know when she came in, when she started talking, or what she was previously talking about, but she couldn't ignore the woman whose sharpness was only rivaled by her intensity.

"Once you sign your name on the dotted line, make no mistake: we own you, body and soul. You cannot go back on it. Buyer's remorse does not exist in AEX."

Through puffy and tired eyes, Thorn had looked at the woman in front of her, couldn't look away, mesmerized by those eyes.

Purple fire.

Thorn shook her head.

Her hands were still trembling with the aftereffects of the hospital drugs, but she clasped them together as tightly as she could.

"Do you understand? We. Will. Own. You. Your mind will be our research, your skills become ours, and your decisions will be ours.

You will be our limb to the outside world."

"Are you sure you're selling this off as well as you should?"

Khara had given her a stony look.

"I'm not in the business of hiding the truth. You will be used, in more ways than one. If you cannot handle it, you will be taken care of. This is not temporary. There is no return from this."

Thorn wondered if anyone ever changed their mind after hearing her talk. It wouldn't surprise her.

"You have passed the tests. But if the VOS treatment is not successful, you will become a ward of AEX. There is no guarantee."

Thorn picked up the pen and signed with steady fingers.

Thorn

Hallway
9th Floor, K-Pharma

February 27, 2019
7:20 p.m.

Thorn woke from her reverie, shaking the memories from her head. The breath that exploded out of her made her dizzy, and it obfuscated all the other thoughts in her mind.

She had forgotten how comforting, how whole she felt when she had the voice.

Her hand splayed against the wall.

Thorn forgot what it was like, what VOS had pulled her back from.

She hadn't realized how much VOS served as her crutch, both physically and mentally. Only after having survived because of it, and ignoring it for Streye, could Thorn truly appreciate the strange parasite that had bonded with her.

It brought her back from the brink.

The door she was looking for appeared, large and thick and dark.

She had run away from herself too much. It was time to come back to reality.

Khara

Office of Kharavera Terraza   February 27, 2019
9th Floor, K-Pharma   7:25 p.m.

Khara had turned off her electronics and tucked her phone into her briefcase when she heard the doorknob turn.

On instinct, she grabbed the Ruger she kept holstered under her desk and switched the safety off as she pointed it at the door.

The handle twisted down ninety degrees and the door slowly slid open.

"Hi, Khara."

Thorn stood against the doorframe, her dark red hair framing her tired face. She wore only a black tank top exposing her neck and shoulder, and military cargo pants. A large gauze was taped on her chest.

"I hear you've been looking for me."

It wasn't often that Khara was taken by surprise, but there was no way she could have predicted this.

The barrel of her gun drifted a few centimeters. She didn't think there was any immediate danger, but she couldn't be sure.

"I'm surprised you're here."

Thorn shrugged. Her left hand was holding her right forearm.

"What's the point of running away?"

The girl didn't seem to be hiding anything, but she did have VOS. The barrel stayed on her.

"You did sign away your life to AEX, at any rate. Any decision you make is our decision."

A flash of something entered Thorn's eyes, but it quickly faded away. She covered it with a smile.

"I just dropped by to let you know you can stop sending people after me. I'll be back tomorrow. And you can get on with removing VOS."

Khara didn't let the confusion show on her face. *How did she know?*

Thorn uncrossed her arms.

"You could have just asked. You do own me, after all."

Thorn turned to leave.

The barrel rose again. "How will I be sure you'll be back? What's stopping me from shooting you right here right now?"

Thorn smiled, her eyes narrowing.

"You want me alive, don't you? I give you my word." She turned, presenting her back to Khara.

"Don't worry, I won't do anything drastic. Would I have come here to tell you that otherwise?"

She waved her hand, and began to walk down the hallway. For the entire twenty seconds, Khara's gun was pointed at her back, trigger finger pulled in slightly, muscles wanting to contract.

But as Thorn disappeared around the corner, Khara reset the Ruger into its clipped holster.

She leaned forward, the weight of her torso held up by her two hands perpendicular to the desk. Her elbows were locked.

She sat back down in the chair and her hand dug out the phone from her briefcase.

It rang three times.

"Twice in a day? I'm flattered."

"Anthony is no longer needed."

The silence on the other end was deafening.

"James?"

"Sorry, he's your problem now." He didn't sound sorry at all. "He's been released."

"Ah, fuck."

"Good luck."

Randolph

White House
Washington, D.C.

February 27, 2019
8:00 p.m.

"Yes. Thank you for your support."

As Amanda closed the door behind the group of constituents, Randolph heaved a loud sigh.

"Is that it for the day, Amanda?"

She glanced at the calendar on her desk. "You have one more."

"I do?" He glanced at the clock. It was already 8 p.m. "Isn't it a little late–"

The door opened.

Hannah stood there, her face half in shadow, half in the light.

"Randolph, you need to come with me."

Behind her stood an army.

"Hannah–"

He barely noticed the three lasers on his chest before the bullets entered his body.

Randolph

White House   February 27, 2019
Washington, D.C.   8:01 p.m.

Randolph shot up so quickly the back of his head hit the chair.

He didn't feel the pain.

As fast as his limbs would allow, he ran his hands over his body, feeling for blood and holes where his organs used to be.

It took him two minutes to calm his breathing, to reassure himself that he wasn't just shot, that his treason wasn't discovered.

It was all a dream.

A terrible nightmare.

His office was dark. Right. He told Amanda he was going to take a nap and dimmed the lights. What usually took him hours took him a mere five minutes.

Not a very restful sleep, but it was enough sleep to last him another day. Looking over his shoulder for Khara was wearing on him.

There was a knock on his door.

Thorn

Cemetery Canyon
Castaic, California

February 27, 2019
11:50 p.m.

Flames danced, spiraling, undulating towards the sky. They illuminated the face that stared vacantly past the fire, into the blackness of the trees beyond the light's reach.

The smoke blew straight into the sky, undisturbed by wind. It flew upward, toward the bright crescent moon and the winking stars, slowly circling above where Thorn lay on her back.

She loved nights like this. It was strange, especially to Eve, who reminded her it was on this type of night that she almost died.

Her almost successful suicide.

She turned her arm so she was looking at the underside of her forearm. The scarring had healed enough – she hoped so, it's been two years – but it was still somewhat tender, and the nerves around the new skin still felt soft, exposed.

She grabbed her forearm with her whole hand.

Her head turned sideways, and her eyes landed on the dried bloodstain a few feet away.

Streye…

She held her breath for a while, waiting for VOS to speak.

Nothing.

Thorn was glad, actually. Without the voice, she could face tomorrow without regret.

She was levelling up. Thorn was so tired of replaying this level.

She pressed her back against the cold ground, spreading her arms outwards. She stretched, feeling the ache in her back and her legs. She felt the pounding of her heartbeat against her chest and the dirt.

Clawing the ground lightly, Thorn reveled in the feeling of rocks and dirt underneath her palm.

It was beautiful.

She had forgotten how to enjoy those fleeting moments, when nothing mattered and the beauty was endless.

Thorn smiled to herself.

Things are changing.

She was going to be free again.

Thorn
Memory

Corra Residence   When Thorn was 14
Palmdale, California   (Eleven years ago)

Thorn sat on the living room floor arranging puzzle pieces and watched the man sitting with her mom in the kitchen. Slicked back black hair, angular nose, protruding ears...

Her mom could do better. Much better.

The way his hands touched her mother, the way his eyes widened and focused on her face, the way his body never strayed far from hers.

This man knew how women worked.

Thorn went back to putting together her puzzle.

She heard footsteps coming towards the living room.

"Thorn, I'm going to get some dinner. Jason will keep you company."

Her mother's cheery voice bothered Thorn. It was the voice she reserved for the men who came and went, who she doted on and fawned over.

Thorn murmured an assent as Grace picked up her handbag.

The door opened. They blew kisses at each other. The door closed.

Routine.

Thorn went back to focusing on the picture in front of her. Where was that piece with the light brown fur? Her fingers trailed over the pieces closest to her, her eyes switching from empty spot to piece, empty spot to piece.

She was so intent on finding that one piece that she didn't notice his presence until she could smell his cologne.

"So... What are you working on?"

Here we go.

She turned her head to look at his enlarged nose and weird ears.

"Trying to solve this puzzle."

She turned her head back.

"I used to love these when I was a kid! Now I just don't have time to do them."

If you're trying to butter me up to get closer to my mom, you don't have to. I could literally hate you, and she would still have a spot for you in her bed and in her heart.

He shifted the completed parts of the puzzle towards him. His eyes wandered over the display of corner, middle, and side pieces, and found the one. He dropped it into the spot.

Thorn was mildly impressed. He seemed smart enough, and he could help her finish this puzzle.

"My favorites were the landscapes. They were such a challenge."

She shrugged. "They have their appeal."

He turned to look at her. His eyes scanned her face. "Wow, you look so much like your mother."

Thorn nodded. "People say we look like clones."

He touched a finger to her chin to lift it up.

"Yeah, right down to those amazing eyes."

She narrowed her eyes at him.

Her brain told her that this was wrong, and her gut told her to get away from him."

She batted his hand away and moved to the other side of the table.

Streye

Medical Sector   February 28, 2019
11th Floor, K-Pharma   2:15 a.m.

Streye looked around at the trees, at the fields, at the sky. Everything was vibrant, filled with a color that had been lacking for so long.

The house to his right… why did it look so familiar?

He knew he'd been here before. A long time ago.

Who was that older man on the roof? He felt like he should know.

He should. But everything here was distracting.

He could breathe. His chest was filled with a warmth that was almost unrecognizable, a happiness so explosive it expanded his chest.

What was this feeling?

"Trey! Bro!" He turned just in time to see a fist coming at his face. He ducked just in time, but the other hand came from under and started hitting his stomach. The punches weren't hard or painful, but startling.

His hands came up automatically, hitting the other boy with controlled and feigned anger.

They wrestled to the ground, grappling with feet and hands, grunting, covering their clean clothes with mud and grass, but neither one of them cared.

Alex.

They rolled down a hill, kept rolling.

A dark, dank little store, lit by neon lights. They clambered to their feet, both still trying to knock the other one over.

Ah, the smell of this place. Cheap beer and fresh ink.

Streye closed his eyes as he sniffed the air.

They stood up, Alex first because he wanted to prove himself faster and stronger, and Streye second, because he wanted to make his little brother happy. They both got to their feet too quickly, and held onto each other for balance.

An old bearded man with as many faded tattoos on his arms and neck as he had wrinkles stood behind a glass case filled with jewelry. He leaned on the counter, sagging skin pooling on the surface.

"We want to get tattoos."

"How old are you?"

"I'm 16 and he's 14."

The old man looked between the both of them, his eyebrow arched. "The minimum age for tattoos is 18, unless you have parental consent."

"Sir, we just something small. Please sir. I don't know how long we'll be together, and you're our last hope. We don't want to forget about each other."

The old man calculated them both with his gaze.

"What do you want done?"

They both pointed to the center of their chests.

"Forever brothers, far or apart."

Khara

Research Laboratory
11th Floor, K-Pharma

February 28, 2019
9:05 a.m.

"Ready."

Two nurses ran the scans and checked the IV's, needles already inserted into Thorn's arms and legs. Another nurse adjusted the electrode cap on her head, making sure the gel was evenly distributed on her partially shaved scalp.

The doctors were quiet.

Eve was quiet.

The room had lost the excitement of scientific discovery. It was as if the walls themselves were holding their breath.

And in the middle of the silent room, was Thorn.

They had washed her, shaved her entire body, and injected her with the muscle relaxants. Her body, flat on the table, was covered with a loose wrap. Her face was peaceful, eyes closed, lips curled upwards in a slight smile.

Khara had half-expected Thorn to try to run, to go back on her word. She wouldn't have faulted her.

After all, what kind of person agrees to a procedure that guaranteed death, and not reconsider?

But Thorn had surprised her again.

The agent had been right outside her office when Khara arrived, hours before the sunrise.

Thorn must not have slept, but she looked refreshed.

Ready.

Johann gave her a thumbs up.

She nodded at him.

The lights in the room hummed as the machine purred to life.

Alden

Security Room   March 1, 2019
10th Floor, K-Pharma   10:45 a.m.

The blaring alarm jolted the entire office out of their seat. Even the security guards jumped.

Moments later, bright lights flashed in rhythm to the waling sirens.

There was an initial silence as both the sound and lights stunned everyone into immobility.

The electronic speaker system beeped on.

"Security protocol has been breached. Security protocol has been breached. All employees must exit the building immediately through the stairwell. All employees must exit the building immediately through the stairwell."

People, chatting amongst themselves, began to push their chairs back and leave the room. Some even stopped to get a glass of water before they headed down the stairs.

Alden turned to the woman in front of him.

"Hey, what is going on?"

"It's probably just a broken window in the C-sector. It happens every couple of months. There's nothing to worry about."

"What about my work? Will someone take it?"

She laughed and clapped him on the shoulder. "Honey, your work will be fine. No one will be in the building. They're even making the guards go outside."

"Oh, okay. Thanks."

The woman nodded and went to talk to her friend. No one bothered to take any of their belongings with them.

Alden rose from his seat.

Most of his colleagues were already in the stairwell, and a strange silence hung over the normally full office.

Taking one last look around the room, Alden reached for the newspaper clipping on his desk and tucked it into his pocket, carefully folding it so that the corners didn't wrinkle.

As he headed towards the center of the building, away from the direction of the stairwell, he rubbed the center of his chest with the index and middle fingers of his right hand.

AEX
Day 0

The woman looked at her hands, shaking like she was standing on a moving train.

Her chest beat slowly as her throat closed.

A sudden burst of red flashed in front of her. Every nerve in her body throbbed, every muscle twitched, and even her ears closed itself off to the world.

The only thing she heard was the sound of her heartbeat and her own accelerating breaths.

She fell to her knees, grabbing her head. She clamped down on her ears, hoping to get rid of the blockage. Her teeth clenched so tightly that she felt her jaw click. The sound in her ears cleared for a brief moment, and she swiveled her head, trying to take in her surroundings.

What happened? Where is she? Why couldn't she remember anything?

As she tried to think, she found that she couldn't. There was a block in her memory, and the more she tried to fight it, the stronger it became.

She looked at her arms and hands. They were covered with bandages and wraps, two IV's plugged into each of her forearms. Her left arm dangled from her shoulder, unresponsive to her commands.

The woman began to panic, even as a part of her told her she shouldn't. Her brain wasn't telling her anything, but her heart told her to move, to keep moving.

She slammed her left arm against the wall, and pulled her right arm towards her face.

Everything hurt.

There were bruises, bandages and wraps everywhere, and so much blood. Both dried and fresh.

She winced as her right arm slowly inched towards her face. Her bicep felt like it was being pulled in two different directions. As her mouth touched the plastic tubing, she ripped it out with her teeth.

Fresh blood gushed out of the wound, and she cried out, leaning her forehead against the wall.

A few drops dripped onto the ground, and a part of her wanted to wipe it off but she had no energy to do that. Everything was exhausting.

There was something that she had to do, but she had no idea what. All she knew was that she needed to get out of here, go... go... somewhere without the walls around her.

Why was it so noisy?

She blinked, turning her back to the wall. Her head felt bloated, like air was trying to escape from each pore on her scalp. She heard people screaming underwater, gurgling, and the occasional car alarm.

But there was no one in the hallway.

She bumped her head against the wall a few more times to distract herself from the head pressure. She tried again to think about why she was here.

She found herself on the ground in a different hallway.

It was still the same white walls, but this part had windows and numbers on the doors. The other section... did it have numbers? Were they completely unmarked rooms and hallways in the place where...

Wh...What was she just thinking about?

As she pushed away from the floor, she noticed the red handprints she left. She looked at her trembling hands.

Her left hand was still dead weight and her right hand was bloody.

Was it hot? Was it cold? She couldn't tell.

She couldn't understand why her hands were trembling.

Where was she? What is this? The screaming and alarms in her head came back, but this time, one voice stood out as the loudest, harshest and most grating. It was so discordant that she could feel the vibrations of the voice inside her head.

Why, what was it saying, what was happening-

What do you think you are? Ugly, ugly, worthless, ugly worthless, ugly, worthless, ugly-

The voice was so confident, speaking to her like it was right next to her. But it also sounded disjointed and mechanical, like someone had been told to say it verbatim. Thorn had never been called ugly before, has she–

You make me sick. It's a shame we spent so much money on you, money that could be used for better things. You probably won't even wake up–

The voice was getting clearer and less mechanical, taking on a songlike quality. She couldn't pinpoint where the voice was coming from, but it seemed to be exploding out of her head. Didn't she have hardwood floors at her home–

Die. Die. Die. Die. Die. Die. Die. Die. Die. Die.

The woman's eyes flew open.

Her arms still throbbed and ached. It felt like needles were being pushed into every inch of her skin, but her mind was finally clearing up the cobwebs. That wasn't a mechanical voice.

It was her own voice.

How could she have two voices going on in her head? She couldn't possibly be experiencing the side effects of– what?

She blinked and kept her eyes closed.

When her eyes reopened, she was in a different area of the white building, this time with long cables running overhead. The long black cables entered each of the pre-marked doorways, and slid along the walls towards some center office.

Vibrations. Strange voices.

"Where the hell is she? She cannot leave this building in that state! We have no idea what she can do."

It was a woman's voice, older, firm. It also sounded like the voice telling her to die. But the voice inside her head was her… voice, wasn't it?

The woman dragged herself up and limped along, towards this unknown destination she felt was safe. Where she got that idea, she wasn't sure–

"How the hell did she even get out of the goddamn room? I told you to triple-seal it!"

A man's voice… Brusque, rude… A face flashed into her mind but disappeared as quickly as it came. As she tried to remember what the face looked like, the screams inside her head tripled in intensity.

She walked faster, as fast as her weak legs could carry her. Why was she so weak? She had a vague recollection of being strong enough to break doors and hold up two guns–

You'll wish you had your guns when I'm through with you.

Who was that voice? What was she even thinking about? She didn't know anything except to keep walking towards the center of the building, where the cables would join. She didn't know what was there but it would be the right place.

She saw the room at the same time her pursuers turned the corner behind her.

"How the fuck is she still standing? Didn't you tell me–"

Were they going to shoot her down? Tackle her? Something worse? She didn't have a good feeling. A part of her knew that they were going to put her back…where the memory loss came from…

She ran.

She ran as fast as her feet could take her, without regard for whether her limp arm was hitting any surfaces along the way.

"Goddamn it, take her down!" Feet pounded on the ground behind her. She put all her energy into reaching that door, the door that seemed to be getting farther and farther away.

Her vision swam, the floor and walls became hazy, but she kept running. Her lungs hurt, her chest ached, the voices' screeching got louder and louder, but she knew in her gut…

She knew what she needed was just beyond that….

"TAKE HER DOWN!" She heard the metal pinging around her – bullets she realized – and a sharp pain struck her calf just as her hand touched the door handle.

She used the last of her strength to rip the door open, throw her body into the welcoming darkness, and lock the door behind her.

Anthony

Medical Sector   March 1, 2019
11th Floor, K-Pharma   11:00 a.m.

Anthony bit the cloth as hard as he could.

Involuntary tears leaked from his eyes as the scalpel sliced into his foot. Blood dripped out of the meaty part of his heel.

His groans were muffled by the makeshift gag, but the veins on his face popped as he turned a bright beet-red.

While he had an almost absent tactile pain response, the appearance of the skull seemed to have sensitized certain nerves in areas of his body, particularly where it knew foreign objects had touched.

You must remove all external devices. It is taking away your power of dissociation.

He made one last cut, and slammed the scalpel onto the silver tray by the bed. Ignoring the blood that was pooling on the floor, he took the plyers from the tray and peered into the cut flesh.

Three seconds later, the plyers came out with a small gold chip between its teeth. He set both on the silver tray, right next to another set of plyers and a green chip.

He doused his foot in alcohol, squeezing his eyelids shut, and wrapped it in several inches of bandage gauze and tape.

That will have to do for now.

The skull stared at him from the doorway, its eye sockets no longer as black, its jaw no longer as alien.

Anthony touched the back of his neck, making sure that the gauze covering the other open wound was still there. Despite his sweating, the bandage held.

He unclenched his hands and looked straight across the room to the bed where Streye lay, unresponsive and dead to the world except for the consistent beeping of the heart rate monitor.

"I was going to kill you today."

The pain slowly faded from Anthony's neck and foot.

"But that would be too easy."

As he turned to leave, he kicked one of the two bodies on the ground.

"Whoops."

He stepped over the one he kicked, an older Asian woman, and navigated around the little brown-haired one.

"No hard feelings. You were merely in my way."

Anthony strolled out of the room, into the completely deserted hallway and sector, not favoring the left foot at all.

"Now. Where's our precious Thorn?"

The skull led the way.

AEX
Day 0

She was going to die alone.

She didn't know how she knew that, but she felt it. She couldn't remember where she was, who she was, or what she was doing here, but the thought of dying alone... that was something she recognized.

The thought felt comfortable, like home.

As she clung to the darkness, as her head spun, arms bled, and stomach roiled, she had a moment of peace. It felt like she was moving, but she didn't care.

At this very moment, there was no one threatening her, no one trying to kill her, and definitely maybe...

Her stomach and body jerked.

As her head rolled back on her neck, her eyes fell on the panel in front of her. It had numbers and arrows on buttons.

What was it called?

An e....e...elevator.

The only way to access the elevator was through the main security room and the panel on the first floor.

But why did she not remember how she got into the elevator? And how did she know? Where was she?

Before she could properly locate the memory and answer, the elevator jerked again. She realized the metal box had stopped.

Her eyes fell on the floor indicator - eight- and the button that was still lit on the panel. Two.

Someone had manually stopped the elevator.

She leaned toward the doors, but heard nothing. She leaned closer.

A thud landed on the outside of the doors, making her jump backwards. She scooted back as far as she could, her spine aligning completely with the wall. She patted her entire body, trying to find anything sharp or heavy, any weapon that she could use.

But she couldn't find anything.

Another thud on the outside of the doors. The sound of metal crunching against gears and the squealing of metal sliding against plastic.

Everything hurt. Her chest, her arms, her legs, her head.

Why was she running away anyway?

She still didn't remember anything. Whatever happens, will happen. She's had enough. She was tired, tired of running, tired of trying to remember. Tired of living this life that was never going to bring her happiness.

Where did that thought come from?

The metal squealing quieted.

A soft whoom.

The first set of doors was open. She still couldn't anything. Had the chasing and yelling happened? Did she imagine it?

Agents to hunt her down?

Who were agents?

She watched as a metal crow bar jammed between the doors. It awkwardly shifted left and right. She watched in fascination as light pierced through the dark enclosed space.

Why was the elevator pitch black? Did she cut the lights? Did they turn it off?

She had too many questions whose answers she could not recall, and blank spaces where there should be memories.

Another inch open, another inch of light.

She didn't even attempt to retreat into the corner. At the very least, she needed to see the face of her killer.

Maybe remember something before nothing at all.

A grunt from the other side.

She set her arms on her bent knees, feeling the soreness of her muscles and the protestations of her joints.

She didn't want to watch, but she couldn't turn away.

The doors were almost completely open.

The figure leaned his body into one door as his hands and feet kept the other side from slamming shut. His body arched, contorted with effort.

"Get your ass out of there." That voice. Why did it-

"I'd say this more than repays for that croissant. What do you think?"

Adrian Eller

ABOUT THE AUTHOR

Adrian Eller is a graduate student in Northern California studying psychology. She enjoys post-apocalyptic stories, exploring the dark side of human nature, and characters who struggle to find happiness while recovering from a painful past. In her free time, Adrian enjoys riding her motorcycle, baking, and checking off stuff on her bucket list.

Visit her at adrianeller.com.

www.ingramcontent.com/pod-product-compliance
Lightning Source LLC
Chambersburg PA
CBHW060416260626
47161CB00012B/2457